*I*f it was true that *Brambleclaw* wanted to be deputy, that must mean he thought Firestar was wrong to insist that Graystripe might still be alive. Worse than that, it was only one step from being deputy to being Clan leader. Was Brambleclaw looking ahead to the time when Firestar would lose his last life?

A shiver ran through Squirrelflight's pelt as she thought of her father's death, and cold gripped her with icy claws as she remembered the stories she had heard about Tigerstar. He had been prepared to kill to become deputy, and then Clan leader. Did his son, Brambleclaw, share the same ambitions? And would he be prepared to take the same murderous path to achieve them?

WARRIORS

THE PROPHECIES BEGIN

Book One: Into the Wild

Book Two: Fire and Ice

Book Three: Forest of Secrets

Book Four: Rising Storm

Book Five: A Dangerous Path

Book Six: The Darkest Hour

THE NEW PROPHECY

Book One: Midnight

Book Two: Moonrise

Book Three: Dawn

Book Four: Starlight

Book Five: Twilight

Book Six: Sunset

POWER OF THREE

Book One: The Sight

Book Two: Dark River

Book Three: Outcast

Book Four: Eclipse

Book Five: Long Shadows

Book Six: Sunrise

OMEN OF THE STARS

Book One: The Fourth Apprentice

Book Two: Fading Echoes

Book Three: Night Whispers

Book Four: Sign of the Moon

Book Five: The Forgotten Warrior

Book Six: The Last Hope

DAWN OF THE CLANS

Book One: *The Sun Trail*
Book Two: *Thunder Rising*
Book Three: *The First Battle*
Book Four: *The Blazing Star*
Book Five: *A Forest Divided*

EXPLORE THE
WARRIORS
WORLD

Warriors Super Edition: Firestar's Quest
Warriors Super Edition: Bluestar's Prophecy
Warriors Super Edition: SkyClan's Destiny
Warriors Super Edition: Crookedstar's Promise
Warriors Super Edition: Yellowfang's Secret
Warriors Super Edition: Tallstar's Revenge
Warriors Super Edition: Bramblestar's Storm
Warriors Field Guide: Secrets of the Clans
Warriors: Cats of the Clans
Warriors: Code of the Clans
Warriors: Battles of the Clans
Warriors: Enter the Clans
Warriors: The Ultimate Guide
Warriors: The Untold Stories
Warriors: Tales from the Clans

MANGA

The Lost Warrior
Warrior's Refuge
Warrior's Return
The Rise of Scourge

NOVELLAS

Also by Erin Hunter

SEEKERS

RETURN TO THE WILD

MANGA

NOVELLAS

THE NEW PROPHECY
WARRIORS
TWILIGHT

ERIN
HUNTER

HARPER

An Imprint of HarperCollins*Publishers*

Twilight

Copyright © 2006 by Working Partners Limited

Series created by Working Partners Limited

Map art © 2015 by Dave Stevenson

Interior art © 2015 by Owen Richardson

www.harpercollinschildrens.com

Library of Congress Cataloging-in-Publication Data

Hunter, Erin.

Twilight / Erin Hunter.— 1st ed.

p.   cm. — (Warriors, the new prophecy ; #5)

Summary: After the warrior cat Clans settle into their new homes, the harmony they once had disappears as the Clans start fighting each other, until the day their common enemy—the badger—invades their territory.

ISBN 978-0-06-236706-8 (pbk.)

[1. Cats—Fiction. 2. Badgers—Fiction. 3. Fantasy.] I. Title.
II. Series.

PZ7.H916625Tw 2006   2006000447

[Fic]—dc22   CIP

                                                          AC

Typography by Karin Paprocki

16 17 18 19   CG/OPM   10 9 8 7 6 5

❖

Revised paperback edition, 2015

Special thanks to Cherith Baldry

ALLEGIANCES

THUNDERCLAN

LEADER
: **FIRESTAR**—ginger tom with a flame-colored pelt

DEPUTY
: **GRAYSTRIPE**—long-haired gray tom

MEDICINE CAT
: **CINDERPELT**—dark gray she-cat
  APPRENTICE, LEAFPOOL

WARRIORS
: (toms and she-cats without kits)

  DUSTPELT—dark brown tabby tom

  SANDSTORM—pale ginger she-cat

  CLOUDTAIL—long-haired white tom

  BRACKENFUR—golden brown tabby tom
  APPRENTICE, WHITEPAW

  THORNCLAW—golden brown tabby tom

  BRIGHTHEART—white she-cat with ginger patches

  BRAMBLECLAW—dark brown tabby tom with amber eyes

  ASHFUR—pale gray (with darker flecks) tom, dark blue eyes

  RAINWHISKER—dark gray tom with blue eyes

  SOOTFUR—lighter gray tom with amber eyes

  SORRELTAIL—tortoiseshell and white she-cat with amber eyes

  SQUIRRELFLIGHT—dark ginger she-cat with green eyes

  SPIDERLEG—long-limbed black tom with brown underbelly and amber eyes

APPRENTICES (more than six moons old, in training to become warriors)

LEAFPOOL—light brown tabby she-cat with amber eyes

WHITEPAW—white she-cat with green eyes

QUEENS (she-cats expecting or nursing kits)

FERNCLOUD—pale gray (with darker flecks) she-cat, green eyes, mother of Dustpelt's kits

ELDERS (former warriors and queens, now retired)

GOLDENFLOWER—pale ginger she-cat

LONGTAIL—pale tabby tom with black stripes, retired early due to failing sight

MOUSEFUR—small dusky brown she-cat

SHADOWCLAN

LEADER **BLACKSTAR**—large white tom with huge jet-black paws

DEPUTY **RUSSETFUR**—dark ginger she-cat

MEDICINE CAT **LITTLECLOUD**—very small tabby tom

WARRIORS (toms and she-cats without kits)

OAKFUR—small brown tom
APPRENTICE, SMOKEPAW

CEDARHEART—dark gray tom

ROWANCLAW—ginger tom
APPRENTICE, TALONPAW

TAWNYPELT—tortoiseshell she-cat with green eyes

QUEENS (she-cats expecting or nursing kits)

TALLPOPPY—long-legged light brown tabby she-cat

ELDERS (former warriors and queens, now retired)

BOULDER—skinny gray tom

WINDCLAN

LEADER **ONESTAR**—brown tabby tom

DEPUTY **ASHFOOT**—gray she-cat

MEDICINE CAT **BARKFACE**—short-tailed brown tom

WARRIORS (toms and she-cats without kits)

TORNEAR—tabby tom

WEBFOOT—dark gray tabby tom

CROWFEATHER—dark gray tom

OWLWHISKER—light brown tabby tom

NIGHTCLOUD—black she-cat

WEASELFUR—ginger tom with white paws

QUEENS (she-cats expecting or nursing kits)

WHITETAIL—small white she-cat

ELDERS (former warriors and queens, now retired)

MORNINGFLOWER—tortoiseshell she-cat

RUSHTAIL—light brown tom

RIVERCLAN

LEADER **LEOPARDSTAR**—unusually spotted golden tabby she-cat

DEPUTY **MISTYFOOT**—gray she-cat with blue eyes

MEDICINE CAT **MOTHWING**—dappled golden she-cat

WARRIORS (toms and she-cats without kits)

BLACKCLAW—smoky black tom
APPRENTICE, BEECHPAW

HAWKFROST—dark brown tabby tom with a white underbelly and ice-blue eyes

VOLETOOTH—small brown tabby tom

SWALLOWTAIL—dark tabby she-cat

STONESTREAM—gray tom

REEDWHISKER—black tom
APPRENTICE, RIPPLEPAW

QUEENS (she-cats expecting or nursing kits)

MOSSPELT—tortoiseshell she-cat with blue eyes

DAWNFLOWER—pale gray she-cat

ELDERS (former warriors and queens, now retired)

HEAVYSTEP—thickset tabby tom

IVYTAIL—brown tabby she-cat

THE TRIBE OF RUSHING WATER

BROOK WHERE SMALL FISH SWIM (BROOK)—brown tabby she-cat

STORMFUR—dark gray tom with amber eyes

OTHER ANIMALS

SMOKY—muscular gray and white tom who lives in a barn at the horseplace

DAISY—she-cat with long creamy-brown fur who lives at the horseplace

FLOSS—small gray and white she-cat who lives at the horseplace

PIP—black and white terrier who lives with Twolegs near the horseplace

MIDNIGHT—a star-gazing badger who lives by the sea

THE NEW PROPHECY

WARRIORS

TWILIGHT

CAT VIEW

TWOLEG NEST

GREENLEAF TWOLEGPLACE

TWOLEG PATH

TWOLEG PATH

CLEARING

SHADOWCLAN CAMP

SMALL THUNDERPATH

HALFBRIDGE

GREENLEAF TWOLEGPLACE

HALFBRIDGE

ISLAND

STREAM

RIVERCLAN CAMP

HORSEPLACE

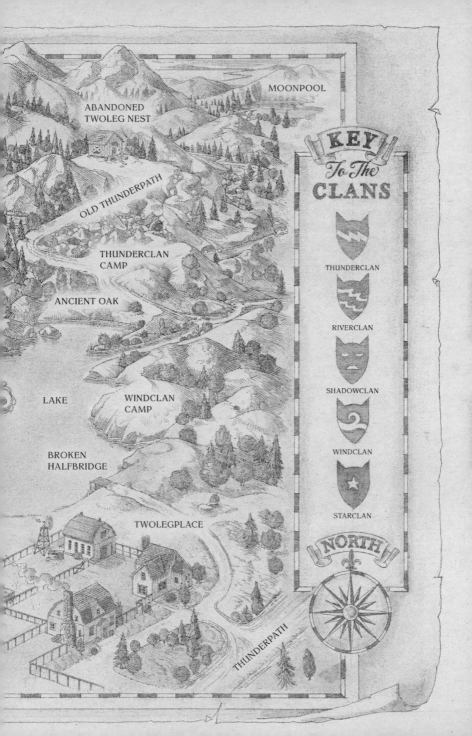

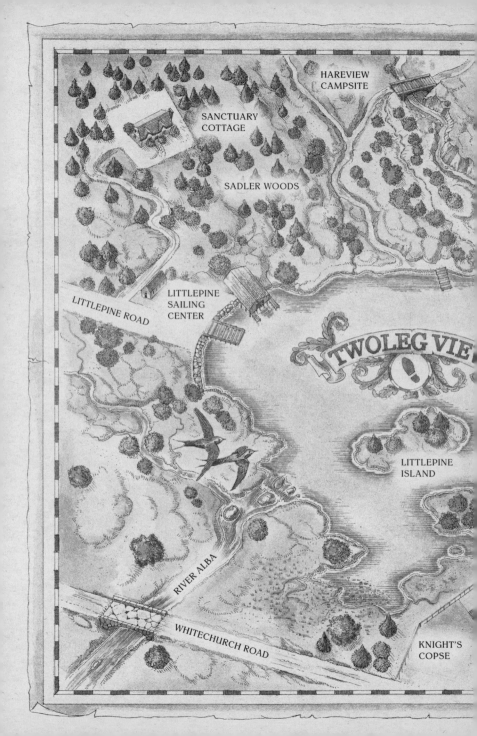

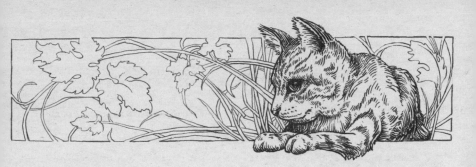

PROLOGUE

"No! There must be some mistake!" The cat looked up from where it crouched by the water's edge, its fur glowing in the moonlight. "There is still so much I have to do!"

A broad-faced cat with blue-gray fur padded around the pool, her eyes soft with sympathy. "I'm sorry," she meowed. "I know you expected many more moons with your Clanmates before coming to join us."

The crouching cat looked down into the water. The moon's reflection trembled like a floating leaf, and the surface of the pool glimmered with starlight cast by the countless shining shapes that lined the hollow. For a moment the only sound was the waterfall that splashed down the steepest part of the rocks. The cats of StarClan waited in watchful silence, as if each one shared the grief of the cat at the water's edge.

"You have served your Clan more faithfully than some cats manage in a long lifetime," the blue-furred cat went on. "It must seem very unfair that you should have to leave them."

The crouching cat raised luminous eyes to face the starry warrior. "Bluestar, I know this isn't your fault. There's no need to apologize."

Bluestar twitched her tail. "Of course there is. You should know how much your Clan owes to you."

"*All* the Clans." A black and white tom with a long tail rose to his paws and padded around the edge of the pool to stand beside Bluestar. "StarClan too. None of us would have found our new home without your help." He dipped his head in a gesture of respect, and the starlight on the surface of the pool wavered.

The cat blinked at him. "Thank you, Tallstar. I've made mistakes, but I have always tried to do what I believed to be right."

"StarClan asks no more from its warriors." A lean, black tomcat began to pick his way over the moss-covered rocks. "If we could change your fate, we would."

"But remember," Bluestar warned, "not even StarClan can turn aside the paws of destiny, however much we might want to."

The cat at the water's edge nodded. "I understand. And I will try to have courage. Can you tell me when—"

Bluestar shook her head. "No. Even we cannot see the future so clearly. But when the time comes, you will know, and we will be waiting for you."

A fourth warrior spirit rose from his place farther up the slope and padded down between the shimmering ranks of StarClan. He was a light-colored tabby with a twisted jaw. "Whenever the Clans tell stories of the great journey, your name will be honored," he promised.

"Thank you, Crookedstar," the cat meowed.

All four of the shining warriors gathered around, four who had been Clan leaders when their paws walked the earth.

"Know that the strength of StarClan will be with you," Bluestar meowed. "We will not leave you to face this alone."

The cat looked up to meet the intense blue gaze. "StarClan has always been with me."

"You say that, even though your life has been so hard?" Tallstar's voice was surprised.

"Of course." The cat's eyes glimmered in the starlight. "I have made good friends in all the Clans. I've seen kits born and watched elders leave on their final journey to Silverpelt. I've made the long journey to the Clans' new home. Believe me, I wouldn't change a single day." The cat paused and looked down into the pool again. "I know it is not in your power to give me longer with my Clan. But I can't help wanting more."

Bluestar's eyes narrowed. "It hurts us all when a young cat is called to join StarClan. I know you would continue serving your Clan loyally for many seasons more." Her voice rasped with pain, and the cat looked up at her, stretching out one paw in a comforting gesture.

"Don't grieve, Bluestar. I know my Clan will be well cared for after I am gone."

A murmur of respect rose up from around the hollow. Bluestar bent her head over the crouching cat, bathing the moon-bright fur with her scent. "We are with you always," she mewed.

In turn, each of the others bent over and added their scent, filling the air with the tang of stars and ice and the night wind. More warriors followed—a graceful tortoiseshell, a sturdy bracken-colored tom, a tabby she-cat with a silver-striped pelt—wreathing the cat with the strength and courage of StarClan.

Their voices swelled to a low keening of sorrow that drifted up to the stars. The shimmering forms began to fade one by one, until the hollow was empty.

And the stars shone down on a single cat who crouched unmoving beside the pool.

CHAPTER 1

"Let all cats old enough to catch their own prey join here beneath the Highledge for a Clan meeting."

Squirrelflight woke with a start as the ThunderClan leader's yowl rang out across the stone hollow. Cloudtail was already pushing his way out through the thorny branches that screened the warriors' den. His mate, Brightheart, uncurled herself from their mossy nest and followed him.

"What does Firestar want now?" Dustpelt muttered, pulling himself stiffly to his paws and shaking scraps of moss from his fur. With an irritated flick of his ears, he thrust his way into the open after his Clanmates.

Stretching her jaws in a yawn, Squirrelflight sat up and gave herself a quick grooming. Dustpelt's temper was even shorter than usual this morning; Squirrelflight could see from his awkward movements that the wound he'd received in the battle against Mudclaw was still painful. Most of the ThunderClan cats still bore the rebels' claw marks; Squirrelflight's side stung from a wound of her own, and she drew her tongue over it in rapid, soothing strokes.

Mudclaw had been deputy of WindClan until the Clans

arrived in their new territory around the lake. The previous leader, Tallstar, had appointed Onewhisker to succeed him instead just moments before he died; furious, Mudclaw had led a rebellion against Onewhisker before he had the chance to receive his nine lives from StarClan. And Hawkfrost of RiverClan had helped him. Squirrelflight felt a surge of anger as she remembered how Brambleclaw still insisted on trusting his half brother, even after he had seen that Hawkfrost was up to his ears in Mudclaw's treachery.

Thank StarClan, Squirrelflight thought, *that ThunderClan discovered the plot in time, and joined the battle against Mudclaw and his supporters.* StarClan had proved who the true leader was when lightning struck a tree that fell on Mudclaw and killed him.

Giving a last lick to her dark ginger fur, Squirrelflight slid through the branches and padded into the clearing, shivering in the cold air. The pale sun of leaf-bare was just showing above the trees around the stone hollow where ThunderClan had settled at the end of their long journey. Wind rattled in the bare branches, but down here all was still. The air smelled crisp, and frost still edged the grass and bushes with white. Yet Squirrelflight could pick up a faint hint of growing things that told her newleaf could not be far away.

Digging her claws into the earth, she stretched luxuriously. Her father, Firestar, was seated on the Highledge outside his den, about halfway up the cliff. His flame-colored pelt gleamed in the slanting rays of sun, and his green eyes shone proudly as his gaze swept across his Clan. Squirrelflight guessed he wouldn't look so confident if he needed to warn them about more trouble.

The cats gathered in the clearing below him. Mousefur and Goldenflower emerged one after the other from the elders' den; Goldenflower was guiding blind Longtail behind her, the tip of her tail resting on his shoulder.

"Hi." Squirrelflight's sister Leafpool padded up and touched noses with her. "How are those scratches? Do you want some more marigold?"

"No, I'll be fine, thanks." Leafpool and her mentor, Cinderpelt, the ThunderClan medicine cat, had been busy ever since the battle, finding the right herbs and treating the cats' wounds. "There are plenty of cats who need it more than I do," Squirrelflight added.

Leafpool sniffed Squirrelflight's scratches and gave a nod of satisfaction. "You're right. They're healing well."

An excited squeal came from the nursery as Birchkit pelted out, tumbled over his own paws, and picked himself up in a scramble of light brown fur to take a place beside his father, Dustpelt. His mother, Ferncloud, padded after him and sat next to him, turning her head to smooth his ruffled fur.

Squirrelflight let out a *mrrow* of amusement. Her gaze drifted past them to the tunnel through the thorn barrier at the entrance to the camp. She felt the muscles in her shoulders tense. It looked like the dawn patrol had just returned: Brambleclaw was padding out of the tunnel, followed by Sandstorm and Rainwhisker.

"What's the matter?" Leafpool asked.

Squirrelflight suppressed a sigh. She and her sister were

much closer than most littermates, and each one was always aware of what the other was feeling. "It's Brambleclaw," she mewed reluctantly. "I can't believe he's still friends with Hawkfrost, after the way he supported Mudclaw."

"Many cats supported Mudclaw," Leafpool pointed out. "They did it because they truly believed Onewhisker wasn't the right cat to lead WindClan. After the tree fell, Hawkfrost admitted he was wrong, and that Mudclaw had tricked him into helping. Onewhisker has already forgiven him, and all the other cats who fought against him."

Squirrelflight lashed her tail. "Hawkfrost *lied*! He was part of Mudclaw's plot all along. I heard what Mudclaw said before he died—Hawkfrost was trying to become powerful enough to take over RiverClan."

Leafpool's troubled gaze seemed to pierce Squirrelflight's fur. "You have no proof of that, Squirrelflight. Why should we believe Mudclaw over Hawkfrost? Are you sure you're not judging Hawkfrost because of who his father was?"

Squirrelflight opened her jaws for a swift retort, but there was nothing she could say.

"Remember, Tigerstar was Brambleclaw's father too," Leafpool went on. "He may have been a murderous traitor, but that doesn't mean his sons have to follow his pawsteps. I don't trust Hawkfrost any more than you do, but we can't assume he's as evil as his father without proof. And even if Hawkfrost is dangerous, it doesn't mean that Brambleclaw has to be like him—or like Tigerstar."

Squirrelflight twitched her tail uneasily. "I guess you're

right." The three tabby toms were tangled together like the tendrils in a bramble thicket, and she wondered if either of Tigerstar's sons could ever be free of their father's treacherous legacy. "It's just—Brambleclaw won't listen to a word I say! He cares about Hawkfrost far more than he cares about me. I don't understand why he would take Hawkfrost's word over mine."

"Hawkfrost *is* his brother," Leafpool reminded her. Her amber gaze was warm and sympathetic. "Don't you think you should judge Brambleclaw by what he does now, instead of what his father did—or what you're afraid he might do in the future?"

"Do you think I'm being unfair?" Squirrelflight asked. On the journey to the sun-drown-place, where StarClan sent them to learn about the danger threatening all the Clans, she had trusted Brambleclaw with her life. Since she had witnessed his growing friendship with his half brother, Hawkfrost, she had felt her trust melt away like dew.

"I think you're upsetting yourself for no reason," Leafpool replied.

"I'm not upset." Squirrelflight couldn't bear to admit, even to her sister, the ache inside her when she thought of what she had lost. "I'm worried about the Clan, that's all. If Brambleclaw wants to go off with Hawkfrost, it's none of my concern," she growled.

Leafpool rested the tip of her tail on her sister's shoulder. "Don't pretend that you don't care," she meowed. "Especially not to me." Her voice was light, but her eyes were still serious.

"Hi, Squirrelflight!" Ashfur joined them before Squirrelflight could reply. The gray tomcat gestured to her with his tail. "Come sit by me."

Squirrelflight padded to his side, noticing that his dark blue eyes gleamed as she joined him. Leafpool followed and gave her ear a quick lick. "Try not to worry," she murmured. "Everything will be all right." She gave Ashfur a friendly nod before padding over to sit with Cinderpelt beneath the Highledge.

Out of the corner of her eye, Squirrelflight saw Brambleclaw take a few steps toward her. The uncertain look in his eyes darkened when she settled down next to Ashfur, and he veered abruptly away to sit beside Brackenfur and Sorreltail. Squirrelflight's fur tingled; she couldn't tell if it was from relief or disappointment. As Firestar began to speak, she stared straight ahead, feeling Brambleclaw's amber gaze burning into her fur.

"Cats of ThunderClan, three sunrises have passed since the battle with Mudclaw," he meowed. "Two dead warriors still lie outside our camp. Now that we have rested, they must be returned to ShadowClan."

A shiver passed through Squirrelflight's pelt. She had discovered the stone hollow by falling into it when she and four other cats had first explored the forest; it was pure luck that the part of the cliff where she had slipped over had been too low for the fall to hurt her. But during the battle, two fleeing ShadowClan cats had hurtled over the precipice at its highest point and broken their necks in the clearing below.

"Do you think ShadowClan will want them?" Cloudtail meowed. "They were helping that traitor, Mudclaw, after all."

"It's not for us to decide another Clan's loyalty to its warriors," Firestar warned. "Mudclaw was no ordinary traitor. Even cats from other Clans believed he was the true leader of WindClan."

Cloudtail twitched the tip of his tail, clearly dissatisfied, though Squirrelflight saw Brambleclaw nod as if he were thinking of Hawkfrost.

"The dead cats were ShadowClan's warriors," Firestar went on, "and their own Clanmates will want to honor them on their journey to StarClan. A patrol must take the bodies to the ShadowClan border."

"I'll go," Thornclaw offered.

"Thank you." Firestar dipped his head. "Brackenfur, will you go as well, and . . ."

He hesitated, his gaze traveling thoughtfully over his senior warriors. Squirrelflight realized this mission could be dangerous. Though only a few ShadowClan cats had been involved in the battle, their leader, Blackstar, might blame ThunderClan for the deaths of his warriors and use it as an excuse to attack.

"Dustpelt and Cloudtail," Firestar decided. "Take the bodies to the border by the dead tree, then find a ShadowClan patrol and tell them what happened. But *don't* look for trouble." His gaze rested on Cloudtail for a moment, as if he were afraid the headstrong white warrior might say the wrong thing. "If ShadowClan seems hostile, get out of there fast."

Thornclaw rose to his paws and beckoned the rest of the patrol with a sweep of his tail. Together they headed for the thorn tunnel. The bodies of the ShadowClan warriors lay just outside, hidden in a dense patch of brambles where they had been protected from foxes and other carrion eaters.

Firestar waited until the branches had stopped rustling behind the patrol before going on. "Last night Onewhisker should have traveled to the Moonpool to receive his nine lives and his name. But his leadership won't be secure unless he is accepted by every one of his Clanmates. I'm going to lead a patrol to WindClan to check."

"Surely that's WindClan's problem!" Mousefur protested. "ThunderClan warriors have already had their fur ripped off once helping Onewhisker. Haven't we done enough?"

Squirrelflight, though she felt a twinge in her wounded side, couldn't agree. "But if we risked our lives for Onewhisker," she argued, "why not make certain it was worth the effort?"

Mousefur shot a glare at her, but Firestar waved his tail to stop the quarrel before it went any further.

Cinderpelt rose to her paws. "Whoever leads this patrol, it won't be you, Firestar. You wrenched your shoulder in the battle, and you need to stay in the camp until it's healed."

Firestar's neck fur bristled; then he relaxed and dipped his head to the medicine cat. "Very well, Cinderpelt."

"I'll lead the patrol." That was Brambleclaw, springing to his paws.

"Thanks, Brambleclaw," mewed Firestar. "You'd better not go onto WindClan territory, though. We must show that we respect their boundaries. Take the patrol along the border, and see if you can spot any of their cats."

Brambleclaw nodded. "Don't worry, Firestar. I'll make sure no cat sets a paw over the border."

Spiderleg, sitting on Ashfur's other side from Squirrelflight, snorted. "Bossy furball," he muttered. "Who does he think he is? Clan deputy?"

"Brambleclaw is a good warrior," Ashfur mewed. "There's nothing wrong with wanting to be deputy."

"Except that ThunderClan already *has* a deputy," Spiderleg pointed out.

"But Graystripe isn't here," Ashfur replied. "And sooner or later Firestar is going to have to decide how long he's prepared to wait for him."

A sharp thorn of grief stabbed Squirrelflight. Twolegs had captured the ThunderClan deputy just before the Clan fled their old forest home; Squirrelflight still remembered the shock of watching Graystripe being carried away inside the growling, mud-spattered Twoleg monster. No cat knew what had happened to him, yet Firestar refused to believe he was dead, or to appoint another deputy in his place.

Does Brambleclaw really want to be deputy? Squirrelflight wondered. She couldn't help thinking *just like Tigerstar,* and remembering how far the murderous tabby had been prepared to go to achieve his ambition.

Firestar called her name, dragging her back to the hollow. "Squirrelflight, you can go with Brambleclaw to WindClan. You too, Ashfur and Rainwhisker."

Squirrelflight pricked her ears; a run through the woods would blast away these troubling memories. Ashfur was on his paws already, his tail bolt upright.

"Let's go!" Squirrelflight meowed, bouncing over to Brambleclaw.

"Not yet," Brambleclaw replied crushingly, his gaze sweeping over her and Ashfur as if he hardly knew them. "I want to hear the rest of the meeting."

Glaring at him, Squirrelflight sat down again.

"We need hunting patrols too," meowed Firestar. "Sandstorm, can you organize those?"

"Of course." Sandstorm looked up from where she sat at the bottom of the cliff. "But there's one thing I want to say before we end the meeting." She paused, and Firestar gestured with his tail for her to continue. "ThunderClan has only one apprentice now. It's hard to get all the duties done."

Sorreltail's brother, Sootfur, twitched his tail. "Yes, I'm fed up with fetching moss for bedding. It's not a proper warrior's job," he complained. He hadn't been a warrior for long, and obviously had hoped he'd finished with apprentice duties forever once Firestar had given him his new name.

"That's too bad." Firestar's voice was firm as he stared at the young warrior. "You can't expect one apprentice to do it all."

"Whitepaw works her paws off," put in Mousefur. "She deserves a bit of help."

Whitepaw, the only remaining apprentice, ducked her head and scuffled her forepaws. Squirrelflight could see she hadn't expected praise from the wiry brown elder, whose tongue was as sharp as her claws.

"I'll help!" Birchkit bounced up excitedly. "I'm old enough to be an apprentice!"

"No, you're not," his mother, Ferncloud, told him gently. "Not for another moon."

"I'm afraid your mother's right, Birchkit," meowed Firestar. "But don't worry, your time will come. And there'll still be plenty for you to do. Sandstorm, will you sort out the duties in the meantime so no cat does more than their fair share?"

The ginger she-cat dipped her head in agreement. "I will, and I'll make sure Whitepaw has enough time to train with her mentor as well. That's another thing," she added. "With no apprentices to train, we aren't practicing our warrior skills as much as we used to. If there's another battle, we could have problems."

"There's not going to be another battle," Spiderleg meowed. "Mudclaw is dead, so where's the threat?"

"Yeah, we've got enough to do," Sootfur muttered.

"And Mudclaw is the only cat who ever caused trouble?" Mousefur asked scathingly, with a contemptuous twitch of her whiskers. "When you've lived as long as I have, you'll know there's *always* some kind of threat."

"Exactly, Mousefur," Firestar mewed. "The four Clans are drawing apart again, and sooner or later we'll find that we have no choice but to fight. We need one cat to be responsible for keeping up our battle skills."

Ashfur opened his jaws to volunteer, but before he could

speak Brambleclaw cut in. "I can do that, Firestar."

Squirrelflight's fur prickled. The Clan deputy would normally do this kind of job; it looked as if Brambleclaw really was trying to take Graystripe's place.

"Starting tomorrow, I can spar with two or three cats every morning," the tabby warrior went on. "Ashfur, I'll start with you and Spiderleg."

Ashfur's blue eyes narrowed. "Claws sheathed?"

Brambleclaw's gaze met his. "Claws sheathed, but that's all. We're not kits play fighting."

"Ashfur never said we were!" Squirrelflight sprang up, her fur bristling along her spine. "*I'll* fight with you, and see if you think I'm playing!"

Brambleclaw blinked at her. "I'm sure Ashfur doesn't need you to fight his battles, Squirrelflight. Why not let him speak for himself?"

Squirrelflight ignored Ashfur's tail, laid warningly on her shoulder. She was too furious to remember she was in the middle of a Clan meeting. "You think you're so great, Brambleclaw—"

"That's enough!" Firestar lashed his tail. His green gaze scorched Squirrelflight's fur; ashamed, she sat down again.

"Told you he's a bossy furball," Spiderleg whispered in her ear.

"Thank you, Brambleclaw," Firestar meowed. "Make sure every cat has a chance to practice as soon as possible." His gaze traveled over the cats below him as if he were taking in every claw mark and patch of missing fur, assessing how soon they'd be battle-fit again.

Brightheart stood up. "There's a sheltered clearing not far from here." The ginger and white she-cat pointed with her tail. "I was hunting there yesterday. The ground is flat and mossy, and it could be a good place to train, like the sandy hollow back in the forest."

"Sounds ideal," meowed Firestar. "Show me after the meeting. Brambleclaw, don't forget to report to me as soon as you get back from WindClan."

The tabby warrior gave a brisk nod. He turned to Squirrelflight. "We can go now, if you're ready."

Squirrelflight sprang up, her eyes narrowing. "Don't tread on my tail, Brambleclaw."

"Then start behaving like a warrior, not a mouse-brained apprentice. Unless you think Firestar should have chosen another cat to lead this patrol?"

His voice was as cold as his eyes. Squirrelflight felt a sting of dislike run through her fur. This was not the same cat who had traveled with her and the others to the sun-drown-place. He had been her closest friend on that journey, the cat who meant more to her than any of the others, and now she scarcely recognized him.

"Firestar can choose whichever cat he likes," she replied, spitting each word out like grit. "You are one of his senior warriors, after all."

"But that's not what you really think," Brambleclaw flashed back at her. His amber eyes blazed and his ears were flattened in fury. "You think I'm disloyal, because I have kin in another Clan. I saw you watching me when I was with

Hawkfrost by the lake."

"It's a good thing I did," Squirrelflight retorted. "Otherwise no cat would know that Hawkfrost was plotting to become WindClan deputy and then take over RiverClan. I heard what Mudclaw said."

"Mudclaw was lying!" Brambleclaw hissed, his neck fur bristling with fury. "Why should we believe that traitor?"

"Why should we believe Hawkfrost?" Squirrelflight clawed the ground in frustration.

"Why shouldn't we?" Brambleclaw countered. "Because Tigerstar was his father? Like he was my father too?"

"That's not fair," Ashfur protested, coming to stand at Squirrelflight's shoulder. "Squirrelflight didn't say—"

"Keep out of this!" Brambleclaw rounded on the gray tomcat, tail lashing. "It's got nothing to do with you!"

Squirrelflight's claws slid out; she was within a heartbeat of slashing at Brambleclaw's muzzle. Then she saw Firestar heading out of the camp with Brightheart, and she thought how angry her father would be if his warriors started fighting among themselves. She dug her claws deep into the peaty soil instead. "I don't care who his father was!" she hissed. "I don't trust Hawkfrost because he plotted to kill Onewhisker. He'll do anything for power. A blind hedgehog could see it."

Brambleclaw glared at her for a heartbeat. "You say that, yet you don't have any proof. Hawkfrost is my brother. I'm not going to turn my back on him when he hasn't done anything wrong."

"Fine!" Squirrelflight exclaimed. "You're so besotted with him you wouldn't know the truth if it sat up and bit you. Why not join RiverClan too, if it makes you happier? You obviously don't care about ThunderClan—or me."

Brambleclaw was about to spit back a retort when Birch-kit lost his balance chasing his tail and stumbled between the tabby warrior's front paws. His eyes stretched wide as he noticed the two cats glaring at each other with bristling neck fur and twitching tails. "Sorry!" he squeaked and fled for the nursery.

Brambleclaw took a pace back, his lip curled. "Come on, we're wasting time. We won't reach WindClan before night-fall at this rate."

Without waiting to see if the rest of the patrol was following him, he whipped around and stalked toward the entrance, his tail high.

Squirrelflight exchanged a glance with Ashfur and saw concern and gentleness in his blue eyes. After Brambleclaw's hostility, it was like cool water on a hot day.

"Are you okay?" he asked.

"I'm *fine*," Squirrelflight insisted as she set off after Bramble-claw. She brushed past Rainwhisker, who was staring at her as if she'd sprouted rabbit ears. "Hurry up, or we'll never catch him."

Brambleclaw didn't wait for them, but plunged into the thorn tunnel without looking back. As he vanished among the trembling branches, Squirrelflight felt hollow inside; it was almost as if Brambleclaw was deliberately walking out of her life. Would they ever be friends again? She couldn't see how, after a fight like that.

She just had to accept that whatever they once had, the friendship that had lasted through their long journey was over.

CHAPTER 2

It was the first time Squirrelflight had left the camp since the battle with Mudclaw, and she found herself enjoying the feel of wind in her fur and the crackle of leaves underpaw. Here and there she glimpsed early signs of newleaf: a few pale snowdrops scattered under a tree, and a single early coltsfoot flower like a splash of sunlight against a mossy green trunk. Squirrelflight reminded herself to tell her sister, Leafpool, where it could be found. Coltsfoot was a good remedy for shortness of breath.

Once they were well away from camp, Brambleclaw stopped. "Why don't you two take the lead?" he suggested, nodding to Ashfur and Rainwhisker. "Let's see how well you know the territory."

"Sure," Rainwhisker agreed enthusiastically, picking up the pace.

But Ashfur gave the tabby warrior a hard stare before sliding through the bracken after Rainwhisker. Squirrelflight knew why.

"What did you say that for?" she mewed crossly to Brambleclaw when they were alone. "You're treating them as if they're your apprentices. Ashfur's older than you, don't forget."

"And I'm leading this patrol," Brambleclaw pointed out. "If you don't like my orders, you'd better go back."

Squirrelflight opened her mouth for a stinging reply, then closed it again. She didn't want to get dragged into yet another quarrel. Instead, she whisked past Brambleclaw and bounded around the edge of a clump of brambles, following the scent trail Rainwhisker and Ashfur had left.

Ashfur must have heard her brushing through the bracken; he waited for her to catch up and slowed his pace to pad next to her. "The buds on the trees are swelling," he remarked, flicking his tail toward the branches of an oak. "Not long now till newleaf."

"I can't wait," Squirrelflight mewed. "No more ice and snow, lots more prey."

"The Clan could do with some extra fresh-kill," Ashfur agreed. "Talking of fresh-kill, how about we hunt? Do you think Brambleclaw would mind?"

"I don't give a mousetail whether Brambleclaw minds or not," Squirrelflight hissed.

She opened her jaws to taste the air. At first she thought she caught a trace of badger, and wondered if she should mention it to Brambleclaw—badgers were trouble, especially if their territory overlapped with a Clan's. But he was the last cat in the forest she wanted to speak to right now, and she guessed he wouldn't listen to anything she had to say anyway.

She tasted the air again; the scent of squirrel flooded over her, and when she spotted the bushy-tailed creature stooped busily over a nut a few fox-lengths ahead, she pushed the badger to the back of her mind. Checking the direction of the wind, she dropped into a hunter's crouch and crept up on her prey. As she launched herself forward the squirrel leapt for a nearby tree trunk, but Squirrelflight sprang quickly. Her claws sank into its shoulder and she dispatched it with a swift bite to the neck.

A loud alarm call made her swing around to see a blackbird fluttering up from a clump of bracken while Ashfur watched it in frustration.

"Bad luck!" Squirrelflight called. "I probably startled it by going after the squirrel."

Ashfur shook his head. "No, I stepped on a twig."

"Never mind, you can come and share this." Squirrelflight waved her tail invitingly. "There's plenty."

As Ashfur joined her beside the fresh-kill, Brambleclaw appeared from the undergrowth. "What are you doing?" he growled. "We're on our way to see WindClan, or had you forgotten?"

Squirrelflight swallowed a mouthful of prey. "Come on, Brambleclaw—lighten up, for StarClan's sake. None of us have eaten this morning." Awkwardly, not sure how Brambleclaw would react if she tried to be friendly, she drew back from the squirrel. "You can have some if you want."

"No thanks." The tabby warrior's voice was curt. "Where's Rainwhisker?"

"He went on ahead," meowed Ashfur, with a wave of his tail.

Without another word, Brambleclaw strode off in the

direction the gray tom had indicated, shouldering through the long grass until his dark pelt was swallowed up by damp green fronds.

Squirrelflight let out a hiss of annoyance.

Ashfur flicked her ear lightly with the tip of his tail. "Don't let him get to you so easily."

"He doesn't," Squirrelflight muttered, trying to convince herself it was true. Once more she remembered how close she and Brambleclaw had been on their journeys, how they had relied on each other and come to need each other. *How did we get from there to here?* she wondered despairingly.

Glancing up at Ashfur, she saw that his eyes were dark with concern. She knew he wanted to be closer to her, more than just fellow warriors. It was tempting to tell him she felt the same way, but it was too soon for her to be sure her feelings were real. She needed to get over the quarrel with Brambleclaw first. *And in the meantime we have a job to do*, she reminded herself with a flash of impatience. *You're a warrior, not a moonstruck rabbit!*

She and Ashfur finished the squirrel in a few swift bites and set out again toward the WindClan border. Soon they overtook Brambleclaw and Rainwhisker. Brambleclaw had brought down a starling and was tearing into it hungrily, while Rainwhisker was gulping down a vole. He glanced up as his Clanmates appeared.

"I thought you'd got lost," he meowed.

Brambleclaw took his last mouthful of starling and rose to his paws. Without saying a word, he turned and stalked off.

Squirrelflight exchanged a glance with Ashfur, shrugged, and followed.

The trees were thinning out when Squirrelflight began to hear the chattering of water over stones. The patrol emerged at the top of a slope that led down to the stream bordering WindClan. Gusts of WindClan scent drifted across on the breeze, but there was no sign of any cats.

"We must have just missed a patrol," Ashfur meowed quietly. "Those scent marks are fresh."

That was a good sign, Squirrelflight thought. If WindClan was organized enough to be patrolling their boundaries, they must be on their way to recovering from Mudclaw's rebellion. Did that mean Onewhisker had been able to travel to the Moonpool to receive his nine lives and his leader's name from StarClan?

"Let's head for the stepping-stones," Brambleclaw suggested. "We might catch up to them."

He bounded down the slope and headed upstream with the rest of the patrol hard on his paws. The trees soon gave way to open moorland; Squirrelflight turned her head to look at the gray sweep of leafless branches below her. Beyond them, the lake reflected the pale blue sky, where the sun had nearly reached its peak.

The stream tumbled more steeply here, between banks fringed by sedge and reeds. Water foamed around stepping-stones that formed a path to the moorland on the other side, easy for a cat to leap, even when the stream was full.

Wind gusted into Squirrelflight's face, buffeting her fur

and making her eyes water. "I don't know how WindClan puts up with it," she grumbled to Ashfur. "There isn't a tree in sight!"

Ashfur let out a small *mrrow* of amusement. "They probably wonder how ThunderClan puts up with all those branches blocking out the sky."

"Ask me that when it rains," Squirrelflight muttered.

A flash of pale brown caught her eye: a rabbit fleeing over the crest of the hill. Squirrelflight's paws itched to dash after it, but it was well inside WindClan's territory. Heartbeats later a lean, gray-black cat appeared, racing after the rabbit with his belly brushing the turf. Blinking to clear her watering eyes, Squirrelflight recognized Crowfeather. Like Brambleclaw, he had been one of the cats chosen by StarClan to make the journey to the sun-drown-place.

Hunter and prey disappeared into a hollow and a high-pitched squeal, quickly cut off, told Squirrelflight that the WindClan warrior had made his kill.

"Hunting patrol," meowed Rainwhisker, nodding to the top of the hill.

Two more WindClan cats followed Crowfeather more slowly over the crest. Squirrelflight made out the dark gray tabby pelt of Webfoot; the smaller cat behind him was his apprentice, Weaselpaw. A third cat, Whitetail, joined them as they stood looking down at the ThunderClan patrol.

Brambleclaw called out, "We've brought a message from Firestar!"

Webfoot and Whitetail exchanged a glance, then Webfoot led the way down the slope until all three cats stood on the opposite side of the stream.

"What message?" Webfoot demanded.

Squirrelflight studied the WindClan warrior. He had been one of Mudclaw's fiercest supporters, and he still showed marks of the battle in a torn ear and a patch of fur missing from one shoulder. But Onewhisker must have decided to trust him again, if he had been put in charge of this patrol.

Brambleclaw dipped his head in greeting. "Firestar sent us to make sure everything's okay," he mewed. "He asked us to check that Onewhisker had made his journey to the Moonpool."

"One*star*," Whitetail corrected him.

Squirrelflight's belly lurched. Calling the Clan leader by his ordinary warrior name had been a really bad mistake, as if Brambleclaw didn't expect him to have received his new name from StarClan.

"Sorry—Onestar." Brambleclaw twitched one ear, but his voice remained steady. "That's good news. Congratulate him for us, will you?"

Webfoot's eyes narrowed. "Why did Firestar send you? Does he think StarClan wouldn't give nine lives to Onestar?"

Squirrelflight's eyes stretched wide. Had Webfoot forgotten that Onestar might have been crow-food by now if it wasn't for Firestar and ThunderClan?

Brambleclaw blinked. "He just wanted to be sure."

"Perhaps Firestar should concentrate on ThunderClan, and let WindClan get on with their own lives," Webfoot suggested.

"Onestar wouldn't be leader if it wasn't for ThunderClan!" Squirrelflight pointed out hotly. "You know that as well as any cat, Webfoot. You and Mudclaw—" She broke off, choking on a mouthful of fur as Brambleclaw flicked his tail across her mouth.

Webfoot's eyes burned. "I wasn't the only cat to believe Mudclaw was our rightful leader," he snarled. "But since StarClan killed him with the falling tree, and gave Onestar his nine lives and his name, I know that I was wrong."

"If Onestar trusts *him* he's got bees in his brain." Squirrelflight dropped back to mutter in Ashfur's ear. "If I was Onestar, I'd watch my tail."

To her relief, she spotted Crowfeather appear over the rim of the hollow, dragging the rabbit's body. Even though the WindClan warrior was as prickly as a holly bush, he wouldn't be as cold and suspicious as Webfoot among his old friends.

"Hi, Crowfeather," she meowed. "Good catch!"

To her surprise, the dark gray warrior gave her a curt nod and glanced away without saying anything. He kept his jaws clamped on his fresh-kill, his nostrils flaring.

"If that's all," Webfoot meowed, "you can all go home."

"Don't tell us what to do on our own territory!" Squirrelflight snapped.

"Leave it," Brambleclaw warned in a low growl. Squirrelflight knew he was right—this was not the time to pick a fight, however hostile the WindClan cats were being.

Webfoot and the other WindClan warriors watched silently from their side of the stream as Brambleclaw turned and led his patrol back toward camp. Squirrelflight felt the WindClan cats' gaze pricking her pelt all the way down the hill, and when she glanced back at the edge of the trees, the four cats were still there. She bounded forward, not stopping until she had put a thick bramble thicket between herself and WindClan.

"Thank StarClan!" She skidded to a halt in a clearing and shook herself as if she had just climbed out of icy water. "I don't know what's got into them."

"Me neither," Rainwhisker agreed.

"I would have thought it was obvious," Brambleclaw meowed. "WindClan doesn't want to be allied with Thunder-Clan anymore. Everything's different now."

"After all we did for them!" Squirrelflight's frustration and anxiety spilled over into anger; she couldn't believe Brambleclaw was accepting WindClan's new hostility without question. "I was a whisker from clawing Webfoot's ears off back there."

"It's a good thing you didn't," Brambleclaw pointed out dryly. "There's more than one cat in ThunderClan who'd say that Firestar shouldn't interfere in another Clan's business."

"Mouse dung! Does that mean you think Firestar should have done nothing, and just let Mudclaw take over?" Squirrelflight sprang forward, but before she could reach Brambleclaw, Ashfur pushed his way between them.

"There's no need for this," he meowed. "WindClan probably wants to prove they're strong again, now that they have their new leader. Give them time. They'll calm down."

Squirrelflight suspected the gray tomcat was right, but that didn't mean she was willing to let Brambleclaw get away with insulting her father. She forced her neck fur to flatten again, but she still quivered with fury as they set off toward the ThunderClan camp.

"Firestar will always want to help Onestar." She addressed the back of Brambleclaw's head as he slipped through a patch of ferns ahead of her. "They've been friends forever."

"Maybe, but Onestar clearly doesn't need his help anymore," Brambleclaw mewed without looking back. The certainty in his tone infuriated Squirrelflight all over again. "It's natural for Clans to be rivals. We were right to help WindClan when they were in trouble, but we can't keep on looking out for them."

"Stupid furball!" Squirrelflight growled, not loud enough for Brambleclaw to hear her. She hated the way the Clans had separated like flowing water into their new territories; what had happened to their closeness during the journey from the forest, when every cat had tried to help each other without stopping to remember which Clan they belonged to? It felt much too soon to turn their backs on that and let hostility and Clan rivalry take over. How would they survive in this new and unfamiliar place if they couldn't rely on each other?

"And what will happen if ThunderClan needs WindClan's

help?" Rainwhisker meowed ominously, as if he had followed Squirrelflight's thoughts. "Have any of you thought of that?"

Brambleclaw led the patrol home by a different route, hunting on the way to take fresh-kill back for the Clan. Pausing underneath an oak tree, Squirrelflight once again picked up the scent of badger. It was stronger this time, and fresh; she guessed that it was not long since the creature had passed that way.

"Brambleclaw, do you smell that too?"

The tabby warrior padded up with a squirrel he had just caught. He put the fresh-kill down and swiped his tongue around his jaws before drawing in a stream of air. Alarm flared at once in his amber eyes. "Badger! Close by, too."

Squirrelflight's pelt prickled. A badger in their territory was the last thing any cat wanted. Hawkfrost had already driven one away from RiverClan, and it looked like Thunder-Clan had been lucky not to encounter one before now. "We'll have to do something," she mewed.

Brambleclaw nodded. A badger would make a tasty meal of a young kit if it had the chance. They were unlikely to prey on an adult cat, but that didn't mean full-grown warriors were safe if they met one. A badger would kill out of pure savagery, trampling its prey into the ground or clamping it in its jaws and never letting go until its victim was dead.

Squirrelflight reminded herself that not all badgers were like that. Her first journey from the forest had led her to Midnight, the wise badger who lived at the sun-drown-place.

Midnight had warned them that Twolegs would destroy the forest, and told them that the Clans would have to leave. But Midnight was unique; the rest of her kin could be bloodthirsty marauders if the mood took them.

"Is there a problem?" Ashfur came to join Squirrelflight and Brambleclaw; his words were indistinct because he carried a mouthful of mice, dangling from their tails.

Brambleclaw beckoned with his tail to Rainwhisker, who had just brought down a blackbird; the young warrior came trotting over with a satisfied look on his face and a feather on his nose.

"A badger—maybe more than one—has been here," Brambleclaw meowed. "We can't go back to camp without checking it out."

"You mean, follow the trail?" Rainwhisker mewed in alarm. "Are you sure?"

"We have to find out if it's left our territory. Squirrelflight, can you tell which way it went?"

Squirrelflight nosed at the scent the badger had left in the grass. "That way." She pointed with her tail.

Brambleclaw padded over to sniff the trail. "Keep quiet, all of you. I don't want them to know we're here until we see how many there are and decide what's best to do. We're lucky that the wind's in the right direction, so it won't carry our scent to them."

The cats left their prey among the roots of the oak tree, scratching earth over the pile until they could come and collect it later. Then with Brambleclaw in the lead, they set out after the badger.

The trail led them deeper into the forest, in the direction of the ShadowClan border. Here and there were freshly turned patches of earth, as if the badger had been digging for grubs. Squirrelflight felt a pang of concern for her friend Tawnypelt and the rest of ShadowClan; if they failed to track the badger down in their territory, some cat would need to warn Blackstar.

The scent grew steadily stronger, a powerful reek that swallowed up all other scents of the forest. Squirrelflight felt her fur stand up along her spine. It looked as if ShadowClan would be safe after all; the badger was still close by.

Suddenly Brambleclaw halted in the shadow of a boulder and held up his tail as a sign for the others to stay back. He clawed his way silently up the rough stone until he could poke his head above it and see to the other side.

Instantly he ducked down again. Squirrelflight crept forward until she could peer around the side of the boulder.

The ground on the other side was flat and pebbly, leading to a scattering of more smooth gray boulders. Between two of the rocks there was a gaping hole flanked by piles of freshly dug earth; Squirrelflight almost sneezed as a harsh scent reached her from the damp soil, a mingled reek of badger and fox. *The badger must be building a set in an old fox den*, she thought.

In front of the hole, three badger cubs scuffled about, making high-pitched fretful noises as if they didn't like having to trek through the forest in daylight. Squirrelflight stared, her neck fur rising in horror, then she slid back to join Ashfur and Rainwhisker in the shelter of the rock.

"There's a whole family of them!" she hissed. "Great StarClan, they'll be all over the territory in a couple of seasons!"

Ashfur looked puzzled. "It's unusual for a badger to move with cubs."

"Maybe they were forced out of their old home," Rainwhisker suggested.

Brambleclaw slid down from the top of the boulder and crouched beside them. "We can't do anything until we know how many adults there are," he meowed. "We'll stay here and keep watch. Don't do anything unless I say so, okay?"

All three cats nodded, though Squirrelflight seethed at the way Brambleclaw was ordering them about like wet-eared apprentices.

"Badgers mostly come out at night," Brambleclaw went on. "If they're in the set now, there's not much we can do. No cat is going in there." His amber gaze rested on Squirrelflight.

"I'm not stupid!" she hissed.

"I didn't say you were," Brambleclaw retorted. "But there are times when you do stupid things."

Ashfur took a breath as if he were going to leap to her defense, but she flicked her tail at him for silence. "Really, it's not worth it," she muttered.

"If we find there's just one full-grown badger with the cubs, we'll attack," Brambleclaw mewed. "We can't let them settle in our territory. Four of us should be able to cope with one badger. Hawkfrost managed to drive one off, after all. This could even be the same badger."

Squirrelflight's neck fur began to rise again at the mention of Brambleclaw's half brother. It was bad enough that Brambleclaw refused to admit that Hawkfrost was untrustworthy, without having him held up as a model of courage and fighting skill as well.

"We might drive it into ShadowClan territory," she pointed out.

"Then ShadowClan's warriors will have to deal with it." Brambleclaw's eyes were intense, and his voice cold. "We have to protect our own Clan first."

"And if there's more than one badger?" Ashfur wondered.

"Then we'll gather as much information as we can and report back to Firestar. Find somewhere to hide where you can see the mouth of the set."

Squirrelflight returned to her vantage point in the clump of fern. The badger cubs were still scuffling in front of the pile of earth. The sun climbed higher, and Squirrelflight would have dozed off if hunger hadn't gnawed at her belly. The squirrel she had shared with Ashfur seemed a long time ago, and she thought longingly of the heap of fresh-kill left under the oak tree.

Her jaws gaped in a yawn, and she clamped them shut again as an even stronger reek of badger flooded into her mouth. The undergrowth on the far side of the clearing rustled briefly before the ferns parted to reveal a powerful, broad-shouldered body and a long muzzle with a white stripe down the middle. The female badger lumbered into the clearing and her three cubs scampered up to her. She dropped a mouthful of beetles onto the ground and the cubs gulped them up with high-pitched cries of joy.

Brambleclaw sprang on top of the boulder and let out a challenging yowl. The female badger's head shot up and she roared in defiance, showing two rows of sharp yellow teeth.

Brambleclaw yowled again. "Attack!" He leapt from the boulder, landing among the cubs who scurried out of the way, yelping with fear. They huddled together in the mouth of the set, staring at the warrior with wide, scared eyes.

Ashfur hurtled out of his hiding place farther around the clearing, with Rainwhisker hard on his paws. Squirrelflight pelted forward to stand beside Brambleclaw. "Get out!" she hissed at the badgers, even though she knew they wouldn't understand what she was saying. "This is our territory!"

Brambleclaw lashed at the badger's muzzle with both fore-paws. She reared backward, swiping at him with massive claws, but Brambleclaw dodged the blow.

Squirrelflight ran forward until she was close enough to rake her claws down the badger's side; blood welled out of the claw marks and she shook her paw fiercely to dislodge the trapped black fur. She ducked to avoid the snapping jaws, then darted back just as Ashfur dashed in from the other side. The badger swung her head from side to side as if she couldn't decide which swift-moving target to attack first.

This is easy! Squirrelflight thought. *She's too slow and clumsy!*

She let out a screech of alarm as a massive white-furred paw slammed down less than a mouse-length away from her haunches. If it had landed on her it would have snapped her spine. Startled and shaking, she rolled out of range in a tangle of paws and tail. She wanted to run all the way back to the camp, but she knew they couldn't give up now. This ferocious creature could not be allowed to make a home in their territory, or no cat would be safe, from the youngest kits to the most battle-hardy warriors.

She scrambled to her feet in time to see Brambleclaw swipe his claws down the badger's shoulder. Leaping up, he tried to fasten his teeth in her throat, but the badger shook him off. He flew through the air, landed with a loud thump, and lay motionless.

Squirrelflight raced to his side, her belly churning in fear. But before she reached him, he shook his head as if he were coming out of deep water, then he staggered to his paws. "I'm okay," he rasped.

Squirrelflight veered away to meet the badger head-on. Rearing up on her hind legs, she clawed her enemy's nose while her other paw slashed for the tiny bright eyes. Ashfur battered at the creature's haunches, angling his body to make room for Brambleclaw, who was biting down on the badger's hind paw. Rainwhisker had his front paws hooked in the badger's rough pelt while his teeth clamped down on her ear.

The badger had had enough. Shaking off Brambleclaw and Rainwhisker, she let out a roar of fury and defeat and turned tail. Lumbering across to the mouth of the foxhole, she nudged her cubs to their paws and herded them in front of her as they fled the clearing.

"And don't come back!" Ashfur yowled.

The badger wouldn't understand his words, but the meaning was plain enough. All four cats stood shoulder to shoulder while the badger's roars and the high-pitched cries of the cubs faded away through the trees.

"Well fought, all of you," Brambleclaw panted. "Let's hope that's the last we see of them."

"And that there aren't any more," Ashfur commented.

Brambleclaw nodded. "We'll fill in the hole and keep watch to make sure they don't come back."

"What? Now?" Squirrelflight protested. "I'm worn out, and my belly's yowling!"

"No, not now. We'll go back to camp and get a couple of other warriors to deal with the set. The regular patrols can keep an eye on it after that."

"Thank StarClan!" Squirrelflight sighed. "Let's go and collect that fresh-kill."

The four cats limped back through the forest. Squirrelflight felt the sting of new wounds on top of her scratches from the battle against Mudclaw. "I won't have any fur left at this rate," she muttered.

Ashfur padded to her side and drew his tongue gently across a claw mark on her shoulder. "You fought well," he murmured.

"So did you." Squirrelflight could see how battered he was, with blood seeping from a patch on his hindquarters where the fur had been clawed off. She touched her nose to his ear. "I

bet that badger wishes she'd never set foot on our territory!"
she mewed.

She pictured the huge creature crashing through the
undergrowth with her cubs stumbling along behind. For a
few heartbeats she shared their fear, and a pang of sympathy
pierced her. She knew what it felt like to lose your home, and
have to travel far to find a new one.

I hope she finds somewhere safe for her cubs, Squirrelflight thought.
But a long, long way from ThunderClan.

CHAPTER 3

"Leafpool! Leafpool, what's the matter with you? That's the third time I've called your name."

The young medicine cat jumped. "Sorry, Cinderpelt."

The gray she-cat bent her head to sniff at the seeds Leafpool was wrapping in a leaf. "What have you got here?"

"Poppy seed."

Cinderpelt sighed. "No, it's not. It's nettle seed. Honestly, Leafpool, what's the matter with you today?"

Leafpool stared down at the leaf. Cinderpelt had asked her to take some poppy seed to Firestar to soothe the pain in his wrenched shoulder. She had no idea how she had taken the wrong herb from the store inside Cinderpelt's den, but the green, spiny seeds on the leaf in front of her were definitely nettle. They might have helped if Firestar had eaten something poisonous, but they wouldn't do anything to help his shoulder.

"I'm really sorry, Cinderpelt."

"I should think so. This morning I caught you trying to put yarrow on Mousefur's ticks instead of mouse bile." Cinderpelt's tone softened. "Is everything all right, Leafpool? Were you hurt when those ShadowClan warriors chased you?"

Leafpool shook her head. "No . . . no, I'm fine."

Her thoughts flew back to the night of the battle, when two ShadowClan warriors had chased her into the undergrowth at the top of the hollow, and plunged over the cliff to their deaths. Leafpool had almost fallen with them, her paws slipping on the rock as she tried to haul herself up. She could still feel the firm grasp on her scruff that had hauled her to safety, still see the intense gaze of her WindClan rescuer as he confessed that he loved her. *Crowfeather!* Every hair on her pelt tingled.

"Leafpool, you're doing it again!"

Shaking her head to clear it, Leafpool carried the leaf back into Cinderpelt's den. She returned the nettle seeds to the crack in the rock and took out some poppy seeds instead.

"If there is anything wrong, I wish you would talk to me about it," Cinderpelt meowed, watching her from the entrance. "We're busier than we've been since we arrived, dealing with wounds from the battle. I need you, Leafpool. You're more than an apprentice now—you should be able to carry out medicine cat duties on your own."

"I know. I'm sorry. But everything's fine, really."

Of course it was—it was better than fine, when Crowfeather loved her! Leafpool wrapped the correct seeds in the beech leaf and picked up the package to carry it to Firestar. She nodded to her mentor as she nudged her way through the curtain of brambles that led into the camp. Part of her wanted to confide in Cinderpelt more than anything, but Leafpool knew she could never reveal her feelings for Crowfeather to any cat. Medicine cats were not supposed to fall in love.

Cinderpelt had suspected a connection between Leafpool and the WindClan warrior before the Clans split up into their new territories. But that was before Crowfeather told Leafpool that he loved her, before Leafpool had admitted her own feelings to herself. Now it would be even harder to hide what she felt from the wise medicine cat.

She scrambled up the rocks that formed a tumbled pathway to the Highledge outside Firestar's den. Looking down into the clearing, she saw Dustpelt slipping into the nursery to visit Ferncloud and Birchkit; the patrol that had taken the bodies to ShadowClan must have returned peacefully.

Leafpool set her leaf packet down on the ledge outside the den. "Firestar!" she called.

"Come in!"

She slid through the narrow cleft for a couple of tail-lengths until it widened out into a cave, dimly lit by the light that shone through the opening. Firestar was stretched on a bed of fern and moss at the far end. Thornclaw sat beside him. Firestar nodded a greeting to Leafpool and turned back to the golden-brown tabby.

"So there was no trouble with ShadowClan?"

Thornclaw shook his head. "We met Russetfur leading a border patrol, and she fetched Blackstar. He *said* he knew nothing about his warriors supporting Mudclaw."

Firestar shrugged, wincing at a twinge of pain from his shoulder. "That could be true."

"Then his warriors took the bodies away to be buried," Thornclaw finished, "and we came home."

"Well done, Thornclaw. I don't want any trouble with ShadowClan." Firestar paused for a moment before adding, "We'd better be careful what we say at the next Gathering. No sense in trailing our tails for Blackstar to pounce on. Pass the word to the rest of the Clan, would you?"

"Sure, Firestar." Thornclaw rose to his paws and left with a farewell flick of his tail.

Leafpool padded across the cave and set down the leaf-wrapped poppy seeds. "Cinderpelt sent you these."

Firestar leaned over and licked up the seeds with one swipe of his tongue. "Thank you, Leafpool. This'll teach me not to take on two warriors at once!"

"You should sleep now," Leafpool meowed.

As she finished speaking, she heard the sound of cats gathering in the clearing below the ledge, and Squirrelflight's voice calling, "Firestar!"

The Clan leader glanced at Leafpool with a gleam of amusement in his eyes. "There goes my nap. Brambleclaw's patrol must be back from WindClan."

He rose to his paws and limped across the den. Leafpool followed him. Excitement rushed through her like a bubbling stream. She wanted to fling herself down the rocks and hurl questions at Squirrelflight. Had the patrol seen Crowfeather? What did he say? Had he been hurt in the battle? Had he mentioned her . . . ?

She stopped abruptly at the entrance to her father's den.

If she asked just one of these questions, Squirrelflight would want to know why she was so interested in the young Wind-Clan warrior. And even her sister wouldn't understand if she knew that Leafpool had broken the code of a medicine cat and fallen in love.

Brambleclaw and the rest of the patrol were waiting in the clearing, while more of the Clan cats gathered around them to hear their news. Leafpool jumped down the tumble of broken rocks and paused, feeling puzzled as she caught a powerful wave of feeling from her sister. Squirrelflight was in even more turmoil than she had been after the quarrel with Brambleclaw, making Leafpool's fur bristle with a whirl of agitation, fear, and sympathy.

Leafpool slid between Dustpelt and Mousefur until she reached Squirrelflight's side. "What's the matter?" she murmured in her sister's ear. "What happened?"

Squirrelflight's claws scraped furiously at the earth in front of her. "WindClan treated us like we were sworn enemies!" she hissed.

Leafpool turned to listen to Brambleclaw, who was reporting to Firestar.

"Webfoot looked as though he'd like to claw our fur off," the tabby warrior meowed. "You would never have thought we were the same cats who helped WindClan fight off Mud-claw a couple of nights ago."

"But did you find out about Onestar?" Firestar asked. "He *is* Onestar now, isn't he?"

"Oh, yes, he's got his nine lives all right, but his Clan doesn't seem to think we're allies anymore."

"I told you," Ashfur broke in. "They have to show us they're strong enough to stand on their own now."

Brambleclaw shook his head. "I think it was more than that."

"And you really can't imagine what the problem is?" Dustpelt meowed, coming forward to stand beside his Clan leader. "Come on, Brambleclaw. You're hardly likely to be the most popular cat in WindClan just now, not after Hawkfrost saved your life at the end of the battle. Onestar probably thinks you and Hawkfrost were working together all along."

"Mouse dung!" Brambleclaw snapped. "Onestar forgave all the cats who fought against him, including Hawkfrost. And every cat knows I fought for WindClan. Onestar can't have any quarrel with me."

Leafpool glanced at Squirrelflight; once her sister would have leapt to Brambleclaw's defense, but now she was just staring at him with narrowed eyes.

Firestar looked from Brambleclaw to Dustpelt and then back again. "I hope Ashfur's right," he mewed at last, "and this is just an example of WindClan trying to prove how strong they are. But I don't think we can trust Webfoot to report on what's happening in his Clan. I'll have to visit WindClan myself once my shoulder is better."

Leafpool exchanged a startled glance with her sister. "He should wait for the Gathering," she mewed quietly. "He could talk to Onestar there."

"You try telling him that," Squirrelflight murmured back.

Leafpool knew she couldn't. Firestar's friendship with Onestar went so far back that none of the Clan cats, even those who had grown up with Firestar, would dare tell him he couldn't visit his old friend. Leafpool heard Mousefur mutter, "Did you ever hear such a mouse-brained idea? A day-old kit could see that WindClan wants to be left alone."

Firestar was about to go back to his den when Brambleclaw stopped him. "Wait, we haven't told you about the badger yet."

"What badger?" Firestar turned back, his green eyes flashing with alarm. "On our territory?"

"Not anymore," Brambleclaw replied, and he described how the patrol had tracked the badger by its scent.

"It was digging out a set in an old foxhole," Rainwhisker added. "And there were *four* of them. Three cubs and their mother."

"The cubs were too small to fight," meowed Ashfur. "But the mother gave us enough trouble." He twisted around to lick a raw patch on his hindquarters.

Squirrelflight remained silent as Brambleclaw finished explaining how the badgers had been driven off. Leafpool picked up mingled feelings of fear, defensiveness, and pity. She could understand why. ThunderClan had been driven from their home too. *But this is our territory now*, she reminded herself. *We can't share it with badgers, especially not four of them.*

Firestar looked around at his Clan. "Dustpelt, take a patrol up there, please, and fill in the hole. Keep at least one of the warriors on watch in case the badger comes back."

Dustpelt beckoned to Rainwhisker, who would be able to

show him the way to the half-built set, and signaled Bright-heart and Cloudtail to follow.

Firestar watched them go. "Every patrol will have to watch out for badgers in the future," he warned. "This family could come back, or more of them might be trying to settle. If one badger is trying to find a new home, there could be others." Grimly he added, "We must make it clear they're not welcome here."

Moonlight glimmered on the rippling stream, and the warm scents of newleaf drifted across Leafpool's fur as she stood gazing into WindClan's territory. Suddenly a lean, dark shape raced down the bank—Crowfeather. He plunged into the stream with a glittering splash as moon-filled drops spun away from his paws. Water brushed his belly fur; then Crow-feather was pulling himself onto the bank beside Leafpool. His scent flooded over her.

"Crowfeather . . ." she murmured.

"What?"

Leafpool opened her eyes to see Cinderpelt poking her head out of her den. "Did you say something?" the medicine cat mewed.

Leafpool sprang out of her nest and gave herself a shake to dislodge scraps of moss from her pelt. "No, Cinderpelt." The last thing she wanted was to be asked what she had been dreaming about. "Do you need me to do something?"

"I've just been checking our stores of herbs," Cinderpelt meowed. "Some of them are getting very low, and—"

"I'll go and gather some," Leafpool offered. "It's almost newleaf, so there's bound to be something growing. Squirrelflight told me where she saw some coltsfoot."

"Good," mewed Cinderpelt. "We could do with some marigold or horsetail too. We used nearly every scrap after the battle. And anything else you see that would be useful."

"Right, Cinderpelt." Leafpool's paws itched to carry her out of the camp so she could be alone with her thoughts. Waving her tail in farewell, she headed across the clearing and through the thorn tunnel.

The sun had not yet cleared the tops of the trees, and clammy, dew-laden grass brushed Leafpool's belly fur, but she scarcely noticed the chill. Her paws tingled with excitement, and she ran faster until she was racing through the trees. The gurgle of water brought her to a halt. She realized her paws had brought her to the stream that marked the border with WindClan, close to the lake where trees grew in WindClan territory too. The place was hauntingly familiar. She had stood here in her dream, and Crowfeather had come to her.

The bank was silent and deserted, the trees casting long shadows over the water. Leafpool stood still, her gaze devouring the undergrowth on the far side of the stream. She half-hoped, half-dreaded what she might see. A WindClan patrol would be hostile if they found her so close to the border, but if Crowfeather appeared . . . But she had no business hoping to meet Crowfeather. She was a medicine cat, and medicine cats *could not* fall in love.

She tasted the air and picked up her own Clan's scent

markers, and those of WindClan from the opposite bank, but not the scent that threw her into such turmoil. A pang of disappointment burned through her, and she knew some part of her had expected him to be waiting for her.

"Stupid furball," she muttered. "It was only a dream."

She stiffened as she heard voices from farther downstream; a heartbeat later ThunderClan scent drifted around her. She didn't want to meet a patrol this far away from the camp. They would ask what she was doing, and she was too confused to explain properly. She glanced around. The only cover close by was a holly bush with branches that swept the ground; Leafpool squeezed under it just as the ThunderClan patrol came into sight.

Peering out between the prickly leaves, Leafpool saw that Brackenfur was leading the patrol. He padded past with Sootfur and Whitepaw behind him, then paused to ask his apprentice what she could scent. Leafpool froze.

"WindClan cats," Whitepaw replied after a moment. "And ThunderClan, of course, and I think a fox went by a while ago—probably yesterday. No sign of any badgers, though."

"Well done," meowed Brackenfur. "If you go on like this, you'll be a warrior in no time."

Whitepaw fluffed out her tail with pride as she followed her mentor and Sootfur upstream. Leafpool relaxed; the apprentice hadn't singled her out from the other Thunder-Clan scents. When the patrol had disappeared she began to wriggle out from her hiding place, only to be flooded by another, crashingly familiar scent.

"Leafpool, whatever are you doing under there?"

Leafpool scrambled the rest of the way out of the holly bush and turned around to meet the curious gaze of her friend Sorreltail. "Looking for berries," she mewed feebly.

"*Holly* berries?" Sorreltail's amber eyes stretched wide in surprise. "I thought they were poisonous."

"Yes, they are. I was . . . er . . . looking for different berries."

Sorreltail's tail curled up, but to Leafpool's relief she didn't ask any more questions. Her eyes were shining, even though she looked tired. "There's something I have to tell you, I think," she meowed.

Leafpool stared at her friend in horror. Had she guessed about Crowfeather? "There are good herbs around here," she began, struggling not to show her panic. She had to make Sorreltail believe she was here on medicine cat business—no other reason. "I always come here when—"

"Leafpool, what are you meowing about? I'm expecting kits!"

Leafpool saw pride and excitement and a flicker of fear in Sorreltail's expression. *Mouse-brain!* she scolded herself. *Call yourself a medicine cat?*

A purr of happiness rose inside her. "Are they Brackenfur's?" The tortoiseshell and golden brown warriors had been inseparable ever since they arrived in the new territory.

Sorreltail nodded. "I haven't told him yet; I wanted to be certain first. Oh, Leafpool, I just know he'll make a wonderful father."

"I'm sure he will." Leafpool pressed her muzzle against her friend's. "And you'll be a wonderful mother."

"I hope so." Sorreltail ducked her head. "I'm a bit scared, but I know I'll be fine if I've got you to look after me."

"I'll do my best," Leafpool mewed, trying not to squirm under the warmth of her friend's praise. Right now, she was as far from being a good medicine cat as she could be. "Just think, Sorreltail, you'll be the first cat to bear kits for ThunderClan in our new home! The first cat to use the new nursery."

Sorreltail blinked happily. The sound of a pawstep behind her made Leafpool turn; Brackenfur had come back to see what was keeping his mate.

"Are you okay?" he asked, padding up to her and giving her ears a lick.

"I'm fine, Brackenfur," Sorreltail replied. "Just a bit tired."

"Come a bit farther," Brackenfur meowed, pointing upstream with his tail. "We've found a nice sunny spot under a tree. You can rest and we'll see how Whitepaw's hunting skills are coming on."

His gentle care of Sorreltail made Leafpool certain that he had guessed her secret. It wouldn't be a secret for much longer.

Sorreltail leaned against his shoulder for a moment, then touched her nose to Leafpool's. "Bye, Leafpool. I hope you find those berries."

Leafpool watched the two cats head upstream, their pelts brushing, until they disappeared among the trees. There was a strange ache in her heart, half joy and half sorrow. She was happy for Sorreltail, but she envied her too. She and Bracken-fur had entered a private world where a medicine cat could never follow.

Leafpool had always known that, ever since she first became apprenticed to Cinderpelt. But she had never thought about what it would mean. She had never realized one cat could long for another the way she longed for Crowfeather with every hair on her pelt. And now Sorreltail was depending on Leafpool to take care of her when her kits were born. Her duties kept her busy enough already. There was no room for forbid-den feelings.

"You're a medicine cat," she told herself. "And Crowfeather's a warrior from another Clan. So stop thinking about him. Stop *dreaming.*"

Head down, she padded away from the stream without looking back at the WindClan border, and went to search for Squirrelflight's coltsfoot.

CHAPTER 4

Squirrelflight used her claws to tear moss from the roots of an oak tree and began patting it into a ball to take back to camp. A quarter moon had passed since the battle with Mudclaw and his followers, and the Clan was beginning to recover. Wounds were healing and the memory of Mudclaw's rebellion was fading.

Brambleclaw had started his training sessions, and Sandstorm had insisted that every warrior take a turn with the apprentice duties. Squirrelflight would rather be hunting or exploring than fetching fresh bedding for the elders, but the job wasn't too boring when you had a friend to share it with.

Casting a mischievous glance at Ashfur, who was gathering moss from another tree nearby, she hooked up her ball with the claws of one paw and hurled it at him. It landed accurately in the middle of his back and disintegrated, covering his pelt with scraps of moss.

Ashfur spun around to face her. "Hey!"

His eyes gleaming with laughter, the gray warrior scooped up his own moss and flung it at Squirrelflight. She dodged behind the tree to avoid it, and crashed straight into Bramble-claw.

"What's going on?" the tabby tomcat demanded. "What are you doing?"

"Collecting moss for the elders' bedding," Squirrelflight replied. Regret for their lost friendship pierced her like a thorn, along with fury that he had to appear at the exact moment she'd stopped working.

Ashfur hurtled around the tree with more moss in his jaws and skidded to a halt when he saw Brambleclaw.

"Collecting bedding? So I see." Brambleclaw used his tail to flick a scrap of moss from Ashfur's shoulder. "Carrying it back on your pelt, are you?"

Ashfur put the moss down. "We were only having a bit of fun."

"Fun?" Brambleclaw snapped. "Wasting time is what I'd call it. Don't you realize how much there is to do?"

"Okay, okay." Squirrelflight felt her neck fur bristle. "There's no need to treat us like lazy apprentices."

"Stop behaving like lazy apprentices, then," Brambleclaw flashed back at her, a glint of anger in his amber eyes. "Being a warrior means putting the Clan first."

Squirrelflight's fury rose like a wave. "Do you think we don't know that?" she spat. "Who died and made you deputy?"

As soon as the words were out she knew she had said some-thing unbelievably stupid. She wanted to snatch it back, but it was too late.

Brambleclaw's eyes blazed, but when he spoke his voice was

icy calm. "No cat knows whether Graystripe is dead or alive. Do you have any idea what Firestar must be suffering?"

"Of course I do!" Deep inside, Squirrelflight wanted to say she was sorry, but she couldn't back down when Brambleclaw was being so unfair. "Firestar is my *father*, for StarClan's sake! Don't talk to me like I don't care."

"Steady." Ashfur stepped forward and pressed his muzzle against Squirrelflight's shoulder.

Squirrelflight struggled to control her anger. "I'd give anything to have Graystripe back."

"Yes, we know," Ashfur reassured her. His breath felt warm against her pelt. "Look, Brambleclaw," he went on, straightening up, "we'll get the moss, okay? You don't need to hassle Squirrelflight."

Brambleclaw twitched his ears. "Okay, but be as quick as you can. And when you've done that, make sure the elders have had some fresh-kill." Without waiting for a reply he turned and stalked off toward the camp.

"Feed the elders yourself!" Squirrelflight yowled after him. There was no need for Brambleclaw to behave like this—not unless he was punishing her for being suspicious about Hawkfrost.

If Brambleclaw heard her, he didn't show it. He just carried on walking until soft green ferns hid him from sight.

"Take it easy," Ashfur meowed. "He's just trying to make sure everything gets done. We're all under pressure, with only one apprentice."

"He should do more himself then, instead of striding

around giving orders," Squirrelflight grumbled. "If he thinks I'm collecting moss for him, he can think again! I'm going hunting."

She spun around and raced into the trees. Behind her she heard Ashfur call her name, but she was too furious to slow down. Part of her wanted to launch herself at Brambleclaw and wipe that look of scorn from his face, while part of her was torn apart with guilt for implying that Graystripe was dead. Every time she and Brambleclaw spoke to each other they seemed to plunge deeper into a pit of anger and mistrust. Squirrelflight wondered if anything could put things right between them.

With these troubled thoughts churning in her head she hardly noticed where her flying paws were taking her. Too late she saw a bramble thicket looming up in front of her; she tried to skid to a halt and stumbled headlong into the prickly tendrils.

"Mouse dung!" she spat.

Thorns tugged at the fur on her back as she struggled to wrench herself free; she couldn't bear the indignity of Bramble-claw or Ashfur coming up to find her stuck. Digging her claws into the ground, she managed to drag herself out of the thicket, leaving scraps of ginger fur on the bramble thorns.

Scrambling up, she saw that the trees around her were unfamiliar—huge gray trunks hung with moss and ivy, packed closer together than in the woods around the camp.

"Squirrelflight! Watch out!"

Ashfur's gasp of alarm came from close behind her. She

spun around, her pelt standing on end. Just beyond the bramble thicket was a clearing where the ground was thick with dead leaves. Squirrelflight's heart started to pound as she spotted a russet-brown, wedge-shaped face peering out at her from a clump of thorns on the far side of the clearing. She watched in horror as the fox stepped delicately out, its jaws parted in a snarl and its eyes gleaming with hunger.

"Back away slowly." Ashfur's quiet meow came from close by.

Squirrelflight's legs felt as if they had turned to stone, but she forced herself to take one step back. At once the fox leapt. Squirrelflight raised her claws to defend herself, but in the same instant a gray streak flashed between the fox and her: it was Ashfur, slashing at the creature's muzzle with both forepaws. He let out a fearsome caterwaul, but the fox stood its ground in the center of the clearing. It wrenched its head toward Ashfur, jaws snapping. Squirrelflight hurled herself at the fox with a furious yowl and raked her claws down the side of its face. It reared up, throwing her off; she hit the ground with a thud that drove the breath out of her. When she scrambled to her paws she saw Ashfur on the ground, battering at the fox with his hind paws as it tried to bite down on his throat.

Squirrelflight sprang again, claws stretched toward the russet fur. As the fox rounded on her, she glimpsed Ashfur trying to drag himself away with blood pouring from his neck. While her attention was distracted, the fox snapped at her, and this time its teeth met in her shoulder. Squirrelflight yowled with pain and tore at the fox's muzzle with her claws. She heard Ashfur's voice calling weakly, "Squirrelflight, run!" But the fox wouldn't let go. Angry and terrified, Squirrelflight fought harder.

The fox gave her a shake that rattled her teeth. Squirrelflight hung limply in its grip, feeling her strength ebbing away. A black wave was rising behind her eyes, threatening to drown her, when she heard a loud yowling close by. Abruptly the fox's jaws opened and let her drop. For a few heartbeats she lay half conscious among the leaves, aware of furious snarls somewhere above her head.

Gasping for breath, she staggered to her paws. The forest swirled around her; when her vision cleared she saw Brambleclaw, his tabby fur fluffed out with rage so that he looked twice his normal size. He was driving the fox back into the trees with slashing claws and bared fangs; Ashfur fought alongside him, looking shaky but determined. Squirrelflight stumbled over to join them, letting out a yowl of defiance. At the sight of a third attacker, the fox backed off rapidly, then turned and vanished into the undergrowth. For a moment they heard rustling as it crashed through the ferns, then silence.

"Thanks, Brambleclaw," Ashfur gasped. "How did you know we were in trouble?"

"I heard you," Brambleclaw replied. His voice was tight with anger. "Great StarClan, what did you think you were *doing* out here? You know we haven't explored this part of the territory properly yet. Surely finding that badger should have made you more careful?"

Squirrelflight was almost speechless with fury. Why did it

have to be Brambleclaw who had come along to help? What made it worse was that he was right; she shouldn't have gone tearing through the forest in a temper without looking where she was going. But he didn't have to be so obnoxious about it. "What is your problem?" she spat. "I don't know what I ever saw in you!"

"We thought we'd hunt," Ashfur explained, brushing his tail across Squirrelflight's mouth before she could say anything else. "I'm sorry we came farther than we meant to."

Brambleclaw's gaze raked over him, fury still burning in his amber eyes.

"It's a good thing we came across that fox," Squirrelflight pointed out. "The Clan needs to know about it."

"And how much would the Clan have known if the pair of you were killed?" Brambleclaw growled. "For StarClan's sake, have a bit more sense next time."

He stepped forward to sniff the wound in Ashfur's neck. To Squirrelflight's relief it had almost stopped bleeding; it looked deep, but not the kind of wound that would kill.

"You'd better get back to camp and let Cinderpelt have a look at that," he advised. "You too, Squirrelflight. You have some pretty bad scratches there."

Squirrelflight twisted her head to see along her flanks and over her shoulders. Several clumps of fur were missing, and blood trickled out in sticky red streams where the fox's teeth had sunk into her flesh. The bitemarks stung fiercely, and every muscle throbbed. Squirrelflight longed to creep back to camp for a pawful of soothing herbs and her soft nest under the thornbush. But they couldn't let the fox go without trying to find its den.

"Shouldn't we follow the scent trail and see if the fox has a den close by?" she suggested. Her voice was cold, hiding the anger that burned inside her. "There's no use going to Firestar with half a story."

"Good idea," Ashfur agreed. "That fox looked thin and desperate, as if it's competing for food with stronger foxes. That makes it dangerous. If it lives in our territory, we need to work out how to get rid of it."

Brambleclaw hesitated, then nodded. "Okay, we'll follow for a while, at least."

He led the way to the thicket where the fox had disappeared. The reek of its scent was still strong.

"What a stink!" Ashfur snarled.

Brambleclaw took the lead as the three cats followed the trail through the undergrowth. Before long it crossed the old, overgrown Twoleg path that led back to the stone hollow and continued into the woods on the other side. As the trees thinned out and gave way to moorland, Squirrelflight realized it was becoming mingled with the scent of cats. Not far off she could hear the gurgling of a stream.

Brambleclaw halted. "This is the WindClan border," he announced.

"If the fox has crossed into their territory, it's not our problem anymore," meowed Ashfur.

"Don't be too sure of that." Brambleclaw glanced from side to side. "Let's just check if we can see its den."

"Its den must be in WindClan territory, mouse-brain," Squirrelflight muttered, but she helped in the search, padding along the border for several fox-lengths in each direction before heading farther back into the trees.

When the three cats joined each other again at the border, none of them had found the den.

"It looks as if the fox crossed the border. WindClan can deal with it now," Squirrelflight mewed.

"I'm not sure Firestar will see it that way," Brambleclaw warned. "He might want to warn Onestar."

Squirrelflight knew he could be right. The awkward meeting with the WindClan patrol a few days before hadn't seemed to change her father's faith in his friendship with Onestar. And a true friend wouldn't keep news of the fox to himself. Besides, even if the fox crossed the border, ThunderClan cats were still in danger.

"Okay," she agreed. "Let's get back to camp and tell Firestar about it."

Squirrelflight lay near the entrance to Cinderpelt's den, gritting her teeth while Leafpool dabbed chewed-up marigold leaves onto her scratches. Nearby, Cinderpelt was applying cobwebs to the wound in Ashfur's neck. He flinched, and Squirrelflight gave him a sympathetic glance.

"That should be fine," the medicine cat told him. "Take it

easy for the next couple of days, though. And make sure you let one of us check the wounds every day, to make sure they're not infected."

"You say the fox went across the WindClan border?" Leafpool asked her sister.

She looked worried. Squirrelflight couldn't imagine why Leafpool should be bothered about a fox in WindClan's territory. It would be much more worrying if it lived on the ThunderClan side of the border.

"That's right," she mewed, wincing as marigold juice seeped into the puncture wounds where the fox's teeth had pierced her fur.

"You didn't see any WindClan cats, did you?" Leafpool went on. Squirrelflight began to pick up embarrassment from her, and some deep, churning feeling she couldn't identify. "Like—like Crowfeather, for instance?"

"No. If we'd seen any WindClan cats we would have told them about the fox, mouse-brain. We wouldn't have to think about visiting them again." Brambleclaw was with Firestar right now, describing what had happened, and Squirrelflight was fairly sure what her father's reaction would be. "Anyway, what made you think of Crowfeather?"

Leafpool was taking a long time to sort through the heap of marigold leaves. "Oh, no reason," she mewed. "I just know he's a friend of yours, from when you went to the sun-drown-place."

"I don't know about a *friend*," Squirrelflight remarked. "I don't think Crowfeather is capable of getting close to another cat—especially now that Feathertail's dead. He really loved her. He must miss her so much."

"I expect he does," Leafpool replied. She sounded as if something was choking her, and Squirrelflight looked at her in concern, but she had bent down to chew up another leaf.

Ashfur hissed at the sting of marigold as Leafpool slapped the chewed-up leaf on his clawed hind leg. Squirrelflight blinked. Her sister was usually gentler than that!

There was a rustle among the brambles that sheltered the den and Firestar appeared, followed closely by Brambleclaw.

"Brambleclaw said you'd be here," the Clan leader meowed to Squirrelflight and Ashfur. "I've decided to go over to WindClan to warn Onestar about the fox, and I want you to come with me."

Squirrelflight wasn't surprised. *But we didn't warn ShadowClan about the badger*, she thought.

Cinderpelt raised her head. "I don't think—"

"I know what you're going to say," Firestar interrupted. "But my shoulder's fine now, and I've made up my mind."

"That's *not* what I was going to say." The medicine cat's blue eyes flashed. "These cats have been hurt in a fight and they need to rest."

"I need them to tell Onestar what they saw," Firestar objected.

"They can tell you, and you can pass on the message," Cinderpelt mewed stubbornly.

"Hang on." Squirrelflight heaved herself to her paws. "What about asking us? I feel strong enough to go over to

WindClan. What about you, Ashfur?"

"Sure." The gray warrior rose and stood beside her.

Firestar's gaze swept over them. "Yes, you look fine to me. You can rest when we get back."

"And if you get into another fight over there?" Cinderpelt challenged him.

"That won't happen," Firestar said calmly. "WindClan cats are our friends."

Cinderpelt let out an angry hiss and stalked into her den, her tail twitching irritably.

Firestar watched her with a warm look in his green eyes. "She gets more like Yellowfang every day," he murmured.

By the time Firestar led his patrol across the WindClan border the sun was beginning to set. There was no sign of any other cats; even the scent of the most recent WindClan patrol was faint. Squirrelflight struggled to pick it out among the rich odors of rabbit that drifted down from the moorland, reminding her that she hadn't eaten since early morning. They had not gone far when she spotted three rabbits hopping slowly along as they nibbled the grass.

"It's as if they know we're not allowed to chase them," she complained to Ashfur.

Ashfur's whiskers twitched. "I know. But just think what Onestar would say if he caught us taking prey in his territory."

Soon they came to a stream that fell steeply over a series of tiny waterfalls. A few stunted thorn trees grew beside it. There were no WindClan cats to be seen until the patrol was climbing the slope that led to the camp. Then Squirrelflight spotted the outline of a single warrior keeping watch on the skyline; the cat whisked around and disappeared as Firestar led the others up the final stretch of turf. A few heartbeats later, Onestar appeared from the thornbushes that surrounded the hollow and stood waiting for them. Webfoot and Crowfeather flanked him, their faces expressionless.

"Firestar." Onestar dipped his head in greeting. "What are you doing in WindClan territory?"

His tone was polite, but he spoke to Firestar as an equal, his head proudly raised and his gaze steady. This was not the cat who had pleaded to Firestar for help when Tallstar first made him Clan leader.

"We came to see how you are," Firestar replied. "I'd have come before, but I wrenched my shoulder in the battle."

"WindClan is fine," Onestar meowed. "Is there any reason we shouldn't be?"

Squirrelflight's jaws gaped in astonishment. How could he ask that, when less than a moon had passed since Mudclaw's rebellion?

Firestar's gaze slid past the WindClan leader to where Webfoot was standing in front of the barrier of gorse bushes. Squirrelflight guessed her father was reluctant to point out that some of the traitorous cats were still members of the Clan—not when one of those cats was in earshot.

Onestar's eyes narrowed. "Every cat in my Clan knows that I am the cat chosen by StarClan to be their leader. There will be no more trouble. You don't need to watch over me as if I were a helpless kit."

"That's not what I was doing," Firestar protested. "We also came to bring you some news," he went on. "Brambleclaw, tell Onestar what happened today."

Brambleclaw stepped forward beside his leader. "These two"—he flicked his tail at Squirrelflight and Ashfur—"surprised a fox."

"A young dog fox," Ashfur put in. "One of the biggest I've seen."

"The three of us fought it off," Brambleclaw explained, "and it crossed the border into your territory. We think it must have a den—"

"—among some rocks near the foot of the hill," Onestar finished. He flicked his tail dismissively. "My warriors have already tracked it. We're keeping an eye on it; don't worry."

"It's more savage than most foxes," Brambleclaw warned. "Look at the wounds on Squirrelflight and Ashfur."

"You can say that again!" Squirrelflight murmured, wincing as she flexed her shoulders.

"WindClan can deal with it," Onestar insisted. "Many seasons have passed since ShadowClan drove us out of our old home, but too many cats still see WindClan as the weakest clan. You act as if we can hardly feed ourselves. But WindClan is as strong as any other Clan and we shall prove it. We do not need help from *any* cat."

Firestar bent his head. Squirrelflight saw pain in his eyes and she longed to be anywhere but here, listening to one of her father's oldest allies rejecting his friendship.

"WindClan did just as much as any other Clan to bring us to our new home," Onestar went on. "We owe nothing to any cat."

Squirrelflight barely stopped herself from yelling, *That's not true! Without ThunderClan, WindClan would have died in their former home, every last cat caught by Twolegs or killed by their gigantic, churning monsters!*

Firestar lifted his head. "I'm sorry if we offended you," he said evenly. He gestured with his tail at his Clanmates, indicating that they should leave. "Good-bye, Onestar," he mewed. "I'll see you at the Gathering."

"Do you want a patrol to follow them to the border?" Webfoot spoke for the first time.

Onestar shook his head. "That won't be necessary." Without saying anything else, he turned and disappeared into the bushes. Firestar watched the place where he had vanished until the leaves stopped trembling. Then without speaking he turned and headed down the slope. Squirrelflight was about to follow when she heard a low voice call her name. She glanced back; Crowfeather was still standing in the shadow of the bushes.

"Squirrelflight, I wanted to ask you—" he began.

Webfoot thrust his head out of the bushes. "Crowfeather!"

"I'll be there in a moment!" Crowfeather called back. "Squirrelflight, listen," he began again.

But Firestar had paused at the foot of the slope. "Come on, Squirrelflight!"

"Can't this wait until the Gathering?" Squirrelflight mewed to the WindClan warrior. "I've got to go."

Crowfeather took a step back, his tail drooping in disappointment. "Okay, I guess it can wait."

Webfoot called out again, and with a last frustrated look at Squirrelflight, Crowfeather turned away.

Squirrelflight bounded after her Clanmates. She still couldn't believe the way Onestar had spoken to her father. Any new leader would want his Clan to be strong and independent, but surely he couldn't have forgotten everything he owed to Firestar?

If that's the way Onestar wants it, she thought as she caught up to her Clanmates, *then fine. It didn't do us any favors to be his allies. But he'll be sorry in the end, when he needs ThunderClan's help again.*

CHAPTER 5

A *ruffled disc of white light* trembled on the surface of the lake, and up above the stars of Silverpelt blazed in the night sky. *StarClan must be pleased with how we're settling in,* Squirrelflight decided as she followed her sister along the lakeshore. Her paws tingled at the thought of taking part in the first Gathering on the island. She couldn't wait to cross the fallen tree and explore.

Firestar led the way with Dustpelt, Sandstorm, and Cloudtail close to his flanks. Ashfur and Spiderleg padded just behind, ahead of Cinderpelt, Goldenflower, and Brackenfur. Brambleclaw brought up the rear, glancing back now and again as if he expected trouble.

His caution reminded Squirrelflight of the uneasy new relationship with WindClan. To reach the tree-bridge and the island, they had to pass through WindClan territory, and as far as Squirrelflight knew they hadn't formally asked for Onestar's permission.

"It was a lot easier at Fourtrees," she meowed to Leafpool, with a sudden pang of homesickness. She would never forget the horror of discovering that Twoleg monsters had destroyed the great oak trees where the Clans met every full moon.

"Back there, we didn't have to cross other Clans' territories to get to Gatherings."

"Cats can't possibly fight on the way to a Gathering," Leafpool mewed.

"I'm not sure. When does the truce start? When we get to the island, or when we're on the way?"

Leafpool shook her head, unable to reply.

Squirrelflight stayed alert as she and her Clanmates slipped through the shadows with the glimmering lake on one side and the steeply sloping moorland on the other. As they drew closer to the Twoleg horseplace, they began to pick up strong WindClan scent, as if a large patrol had just passed that way.

"Onestar and his Clan must be ahead of us," Squirrelflight meowed. Pausing to taste the air, she distinguished another scent, and a moment later she spotted two pale shapes flitting across the field beyond the horseplace fence. "That must be the kittypets who live in the barn," she commented. "Do you remember Smoky and Daisy? We met last time we came to a Gathering. I wonder if Daisy has had her kits yet."

"It's time the ThunderClan queens started having kits," Leafpool mewed. "The Clan is really short of young cats."

Squirrelflight nodded. More kits meant more apprentices, and that meant she wouldn't have to collect any more moss!

They crossed the marshy ground where they had made their temporary camp when they first reached the lake. Just beyond it, a new set of scent marks warned that they had reached the RiverClan border. On the lakeshore ahead of them, Squirrelflight could see a throng of cats; in the bright moonlight it was easy to recognize Onestar and his Wind-Clan warriors.

She remembered how her patrol had first discovered the island. They had always known it would be a perfect place to gather, but they had assumed it would be impossible to reach, except for the strong swimmers in RiverClan. But StarClan had found a way to help them cross the narrow stretch of water that separated the island from the shore. Squirrelflight felt her fur bristle with anticipation as they approached the tree-bridge. It had once been a lofty pine tree, growing close to the edge of the island. Now its roots reared up into the air, while its tip rested on the pebbly lakeshore. As she drew closer Squirrelflight could see its needles were already brown and dry, falling like brittle rain onto the stones.

Cats were bunched together around the topmost branches; their flattened ears and stiffly held tails betrayed their ner-vousness about trusting the tree to support their weight across the cold black water. Squirrelflight watched Webfoot sniff warily at a twig. Suddenly there was an impatient meow and Crowfeather leapt up onto the trunk, close to where it stretched out over the water. He swayed until he found his balance, then started to walk along the trunk, placing each paw carefully until he was near enough to the opposite shore to jump down safely.

Squirrelflight wanted to push forward and scramble along the trunk so she could explore the island too, but she made herself wait, claws scraping impatiently on the stones. She was conscious of Brambleclaw watching her with amber eyes that gave away nothing of what he felt. Turning her back on him, she padded over to Ashfur.

"This is great!" he meowed, touching his nose to her ear. "I can't wait to get over there."

"Me neither," Squirrelflight agreed.

More WindClan cats began to cross, gripping the trunk with their claws as they advanced pawstep by pawstep toward the far shore. When Firestar waved his tail for the Thunder-Clan cats to follow, Squirrelflight started forward eagerly, only to bump into Leafpool, who was gazing across the water to the island.

"What's the matter?" Squirrelflight mewed. "For StarClan's sake, get a move on!"

Leafpool jumped. "Sorry!"

As Tornear leapt up onto the tree-bridge, Onestar padded across and spoke quickly to Firestar before following his war-rior. Firestar beckoned his Clan around him.

"RiverClan and ShadowClan have already crossed," he meowed. "Onestar told me Leopardstar and Blackstar agreed we should all have a chance to explore the island before the Gathering."

"Where will we meet when it starts?" Cloudtail asked.

Firestar twitched his ears. "Only StarClan knows, until we get over there. But you shouldn't get lost. The island's not that big."

He jumped onto the tree trunk, followed by Sandstorm and

Cloudtail. At last it was Squirrelflight's turn. She crouched and sprang into the air; the trunk bounced under her weight as she landed. Her fur fluffed out in alarm and she sank her claws into the bark to keep her balance. Suddenly she was conscious of how narrow the trunk was, and how close the water was, lapping at the half-submerged branches beneath her.

"Go on," Ashfur meowed. "You're keeping every cat waiting."

Cautiously Squirrelflight edged out along the tree trunk. The trunk bounced even harder as more cats sprang up behind her, and the branches scraped her pelt as she wove her way between them. But gradually she got used to the motion, and the trunk grew thicker as she crept out across the lake. Her confidence grew; when the branches came to an end she broke into a run until she hurled herself with a yowl of triumph onto the shore on the other side.

Dustpelt leapt into the air and spun to face her. "Great StarClan, you startled me!" he exclaimed. "Any cat would think you were still a kit, the way you behave."

"Sorry, Dustpelt." Seeing his tail curl up with amusement, Squirrelflight guessed the brown tabby warrior was as excited as she was to be in their new Gathering place.

She waited in the shelter of the tree roots while Ashfur, Leafpool, and then Brambleclaw crossed. As soon as the broad-shouldered tabby warrior landed on the pebbles, he veered away to join another muscular warrior, as much like Brambleclaw as his reflection in the lake.

"Hawkfrost!" Squirrelflight hissed. "I might have known."

"There you are, Brambleclaw," she heard the RiverClan cat meow. "I was hoping you'd be here tonight. Come on—there's something I want to show you."

The two cats padded off side by side.

Squirrelflight turned back to look for Leafpool and saw her racing across the shore to join Hawkfrost's sister, Mothwing, who was the RiverClan medicine cat. The beautiful golden tabby twined her tail with Leafpool's, excitedly telling her something that Squirrelflight was too far away to hear.

Squirrelflight suddenly felt very lonely. Exploring didn't seem like so much fun if she had no one to share it with. Then she heard a voice calling her name, and she glanced around to see Ashfur standing a little way off. She bounded over to him.

"Where do you want to go? That way?" he suggested. He gestured with his tail toward a thicket of trees and bushes in the center of the island.

"No, let's go around the outside first," Squirrelflight meowed. "I want to see every pawstep!" She blinked warmly at him—somehow she knew there was no need to tell him how pleased she was that he wanted to explore the island with her.

They padded along the shore, passing Squirrelflight's mother, Sandstorm, who was sharpening her claws on the trunk of another pine.

"This is good," she mewed happily. "Much safer than where we gathered last time, near the horseplace." Her claws sharpened to her satisfaction, she sat down and stared out across the gently lapping water.

Squirrelflight and Ashfur skirted an outcrop of rocks

leading down to the water and came to a wider stretch of pebbles and sandy earth, broken up here and there by small, gleaming pools. Squirrelflight crouched down beside one, tongue extended to lap, then sprang back with a meow of surprise.

"There are fish in there!"

Ashfur padded up beside her and looked interestedly into the water. "I can't see any."

"Tiny fish—look, there!" She pointed with her paw as a sleek shape flickered from the shelter of one rock to another. "Too small for prey, though," she added regretfully. "Let's keep going."

The island shore grew rockier farther around, where the vast, glittering lake stretched all the way to their own territory. Squirrelflight could just make out the mass of trees with the dark bulk of the moorland rising above them.

"This would be great to sun ourselves on warm days," Ashfur commented, gazing up at a smooth gray boulder splotched with lichen. "We haven't found anything like Sunningrocks in our territory."

"No, but we haven't explored it all yet," Squirrelflight reminded him. "And it would be a very long way to come to warm our pelts!"

As they scrambled over the boulder, claws scraping for balance, she caught a glimpse of Brambleclaw and Hawkfrost nearer the center of the island. They were padding side by side, their heads bent close together as they talked. They didn't seem interested in exploring their surroundings, and they took no notice of the cats from all Clans that swarmed around them. Squirrelflight wrenched her gaze away from Brambleclaw and called a greeting to Tawnypelt, who was peering under a bush with a young ShadowClan warrior Squirrelflight didn't recognize. Tawnypelt acknowledged her with a flick of her tail, but didn't speak; Squirrelflight guessed she had her eye on prey.

The ShadowClan deputy, Russetfur, was sniffing around the bottom of a rock, flanked by her Clanmates Rowanclaw and Oakfur. Squirrelflight changed direction to avoid them; Tawnypelt was the only friend she had in ShadowClan.

"Have you noticed," she mewed to Ashfur, "how we've split up into our Clans again? It's as if the journey from the forest never happened."

"Well, Brambleclaw is over there with Hawkfrost," Ashfur pointed out, turning his ears to where the two tabby toms had reappeared from a clump of bracken.

"Huh!" grunted Squirrelflight.

Ashfur's blue eyes gleamed. "You're worried about him, aren't you?"

"Worried? Me?" Squirrelflight mewed. "Certainly not!" When Ashfur didn't respond, she added, "Honestly, I'm not worried about him."

Ashfur let out his breath in a long sigh. "Good," he murmured. "He's an honorable cat, you know. He may be friends with Hawkfrost, but he wouldn't betray his Clanmates."

Squirrelflight flinched. Was it so obvious that she no longer trusted Brambleclaw? Surely she knew him better than any cat in ThunderClan. Or had she become too close to him to judge properly? She shook her head, confused by the thoughts that buzzed in her ears. She wanted to trust Brambleclaw, she really did, but he seemed determined to make that impossible with everything he said and did.

The moon had risen high in the sky by the time the two cats made a complete circuit of the island. Squirrelflight bounded down to the lake beside the tree-bridge and gulped down a few mouthfuls; the water was icy cold, and as she lapped at the glittering surface she felt as if she were drinking starlight.

"I can see why Hawkfrost wanted this to be the RiverClan camp," Ashfur mewed. "There's everything here a cat could want!"

"Except enough prey," Squirrelflight pointed out. "River-Clan doesn't eat fish all the time. Imagine trying to swim across with fresh-kill in your jaws."

Ashfur shifted uneasily. "I hope RiverClan doesn't change their mind now that the tree-bridge is there."

Squirrelflight stared at him in alarm. "They *couldn't!*" she protested. "StarClan put the tree here for all of us."

"Well, if Leopardstar is planning to claim the island for RiverClan, we'll find out soon. The Gathering must be due to start." Ashfur glanced up at the moon.

Squirrelflight shook starry drops from her whiskers. "We still don't know where we're meeting."

"Let's head for the center," Ashfur suggested. "We should be able to hear the other cats, even if we can't see them."

The two warriors headed for the central thicket. They

hadn't gone far before they heard the gentle murmur of many cats greeting each other after a moon apart.

Ashfur paused to taste the air. "All four Clans are here. This must be the place."

He led the way through a clump of thorns, swerving to avoid a particularly prickly branch. Squirrelflight could hear prey rustling in the leaves around her, but she was too excited to think of hunting. She tried to push her way through the brambles more quickly, but thorns caught in her pelt.

"I'm *not* going to get stuck again!" she muttered.

Ashfur let out a *mrrow* of laughter. "Don't worry. If you do get stuck, I'll help you. We can't have you missing the Gathering."

Squirrelflight crouched down until her belly brushed the crisp dead leaves underneath the brambles, then she wriggled forward until the branches thinned and she broke out into the open.

"Wow!"

She was standing at the edge of a wide circle of grass that shone silver in the moonlight. It looked like a much smaller version of the lake, its surface rippling as the breeze brushed against the stems. A single oak tree grew in the center. Roots thicker than a cat's body clutched at the ground, while branches shifted overhead and cast trembling shadows on the cats below.

"This is perfect!" Ashfur exclaimed, emerging from the bushes beside her.

Squirrelflight looked around for her Clanmates. Goldenflower was stretched out in a clump of longer grass with a couple of elders from other Clans, and Cinderpelt had joined Leafpool and Mothwing near the tree roots. Littlecloud, the ShadowClan medicine cat, was padding over to sit beside them. Cloudtail and Dustpelt were standing in the shelter of the bushes farther around the circle; after a shared glance they went over to Mistyfoot and Blackclaw of RiverClan, dipping their heads in greeting.

Squirrelflight suddenly realized she had been nervous that ShadowClan and RiverClan would be as hostile as Wind-Clan had become since they reached their new home. But this looked more like a regular Gathering back in the forest, with cats from different Clans comfortably sharing news.

She twitched her ears to welcome Leafpool, who had left the other medicine cats and padded across the grass to join her sister.

"I love it here." Leafpool's eyes shone; Squirrelflight guessed she felt especially close to StarClan here. "It's smaller than Fourtrees, but it feels so safe."

As Squirrelflight started to agree, she saw Firestar race across the clearing and leap into the tree. He clawed at the trunk, then pulled himself onto a low branch and stood looking down at the four Clans.

"Blackstar! Leopardstar! Onestar!" he called. "We could sit here for the Gathering."

Blackstar was the next to appear, agile for a cat of his bulk as he swarmed up the tree to crouch on the branch beside Firestar with his tail hanging down.

"I bet Blackstar wishes he thought of sitting in the tree first," Ashfur murmured into Squirrelflight's ear.

Leopardstar settled herself in the fork between two branches not far from Firestar and Blackstar; Onestar climbed a little higher so he could look down on the other three.

Mistyfoot sat tidily on one of the thick, twisting roots at the foot of the trunk. When the other deputies, Ashfoot and Russetfur, joined her there, a pang as sharp as a thorn pierced Squirrelflight's belly. It was blindingly obvious that there was no ThunderClan deputy to sit with them.

Firestar let out a yowl. "Cats of all Clans, welcome to this new Gathering place. StarClan has brought us here, and we thank them." He waited for a moment while the warriors grew quiet, then courteously dipped his head to the Wind-Clan leader. "Onestar, would you like to begin?"

The WindClan leader rose to his paws, balancing confidently on the thick branch. His eyes gleamed in the moonlight, his tabby pelt turned to silver. Squirrelflight remembered how nervous he had been about addressing the Clans when Tallstar died. There was no trace of that uncertainty now. He looked as if he had led his Clan for many moons.

"All is well with WindClan," he reported. "I have made the journey to the Moonpool and received my nine lives and my name from StarClan."

Murmurs of congratulation rose up from the cats in the clearing: from all four Clans, Squirrelflight noticed. Onestar had been popular as a warrior, and his leadership had received powerful approval from StarClan when they made the tree fall, killing Mudclaw. She glanced around to see whether Webfoot and Mudclaw's other supporters were joining in; she couldn't see Webfoot at all, but the black she-cat Nightcloud was crouching under a bush, gazing up at her leader with an unreadable expression on her face.

Onestar bowed his head. "This morning Ashfoot, Tornear, and Crowfeather drove a fox from our territory," he went on. "They fought well, and I'm sure we've seen the last of it."

A yowl of approval came from the cats below—mostly from WindClan, but some from other Clans too. "Ashfoot! Tornear! Crowfeather!"

Squirrelflight didn't join in. "He hasn't mentioned Mudclaw's rebellion at all," she muttered to Ashfur. "Or ThunderClan—how we helped in the battle, and how we warned him about the fox."

Ashfur glanced sideways at her. "Did you really think he would?"

Onestar continued: "We have held warrior ceremonies for two apprentices. Owlwhisker and Weaselfur are here tonight as full warriors of WindClan." He sat down again as the new warriors were welcomed by the other cats.

Leopardstar was on her paws almost before Onestar had finished, impatiently waving her tail for silence. "There is no sign of the badger that we drove out a moon ago," she announced. "We think it has gone for good."

Squirrelflight looked across the clearing to Hawkfrost. He had led the patrol that got rid of RiverClan's badger. Squirrelflight curled her lip when she saw how pleased with himself

Hawkfrost looked. *Like he's the only warrior who ever fought a badger,* she thought resentfully, twisting her head to lick the healing wounds on her flank.

"RiverClan have also made a new warrior," Leopardstar went on. "Voletooth sits vigil in the camp tonight."

"Onestar and Leopardstar seem very keen to report new warriors," Squirrelflight whispered to her sister. "It's as if they're trying to show the other Clans how strong they are."

"It's ridiculous!" Leafpool hissed, startling Squirrelflight with the ferocity of her reply. "Why is it so important for us to be rivals instead of friends? Have they forgotten everything we went through to get here?"

Squirrelflight was a bit surprised that Leafpool felt so strongly; medicine cats usually kept apart from ordinary Clan rivalries, and her friendships with Littlecloud, Barkface, and Mothwing wouldn't change however hostile the Clans became. But then, Leafpool had probably grown as used to living with all the Clans together as Squirrelflight had.

"At the last Gathering," Leopardstar went on, "I agreed that the marshy ground where we first camped could be neutral territory so that we would have somewhere to gather. But now that StarClan have given us this island, I'm claiming the marshes for RiverClan."

Squirrelflight heard several cats muttering discontentedly; Barkface, the WindClan medicine cat, exclaimed, "Mouse dung! Now I won't be able to collect herbs there."

"The rest of the Clans have to agree," Blackstar pointed out, sinking his claws into the bark beneath his paws. "There was neutral territory around Fourtrees."

Leopardstar lashed her tail. "You can't turn this place into the forest. Things are different here. For a start, every Clan but RiverClan has to cross another Clan's territory to reach the island. There's no point in having neutral territory."

"Leopardstar's right," Firestar meowed. "I don't see any reason why RiverClan can't have the marshes."

Leopardstar dipped her head to him, acknowledging his support.

"Onestar, what do you think?" Firestar asked.

Onestar hesitated; Squirrelflight guessed he would like to claim the marshes and their stock of useful herbs for his Clan, but WindClan already had the largest expanse of territory. "Very well," he growled.

Blackstar shrugged. "I won't object, if you all agree."

Leopardstar's eyes gleamed with satisfaction. "Then we will set our scent markers by the horseplace tomorrow."

Yowls of approval rose from the RiverClan cats; Firestar waited for them to die down before he started to speak.

"I don't have much to report," he admitted. "Like River-Clan, we found a badger on our territory, and Brambleclaw led the patrol that sent it away. Apart from that, everything is going well, and we have seen nothing of Twolegs since we moved into the territory." He stepped back and gestured with his tail to Blackstar.

Squirrelflight tensed as the ShadowClan leader stood up. Would he mention the badger? Did he know that Thunder-Clan had driven it into ShadowClan territory? But when

Blackstar spoke, it was to report that prey was plentiful in the pinewoods. "We found an old badger set not far from the Twoleg nest," he rasped. "But we could barely detect the scent. It must have been abandoned long ago."

Squirrelflight exchanged a glance with Ashfur, feeling the fur lie flat on her neck again. The badger and her cubs must have retreated deeper into the forest, well away from any Clan's territory. From the number of old sets being reported, it looked as if several badgers had once lived around the lake. Perhaps the Clans were lucky they hadn't encountered more. "I hope we've seen the last of them," she murmured to Ashfur.

"If they come back, we'll deal with them," Ashfur meowed. "Anyway, I thought you liked badgers," he teased. "What about Midnight?"

"Midnight's different," Squirrelflight told him. "As for the rest—I don't care if I never see another one. Badgers and cats don't mix."

Now that Blackstar had finished speaking, she assumed the Gathering would be over, but the full moon still floated overhead, and Firestar began to speak once more.

"Clan leaders, and cats of all Clans," he began, "there's something we need to decide. This is the Gathering place StarClan has chosen for us, but as Leopardstar said, all of us except RiverClan have to cross another Clan's territory to reach it. We need to decide exactly where cats can travel in each other's territory when it's time to gather."

"Good idea," Squirrelflight commented under her breath.

"Well, there's no need for ThunderClan to cross through our territory to get here," Blackstar meowed instantly. "It's much quicker for you to come across WindClan."

Squirrelflight saw her father stiffen, and she guessed that he was holding back a sharp retort. "Yes, but we still need to discuss it."

"I don't mind any cat coming from either direction as far as the tree-bridge," Leopardstar mewed. "But no cat has permission to take prey from RiverClan."

"The same goes for WindClan," Onestar added, rising to his paws again. "Firestar, you can bring your cats across my territory, but I want you to keep within two fox-lengths of the lake. If my warriors catch you anywhere else, we'll regard it as trespass."

"That sounds reasonable," Firestar replied calmly. "Let's make that a general rule." He raised his voice so every cat could hear. "A Clan may cross another territory to come to Gatherings, but they must stay within two fox-lengths of the lakeshore, and travel without stopping."

"And take no prey," Blackstar added.

Firestar nodded. "Does every cat agree?"

A murmur of agreement hung in the air above the cats; what Firestar proposed sounded fair.

Cinderpelt stood up. "Will the same rule apply to cats who want to visit the Moonpool? Because they would have to leave the lakeshore and cross either our territory or WindClan's to reach the hills."

"WindClan always allowed cats to cross our old territory when they were going to the Moonstone," Onestar pointed out. There was a touch more warmth in his voice; he shared the respect that all cats felt for Cinderpelt.

"True," meowed Firestar. "And I don't see any reason not to do the same here."

"But those should be the only two exceptions," Blackstar put in, with a glare at Firestar. "Otherwise we may as well forget about our boundaries altogether."

"No, wait." Mistyfoot looked up from her root. "Cats who cross borders aren't always hostile. We all need to visit other Clans sometimes. Surely we don't need to be more suspicious here than we were in the old forest?"

Squirrelflight remembered Mistyfoot's urgent visit to Firestar when she discovered that Mudclaw and Hawkfrost were plotting together. She had risked crossing ShadowClan's territory and nearly been caught by a patrol.

"That makes sense," Leafpool agreed softly. "We should be able to visit each other." Her amber eyes gazed unblinkingly across the clearing; Squirrelflight couldn't see what she was looking at.

"If no cat has more to say, we should end this Gathering," Firestar meowed.

"Fine by me," Blackstar replied. Onestar and Leopardstar nodded.

"And we need to make sure the cats who aren't here know what has been decided," Firestar added.

The ShadowClan leader licked one paw and drew it over his ear. "That would be a job for the deputies, don't you think?"

Squirrelflight dug her claws into the ground. That was a cruel taunt, aimed straight at Firestar. There was no way the ThunderClan leader could reasonably object. He nodded curtly and sprang down from the tree.

Squirrelflight sighed. "Blackstar won't let any cat forget that Firestar didn't appoint another deputy when Graystripe disappeared," she complained to Ashfur. "It's obvious he thinks ThunderClan is weaker because of it."

"If he tries to attack us, he'll find out how wrong he is," Ashfur pointed out.

Squirrelflight growled in agreement. As she stood up and stretched, she noticed Brambleclaw still sitting beside Hawkfrost. The RiverClan warrior was mewing something into his ear, and Brambleclaw was nodding slowly.

Maybe he's telling him what a great deputy he'd make, Squirrelflight thought grimly. She hardly recognized Brambleclaw when she looked at him—he certainly wasn't the cat she had traveled with to the sun-drown-place to find Midnight. She couldn't even remember why they had been so close once. Looking at the two warriors again, shoulder to shoulder like a cat beside its reflection in a pool, suspicion prickled through her pelt.

If it was true that Brambleclaw wanted to be deputy, that must mean he thought Firestar was wrong to insist that Graystripe might still be alive. Worse than that, it was only one step from being deputy to being Clan leader. Was Brambleclaw looking ahead to the time when Firestar would lose his last life?

A shiver ran through Squirrelflight's pelt as she thought of her father's death, and cold gripped her with icy claws as she remembered the stories she had heard about Tigerstar. He had been prepared to kill to become deputy, and then Clan leader. Did his son, Brambleclaw, share the same ambitions? And would he be prepared to take the same murderous path to achieve them?

CHAPTER 6

Leafpool stayed sitting down as her sister and Ashfur headed into the bushes toward the lakeshore. She gazed across the clearing to where she had last seen Crowfeather. She spotted the WindClan cat at once; he was looking straight back at her.

Leafpool glanced around. Other cats moved in the shadows; the brambles behind her rustled as they pushed through them on their way back to the tree-bridge. No cat seemed to be paying much attention to her.

She started to circle the clearing, keeping to where the moonlight threw deep shadows.

"Leafpool!"

The young medicine cat froze, feeling her pelt tingle with frustration. She took a deep breath before turning around. "Yes, Cinderpelt?"

"Come on, you're being left behind."

Leafpool narrowed her eyes. Her Clanmates had only just left the clearing. Was Cinderpelt deliberately keeping her away from Crowfeather?

"Okay, Cinderpelt, I'm coming." Leafpool shot a glance

over her shoulder and saw Crowfeather watching her with anguish in his eyes.

Leafpool knew she couldn't do anything but follow Cinderpelt into the bushes.

I'm a medicine cat, she told herself as she ducked under the prickly branches. *I can't love Crowfeather, and he can't love me.*

She repeated it over and over, all the way back to the ThunderClan camp, but all she could think of was the look in Crowfeather's eyes.

A sweet scent drifted around Leafpool and a voice murmured her name. At first she thought Spottedleaf was calling to her; the former ThunderClan medicine cat had often come to her in dreams. But when she blinked open her eyes the cat standing in front of her had a silvery-gray pelt, and eyes of clearest blue. Starlight sparkled around her paws and at the ends of her whiskers.

Leafpool stared at her, bewildered. "Feathertail?"

Beyond her nest among the brambles outside Cinderpelt's den, the hollow was bathed in silvery light. But several days had passed since the Gathering, and the moon was waning. Leafpool knew she was dreaming.

She stood up. "What is it, Feathertail?"

She guessed Feathertail had come to speak to her about Crowfeather. A pang of guilt shot through her. Feathertail and Crowfeather had loved each other so much, but the beautiful RiverClan cat had given up her life to save the

Tribe and her friends from the fierce lion-cat Sharptooth. Was she angry that Crowfeather had fallen in love with another cat?

"I—I'm sorry," Leafpool stammered.

Feathertail swept her tail across Leafpool's mouth. "We need to talk, but not here. Follow me."

She led the way into the clearing. Leafpool tried to walk as lightly as if she were stalking a mouse, then she wondered if the Clan could hear her when this was only a dream.

A bright, unearthly light flooded the hollow. Brightheart and Sootfur, on watch, looked like cats made of stone, their coats the color of moonlight. Neither stirred as Feathertail and Leafpool crept past them and out through the thorn tunnel.

Once they were several fox-lengths away from the camp, Feathertail found a comfortable spot in a clump of long grass and settled down, gesturing with her tail for Leafpool to join her.

"I can guess what you're thinking," she meowed. "You think I'm angry about Crowfeather, don't you?"

Leafpool blinked at her, too ashamed to admit to her suspicion.

"Do you think I wouldn't want to see him happy?" Feathertail asked gently. "You make him happy; I can see that."

"I'm a medicine cat!" Leafpool protested. Her fur tingled with delight that Feathertail wasn't angry—more than that, she seemed to *want* Leafpool and Crowfeather to be together—but she knew it was more complicated than that. "I wish I could make him happy, but I can't."

"That's not why I'm here," Feathertail told her. "There's something I need you to do."

Leafpool pricked her ears. "What?"

"It's Mothwing." Feathertail's expression clouded. "I have an important message for her, but I can't reach her."

Leafpool felt icy water trickle down her spine, making her fur stand on end. When the Clans first came to the lake, the RiverClan medicine cat had confessed to Leafpool that she didn't believe in StarClan. At first, Leafpool had been stunned. How could a medicine cat carry out her duties without the guidance of their warrior ancestors? But she agreed to keep her friend's secret because she knew Mothwing was truly committed to caring for her Clan, and she knew as much about herbs as any of the medicine cats.

But she should have known that StarClan saw into the heart of every cat. There was no hiding the truth from them.

A shiver of alarm swept through Leafpool. Were StarClan angry with Mothwing? Could they stop her being a medicine cat? Would they be angry with Leafpool too, for keeping Mothwing's secret?

"Mothwing's really good with healing herbs," she told Feathertail. "And when she was an apprentice she wanted to believe."

"I know," Feathertail meowed. "We hoped that in time she would find faith in us. But she hasn't, so we can't speak to her to give her the messages her Clan needs."

"But—" Leafpool hesitated. This was so hard to ask, but she *had* to know. "But Mudfur waited for a sign from StarClan before he chose Mothwing to be his apprentice. And one morning he found a moth's wing outside his den. He took it as a sign that StarClan approved his choice. Was he mistaken?"

Feathertail bent her head to lick her chest fur. "You can't expect to understand the signs given to another cat," she replied when she looked up again. More briskly she added, "Leafpool, I need to tell Mothwing something urgently. I can't reach her, so will you take a message to her?"

"What would you like me to say?" Leafpool knew she wouldn't refuse Feathertail's request. She would do anything to help Mothwing.

"Tell her RiverClan is in serious danger from Twolegs."

"Twolegs?" Leafpool cocked her head, puzzled. "But we haven't seen any Twolegs yet. Surely they won't come until greenleaf?"

"I can't tell you any more, except that the danger is to RiverClan alone. But it is real, I promise you that. Will you go and warn Mothwing, please?"

"Yes, of course."

Feathertail gave Leafpool a single lick on the top of her head. Her sweet scent drifted around the younger cat. "Thank you, Leafpool," she murmured. "I know that if things had been different, you and I would have been good friends."

Leafpool wanted to believe it. But they had been in different Clans when Feathertail was alive—and what about

Crowfeather? Would they both have wanted him?

The scent faded. When Leafpool looked up the beautiful silver tabby was gone, and she was waking for real in her nest outside Cinderpelt's den.

Pale dawn light filled the clearing, although the sky was gray with cloud. As Leafpool yawned and stretched, Cinderpelt poked her head out and sniffed the air.

"Rain later," she commented. "You'd better find Ashfur and check that his neck wound is okay. He's healing well, but there's still a risk of infection."

"Sure, Cinderpelt."

As Leafpool set off to find the gray tomcat, she wondered how she could get away long enough to visit Mothwing and give her Feathertail's message. RiverClan's territory was on the opposite side of the lake, and she didn't think she could make it there and back before nightfall. Should she tell Cinderpelt about Feathertail's visit? No, that would mean betraying Mothwing's secret—that she didn't believe in StarClan. Mothwing would have to give up being a medicine cat, and Leafpool didn't want that to happen.

She spotted Ashfur pushing his way through the thorn tunnel with the dawn patrol. "Hi, there," he meowed. "Are you looking for me?"

"Yes, I've come to check your wound." Leafpool parted Ashfur's fur with one paw; the deep puncture wound was scarcely visible. "That's fine. I'll check with Cinderpelt, but I don't think you need any more herbs on it. We'll keep an eye on it for a few more days, though."

"Great!" mewed Ashfur. "I'm lucky it wasn't infected, with that filthy creature's teeth in there."

"Well, let us know if you have any more trouble with it."

"Hi." Squirrelflight had deposited a couple of starlings on the fresh-kill pile and bounded up to Ashfur and her sister. "Leafpool, you'll never guess what we found on patrol!"

"What?"

Squirrelflight's green eyes gleamed. "Catmint!"

"That's impossible! You only find catmint in Twoleg gardens." Leafpool's heart sank into her paws. "Don't tell me you've found Twoleg nests on our territory."

"No, mouse-brain. You remember the abandoned Twoleg nest that Brambleclaw and his patrol found?"

Leafpool nodded.

"Well, it's there. The Twolegs must have had a garden once, but it's all overgrown now. And there are these enormous clumps—only just coming up, but it's catmint, all right."

"That's great!" Catmint was by far the best remedy for whitecough and the dreaded greencough that could be fatal to elders and kits. Back in the forest there had been a steady supply in Twolegplace, but Leafpool hadn't expected to find any here.

"I'll tell Cinderpelt right away. Thanks, Squirrelflight." Halfway to her den, Leafpool realized this could be the answer to her problem. She paused briefly to decide what to say, then she went to find the medicine cat.

Cinderpelt was inside her den, checking the stores of herbs. "Thank StarClan newleaf is coming," she meowed. "We're down to our last poppy seed. I hope no cat gets ill for the next moon or so."

"Then you'll want to hear what Squirrelflight just told me." Leafpool told her about the discovery of catmint.

Cinderpelt purred. "Could you go and collect some?"

"Sure," Leafpool replied. "I'll have a good nose around, and see if there's anything else worth having."

She was about to dart out of the den, but Cinderpelt stopped her. "Do you think you should take a warrior with you?"

Leafpool's heart sank. An escort was the last thing she wanted. Once she might have considered taking Sorreltail, who had shared adventures with her in the past, but the young tortoiseshell had to rest now for the sake of her kits.

"I'll be fine," she promised Cinderpelt. "That old nest is right in the middle of our territory, and we know the fox has gone."

"Okay. Be careful, though. Keep on the lookout for badgers."

"I will."

She hurried across the clearing to the thorn tunnel before anyone else could ask what she was doing. She had never been to the abandoned nest before, but she knew it was near the overgrown Twoleg path that led away from the stone hollow. Brambleclaw thought that Twolegs had once taken stone out of the hollow, leaving their marks on the cliffs, and used the path to carry it away. Leafpool didn't know if he was right, but the stony path made a good clear space where she could race along without being held up by undergrowth.

The morning light was still casting long shadows through the woodland when she came to the Twoleg nest. It was set back from the path, half hidden by sparse trees and thickets of bramble. A shiver went through Leafpool; though Bramble-claw had described it to her, she hadn't known until now just how sinister the nest would feel.

I'd rather face wild foxes than go in there! she thought.

Warily she examined the tumbledown walls and the sagging piece of wood that once had blocked the entrance. Nothing moved, and when she tasted the air there was no scent of Twolegs. However, she could pick out the scent of catmint, and she followed it until she found the clumps Squirrelflight had mentioned, not far away from the wall of the nest. Several stems were long enough to take now, and there would be plenty more later in newleaf. Leafpool bit off a few stalks and padded away from the Twoleg nest.

Instead of following the path back to camp, she cut through the woods in a wide arc until she came to the stream that marked the border with WindClan. She told herself this was the best way around the lake because ShadowClan was more likely than WindClan to be hostile if they found her on their territory.

Slipping along in the shelter of bushes, with her ears pricked for patrols from either Clan, Leafpool followed the stream until she came to the shallow place where ThunderClan had crossed when they first arrived in the territory.

Before she went any farther, Leafpool paused to hunt. She soon brought down a vole that was scuffling in the reeds. She devoured it in a few bites, still listening for the sound of other cats, then she crossed into WindClan territory.

She followed the stream on the other side until she was within two fox-lengths of the lake. Now she could breathe more easily. She was on medicine cat business so she shouldn't encounter any trouble, even if WindClan warriors saw her.

Wishing for the wind in her paws, she raced along the lake-shore. At first she cast anxious glances behind her, in case she was spotted by ThunderClan cats patrolling the stream. Then a fold of the hill hid her from her own territory. She slackened her pace to a brisk trot and began to think about what she was going to say to Mothwing. Suddenly she stopped dead, her heart pounding.

Would Mothwing take the warning seriously, when she didn't believe StarClan existed?

She has to, Leafpool told herself, forcing herself to keep going. Feathertail would be watching her from StarClan, and she had to keep her promise.

Leafpool kept one eye on the moorland slopes, but there was no sign of any WindClan cats. *There's no point in looking for Crowfeather. What could you even say to him if he were here?*

There was no sign of the kittypets at the horseplace, either, but almost as soon as she passed the new RiverClan scent markings Leafpool spotted a patrol approaching her from the higher ground beyond the marsh. Mistyfoot was leading it, with Mosspelt and an apprentice Leafpool hadn't met before.

"Hi, Leafpool" Mistyfoot meowed as she came up. "Is everything all right?"

Leafpool set down her stems of catmint. "I've brought some herbs for Mothwing."

Mistyfoot gave the leaves a good sniff. "Catmint," she mewed approvingly. "Thanks, Leafpool. I think Mothwing's in camp. You can come with us—we're just on our way back."

Picking up her catmint again, Leafpool followed the patrol along the lakeshore until they came to a stream. They turned inland and padded beside the swift-flowing shallow water until a smaller stream joined it on the far side. The land between the two was fringed with reeds and thick with bushes. Even through the scent of catmint, Leafpool could pick up the scents of many cats.

Mistyfoot splashed across and jumped onto the opposite bank. "Welcome," she meowed.

Leafpool picked her way more cautiously through the stream, wishing she were as confident in the water as Mistyfoot and the other RiverClan cats. They passed a bramble thicket where Dawnflower, one of the RiverClan queens, was sunning herself with three tiny kits scrambling over her flank; she acknowledged Leafpool with a wave of her tail. Farther on, a couple of apprentices were wrestling in the shade of a clump of bracken.

Leafpool spotted a well-stocked pile of fresh-kill. "You've settled in well," she commented to Mistyfoot, around the stems of catmint.

Mistyfoot gave a satisfied nod. "This is a good place."

She led Leafpool to a spot where a thornbush overhung the narrower stream. The bank had fallen away, and the current had scoured out a small round pool beneath the bush's roots. Where the earth had been washed away, a smooth-sided hole had been left in the bank; from the piled leaves and berries Leafpool could see inside, she realized this must be Mothwing's den.

Mothwing was crouched on the bank above the pool, sorting through a pile of horsetail.

"Mothwing, you've got a visitor," Mistyfoot meowed.

The golden tabby glanced up and then sprang to her paws with a *mrrow* of delight. "Leafpool! What are you doing here?"

"I brought you this." Leafpool jumped down and laid her catmint stems in front of Mothwing, glancing back to thank Mistyfoot as the RiverClan deputy padded away.

"Catmint!" Mothwing exclaimed. "That's great—I haven't found any in our territory yet."

Leafpool looked around to make sure Mistyfoot had really gone, and that no other cat was in earshot. This was her chance to pass on Feathertail's warning. But her fur prickled and her mouth felt dry. Something about this didn't feel right.

Drawing closer to Mothwing, she mewed, "Actually, the catmint is only one reason I came. I have a message for you from StarClan."

Mothwing's amber eyes stretched wide. Leafpool suddenly wished she hadn't come. It might look like she was suggesting Mothwing couldn't be a proper medicine cat because the warning hadn't come to her directly. But Mothwing said nothing, just pricked her ears as she waited for Leafpool to finish.

"I had a dream," Leafpool told her. "Feathertail came to me."

She hesitated as she saw Mothwing's eyes flood with grief. Of course, since Feathertail had been a warrior of RiverClan, Mothwing would have known her well.

"She . . . she told me she couldn't get through to you. She asked me to bring you a message. RiverClan is in grave danger from Twolegs."

The RiverClan medicine cat sat in silence for several heartbeats, her eyes thoughtful.

"Twolegs?" she meowed at last. "But there aren't any—" She broke off and sprang to her paws. "Leafpool, it's been so quiet along the small Thunderpath that we haven't bothered with it much. Maybe something has happened there. Will you come and check it out with me?"

Leafpool hesitated. She had meant to give Mothwing the message and go straight home. If she stayed much longer in RiverClan she would probably have to spend the night there. But it was important to help Mothwing make sure that her territory held no hidden dangers.

"Yes, of course I'll come," she agreed, pushing aside the thought of the scolding Cinderpelt would give her. She was relieved that Mothwing didn't seem to blame her for bringing Feathertail's message, with all its implications that Mothwing wasn't a true medicine cat. She felt a rush of warmth for her friend and hoped Feathertail was watching them now, seeing how devoted Mothwing was to looking after her Clanmates.

Mothwing led the way upstream until she came to a spot where a single stepping stone broke the surface of the water. Crossing in two graceful leaps, she scrambled up the opposite bank and paused to wait for Leafpool.

"I was afraid you'd think I was talking nonsense," Leafpool confessed in a rush, once she had jumped across the stream. With a surge of hope she added, "Does that mean you're starting to believe in StarClan?"

Mothwing twitched her whiskers. "No, Leafpool. I don't believe the spirits of our warrior ancestors come back to speak with us. Stars are just unseeing specks of light in the night sky, not dead cats looking down on us. We can keep our old friends alive with memories, but if they're not here, they're nowhere. That's what I believe."

"I know." Leafpool paused as she picked her way around a patch of thistles. "But if you don't believe in StarClan, why take any notice of Feathertail's warning?"

The RiverClan cat slowed down to look into Leafpool's eyes. "Because I believe in *you*, Leafpool."

Leafpool shook her head. "That's mouse-brained! How would I know anything, unless StarClan told me?"

"Because you're a good medicine cat. You observe

everything around you. Somehow you've seen or heard or scented something and you know it means danger, though you aren't certain *how* you know. And because *you* believe in StarClan, it all surfaced in a dream about Feathertail. Simple." She turned and padded on.

Leafpool didn't think it was simple at all. But she didn't argue. At least Mothwing had listened to Feathertail's message.

When they reached the Thunderpath, Leafpool glanced around curiously. She had never seen this place before, although Squirrelflight had described it to her. There was a wide space covered by the same hard stuff as the Thunderpath, with a small wooden Twoleg nest in one corner. A halfbridge made of narrow strips of wood jutted out into the water. Everything was quiet.

Mothwing stood on the edge of the Thunderpath and tasted the air. "Yuck. ShadowClan," she meowed, reminding Leafpool that this was the border of the two territories. "And something else . . ."

Leafpool stretched her jaws wide. There was a faint, harsh taint to the air that she had not scented for a long time. She felt the fur on her neck bristle. "Monsters have been here," she mewed.

Mothwing met her anxious gaze. "But not recently. There's stale Twoleg scent too, though that reek from ShadowClan nearly covers it. Honestly, Leafpool, I don't think we can call that 'grave danger.'"

"Then what could the danger be?" Leafpool wondered.

Mothwing twitched the tip of her tail. "You can never tell what Twolegs will do next. Maybe it hasn't happened yet."

Turning away from the Thunderpath, she began to pad along the lakeshore, pausing once or twice to taste the water. "Remember that pool with the dead rabbit?" she called over her shoulder. "How it gave all the elders a bellyache? I won't make that mistake again. But the water here's fine."

When they reached the stream she checked the water there, too, before they followed it back to the RiverClan camp. She ended by taking Leafpool back to her den, where both cats drank from the little pool. The water was cool and sweet tasting, and there was no scent of anything unusual.

The sun was going down, and shadows lay thickly over the pool and stretched into Mothwing's den. As Leafpool had feared, it was too late to go home. "Would you like to stay the night?" Mothwing offered. "You'll never get back to Thunder-Clan before dark."

"Thanks, I would." Leafpool knew Cinderpelt would have missed her long ago, and she knew she would have to answer some awkward questions when she got back. But it would be safer to stay here for the night and go home in the early morning, especially if there might be badgers about.

A RiverClan apprentice brought Mothwing a plump fish, enough for both cats to share. As Leafpool settled down to sleep beside Mothwing in her nest of moss and bracken, she murmured, "You will remember Feathertail's warning, won't you? You'll keep your eyes open for trouble?"

"What?" Mothwing muttered sleepily. "Oh, yes, Leafpool. Of course I will. Don't worry."

But Leafpool couldn't help worrying. Without having heard the warning from Feathertail herself, it would be easy for Mothwing to forget, or decide that it wasn't important. And Leafpool was certain that trouble was coming.

CHAPTER 7

Squirrelflight paused beside a clump of bracken, drawing in the scent of the fresh green fronds. Sunlit dew sparkled on every blade of grass, and the whole forest seemed to be waking up after the long sleep of leaf-bare.

Another deep breath brought the scent of cat. Not ThunderClan, and not ShadowClan either, though she was near their border. Squirrelflight froze, glancing from side to side. A bracken frond waved, and she caught a glimpse of a strange tabby cat creeping along with its belly fur brushing the ground.

Squirrelflight thought at first that a rogue had wandered into their territory; a heartbeat later she realized it must be one of the kittypets she and Brambleclaw had fought with when they first explored the land around the lake. Their Twoleg nest was in ShadowClan's territory, but this crow-food-eating tabby wouldn't give a mouse tail for Clan boundaries.

Dropping into the hunter's crouch, Squirrelflight started to creep up on it, but she hadn't taken more than a couple of pawsteps when she heard the rest of her patrol approaching:

Thornclaw, Ashfur, and Sootfur. *Mouse-brains!* she thought. *Clumping around like horses!*

She warned them to keep back with a flick of her tail, but the tabby had already heard them. Squirrelflight saw the brown shape streak out of the middle of the bracken, and she sprang forward in pursuit. Behind her, she heard Ashfur yowl, "Hey, Squirrelflight, stop!" but she ignored him.

She dashed after the intruder, determined to give it a well-clawed ear to teach it not to come back, but the kittypet had too good a start. "Mouse dung!" she spat when she lost it in a patch of thick undergrowth. She turned back to join the rest of the patrol. To her surprise they were standing bunched together, staring at her with worried looks on their faces.

"Squirrelflight, you mouse-brain!" Sootfur called out.

Before she reached the others, Brambleclaw shouldered his way through the undergrowth, with Sandstorm just behind him.

"Just what do you think you're doing?" he demanded.

"I spotted one of those kittypets from ShadowClan territory." Squirrelflight was puzzled and angry at how hostile he sounded. What was he accusing her of *now*? "We're supposed to chase trespassers on a border patrol, right?"

"Right," meowed Brambleclaw. "What you're *not* allowed to do is cross the border into another Clan's territory. Suppose a ShadowClan patrol had seen you?"

"But I didn't . . ." Squirrelflight's voice trailed off. Suddenly she spotted the dead tree that was one of the boundary markers. She must have chased the kittypet straight past it. "I didn't notice any scent marks," she argued, padding forward until she was on the right side of the border again.

"The markings are really faint." Ashfur had been over to sniff at the roots of the dead tree. "Leave her alone, Brambleclaw. Any cat could have made the same mistake."

Sandstorm gave Ashfur a look from narrowed green eyes. "Squirrelflight can answer for herself," she mewed. "She's not usually lost for words."

Squirrelflight blinked gratefully at Ashfur. She didn't need him or any cat to spring to her defense, but it was good of him to support her. "I'm sorry. I really didn't notice."

"The markings *are* faint," Thornclaw agreed. "I don't think ShadowClan has renewed them for days."

"What's the matter with them?" Sandstorm wondered. "ShadowClan is usually the first to make sure that no cat crosses their borders."

Squirrelflight shrugged. "If they can't be bothered to set their markers, they can't object if some cat crosses the boundary by mistake."

"I suppose you're right," Brambleclaw sighed. "But for StarClan's sake, be a bit more careful next time."

"She will be." Ashfur sprang to Squirrelflight's defense again, unaware of the furious look she gave him this time. She was even angrier when she noticed a surprised glance from Sandstorm, as if her mother couldn't believe she was depending on Ashfur for protection. "Anyway, Brambleclaw," the gray tomcat went on, "it's not your place to tell her what to do."

"It's *any* cat's place," Brambleclaw retorted, his neck fur starting to bristle. "Do you *want* trouble with ShadowClan?"

Ashfur unsheathed his claws. "That's not the point!"

"Hang on!" Squirrelflight protested. "I don't want—"

"That's enough." Sandstorm stalked over and confronted the three quarreling cats. "Let's get back to camp before ShadowClan cats *do* turn up and find us ruffling each other's fur."

She stalked off in the direction of the camp. Sootfur and Thornclaw followed, but Brambleclaw and Ashfur hesitated, still giving each other an angry stare. Squirrelflight felt thoroughly exasperated with both of them.

"You go on ahead," she snapped to Ashfur.

Ashfur looked startled. "Oh—okay. I'll see you back at camp." With a frustrated lash of his tail he padded off after the others.

"You can't blame him for wanting to take care of you." Brambleclaw's words could have been approving, but his tone was critical as if he were remembering all the times on their journey when Squirrelflight had been furious with him for trying to protect her.

"At least there's one cat I know I can trust with my life!" she hissed.

Brambleclaw's eyes widened. "Only one, Squirrelflight?"

"Yes!" she spat back. She felt so far away from him now it was impossible to remember she had once looked at him with warmth. "At least Ashfur doesn't keep going off with a cat from another Clan—a cat who can't be trusted!"

The hurt in Brambleclaw's eyes faded, to be replaced by rage. "That's what you want, is it? A loyal warrior to pad after you and smooth all the thorns out of your path? I never used to think you were like that. I believed better of you."

"Believe what you like!"

Brambleclaw drew his lips back in the beginnings of a snarl. Before he could speak, the undergrowth behind Squirrelflight rustled. She whirled around to see that Ashfur had come back.

"What do you want now?" she growled.

Ashfur looked bewildered. "I'm sorry. I wondered why you didn't catch up, so I came back to make sure you're okay."

Squirrelflight sighed and let the fur lie flat on her neck. Ashfur would have to learn that she could stand up for herself, but at least he was straightforward. He said what he meant, and no cat could doubt his loyalty to his Clan. If Brambleclaw was a deep pool shadowed by forest trees, Ashfur was like the lake, glittering in sunlight. Squirrelflight suddenly found herself longing for the sun.

"I'm fine," she meowed, touching her muzzle to Ashfur's. "Let's go."

She headed away from the border, with Ashfur at her side. But all the while she was conscious of Brambleclaw's amber gaze upon her, until the ferns closed around her and she was hidden from his sight.

* * *

When Squirrelflight returned to camp, the stone hollow was full of activity. Cloudtail and Brightheart were just emerging from the warriors' den; their daughter, Whitepaw, dashed across the clearing to join them, meowing loudly. The elders had already taken their places at the foot of the rocks beneath the Highledge. Firestar was making his way down the stony path from his den to the floor of the hollow.

"What's happening?" Squirrelflight asked as more warriors appeared from their den.

"Firestar just called a meeting." Leafpool spoke behind her. Squirrelflight thought she looked subdued, as if she was still recovering from the fierce scolding Cinderpelt had given her for staying out all night in RiverClan. "It's time for Birchkit to be made an apprentice."

"Great!" Squirrelflight gave a little bounce of delight. For the first time she noticed Ferncloud at the entrance of the nursery, vigorously grooming Birchkit's pelt while the young cat wriggled with excitement. Dustpelt sat close by, looking ready to burst with pride. "The first new apprentice in our new home. Who's going to mentor him?"

"I have no idea," Leafpool meowed, beginning to cheer up. She glanced around the clearing as if she were trying to guess who the new mentor would be.

Squirrelflight and Ashfur found places among the other cats grouped in a semicircle around Firestar. She would have liked to mentor Birchkit herself, but she suspected she hadn't been a warrior long enough to be chosen, when so many more

experienced cats were without an apprentice. Besides, Sandstorm followed Firestar down the rocks from his den, and
she gave Squirrelflight a hard look as she padded past to sit
beside Brackenfur. She must have told Firestar what had happened on the ShadowClan border. Sighing, Squirrelflight
guessed she would have to start thinking before she acted if
she wanted to be trusted with the responsibility of mentoring
an apprentice.

When all the cats had gathered, Firestar summoned
Birchkit with a flick of his tail. The young brown cat padded forward; although he was shaking with nerves he stood
before Firestar with head and tail held high. His pelt gleamed
in the sunlight and his eyes shone. Squirrelflight felt a rush of
admiration for him. His littermates, Larchkit and Hollykit,
had died from starvation when the Twolegs tore up the old
forest. Birchkit had lost his home too, but he had shown great
courage for such a young cat.

Squirrelflight noticed Brambleclaw, crouched by himself a
couple of tail-lengths away from her; ambition flared in his
amber eyes as he gazed at Birchkit. She could see how desperately he wanted the young cat as his apprentice, and she
wondered why he should care so much more than the other
warriors.

Then claws gripped deep in her belly as the answer came
to her. Warriors could not be chosen as deputy unless they
had mentored an apprentice. With Graystripe's fate still
unknown, it couldn't be long before Firestar had to name
another cat in his place. If Brambleclaw were to stand a

chance, he had to have an apprentice. And there were no more kits in the Clan.

Seeing Brambleclaw now, focused on Birchkit as if the young cat were a particularly juicy piece of fresh-kill, Squirrelflight couldn't help asking herself what Brambleclaw would be prepared to do to feed such fierce ambition. Could he really become a killer like his father, Tigerstar?

Firestar waited for the Clan to grow silent. "This is a good day for ThunderClan," he began. "By naming apprentices, we show that ThunderClan will survive and remain strong. Birchkit, from now on you will be known as Birchpaw."

Birchpaw nodded enthusiastically.

"Ashfur, you are ready for an apprentice," Firestar continued. "You will be Birchpaw's mentor."

Squirrelflight saw Brambleclaw's eyes blaze in disbelief. His muscles tensed as if he were about to spring to his paws, but he held himself still. Not even the most ambitious cat would challenge a leader's choice of mentor.

Squirrelflight turned to look at Ashfur. Pride and happiness shone in his eyes as Birchpaw scampered toward him.

"Ashfur," Firestar continued, "you too have known loss and grief, and found the strength to deal with them."

He was talking about the death of Brindleface, Ashfur's mother. She had been murdered by Tigerstar and left as bait for the dog pack to lure them into the old ThunderClan camp. All that had happened before Squirrelflight was born, but every cat in the Clan had heard the story over and over again.

"I know you will pass on your strength to Birchpaw," Firestar meowed, "and teach him the skills that will make him a brave warrior of ThunderClan."

Eyes brimming with excitement, Birchpaw stretched up, and Ashfur bent his head to touch noses with him.

"Birchpaw! Birchpaw!" The Clan welcomed the apprentice with his new name. Ferncloud and Dustpelt bounded over to him, Ferncloud purring too loudly to speak, and Dustpelt gave his son a quick lick of congratulations.

"You never told me Firestar chose you!" Squirrelflight exclaimed to Ashfur, too happy for him to feel really indignant.

Ashfur's blue eyes glowed as he turned and gave her shoulder a swift lick. "I wanted to surprise you," he replied.

With the ceremony over, Birchpaw started to look a bit lost, as if he wasn't sure what happened next. Whitepaw darted across and pressed her muzzle against his. "Come on," she meowed. "I'll show you the apprentices' den. We'll fetch some more moss for your bedding. And I'll ask Brackenfur if we can train together tomorrow."

Birchpaw glanced at his mentor for permission to go with her, and when Ashfur nodded, he followed Whitepaw across the clearing. They both disappeared into the brambles where the apprentices slept.

"I never thought Firestar would choose me," Ashfur murmured, watching him go. "I still can't believe it!"

Squirrelflight pressed her nose into the fur on his shoulder. "You deserve it as much as any cat," she meowed.

But her gaze slid past him to Brambleclaw. The big tabby tom had risen to his paws and was gazing at her and Ashfur with envy and frustration in his eyes. A tremor of fear went through Squirrelflight. What would he do now, when his hopes of becoming deputy had been frustrated yet again?

"Squirrelflight." Sandstorm was calling to her a few tail-lengths away. "Come here a moment."

Squirrelflight padded over to her mother. "What is it?"

"That quarrel today, by the ShadowClan border. Brambleclaw and Ashfur were close to fighting, and that's not good for the Clan."

Squirrelflight's pelt prickled. "It wasn't my fault," she muttered mutinously. "Why tell me about it?"

The tip of Sandstorm's tail twitched back and forth. "Come on, Squirrelflight, you know better than that. Any cat can have problems, but you shouldn't let yours get in the way of your duty to the Clan."

Squirrelflight forced herself to meet her mother's eyes and saw sympathy there in spite of her stern words. "Okay," she mewed. "I'll do my best. But there are times when they *both* behave like furballs."

Amusement glimmered in Sandstorm's green eyes. "That's tomcats for you." She rested her tail on Squirrelflight's shoulder for a moment before heading toward the fresh-kill pile.

Squirrelflight watched Brambleclaw slipping between the thorn branches into the warriors' den. His head was down and his tail trailed on the ground.

The cat Squirrelflight thought she had known would

have accepted his disappointment and moved on, given up his hopes of being deputy, and concentrated on being a loyal ThunderClan warrior.

But Brambleclaw wasn't that cat anymore. Fear tingled through Squirrelflight again as she wondered just how far he would go to fulfill his ambition.

CHAPTER 8

Leafpool and Cinderpelt emerged from the trees beside the lake to see the small figure of a single cat making its way along the shore in ShadowClan territory.

"There's Littlecloud," Cinderpelt meowed, pointing with her tail.

Leafpool let out a faint sigh of relief. The sun had gone down over the lake, and the half moon already shone pale in the darkening sky. It was time for the medicine cats to meet at the Moonpool. Leafpool had been afraid that if she and Cinderpelt had to make the journey alone, the medicine cat would start questioning her about her visit to RiverClan two days earlier.

When Leafpool had returned, Cinderpelt was furious. She wanted to know why Leafpool had stayed away for a whole night.

"Do you realize that Firestar ordered a patrol to search for you?" she hissed. "Do you think cats have nothing better to do? Honestly, Leafpool, I thought you were more responsible."

"I'm sorry." Leafpool scuffled with her forepaws in the dry

leaves outside Cinderpelt's den. "I wanted to take some cat-mint to Mothwing. She gave me the horsetail in exchange." She gestured to the pile of fleshy stalks she had picked on her way back across the marshy ground.

Cinderpelt made an exasperated noise. "Leafpool, the Clans have to start living independently again. I know Moth-wing's your friend, but that doesn't mean you can swap herbs whenever you feel like it. Next time, ask me for permission first."

"Yes, Cinderpelt." Leafpool was pretty sure the permission wouldn't be forthcoming. She knew Cinderpelt would be even angrier if she knew the real reason for Leafpool's visit. But Mothwing deserved to be a medicine cat because of her skill at healing, and if StarClan spoke to her through Leafpool, it didn't matter if Mothwing couldn't believe in them.

Now, as they waited for Littlecloud beside the lake, Cinder-pelt's blue gaze was fixed on her again. "Are you sure you only went to RiverClan that day? There's nothing else I should know about?"

Stung, Leafpool looked up. "No, Cinderpelt. I'm quite sure."

Did the medicine cat suspect her of sneaking off to meet Crowfeather? Leafpool felt even more indignant because she had told Cinderpelt the truth about going to RiverClan. She hadn't seen a single hair on Crowfeather's pelt! Leafpool told herself that her mentor couldn't know for sure about the feel-ings she tried so hard to hide. But it would be hard to defend herself if Cinderpelt made a more direct accusation.

To her relief the ShadowClan medicine cat was close enough to hear them now. Cinderpelt wouldn't say anything about Crowfeather in front of him.

Littlecloud waded through the stream that marked the border, shook water drops off each paw in turn, then bounded along the shore until he reached the other two medicine cats. "May StarClan light your paths," he greeted them. "Is all well with your Clan?"

"Everything's fine," Cinderpelt replied. "How about ShadowClan?"

"Oh, yes, fine, fine."

Leafpool thought that the small tabby tom looked distracted. If Cinderpelt noticed, she didn't say anything, and the three cats headed toward the stream on the WindClan border that they would follow to the Moonpool.

"Mothwing didn't come with you?" Leafpool meowed.

"No." Littlecloud twitched his whiskers. "I expect she's coming through WindClan."

There was no sign of the RiverClan cat traveling along the shore from the other direction. Leafpool's paws felt heavy with secrets as she followed the others upstream through the woodland. She wondered if Mothwing had finally decided that she couldn't be bothered coming to share tongues with cats she didn't believe in. Or maybe the trouble foretold by Feathertail had already come, and the RiverClan medicine cat couldn't leave her Clan.

Her anxiety deepened when they met Barkface, the Wind-Clan medicine cat, at the point where the trees gave way to open moorland. He hadn't seen Mothwing either.

"She can still catch up," Cinderpelt mewed, as she limped farther up the hill.

As they skirted WindClan territory, Leafpool scanned the moorland slopes. She told herself it was Mothwing's golden pelt she wanted to see, not the lean gray shape of Crowfeather.

"How are things in WindClan?" Cinderpelt asked Bark-face. "Onestar seemed confident at the Gathering."

"Onestar will make a strong leader." Barkface's tone was neutral. If there were still difficulties within WindClan, he obviously wasn't going to talk about them, not even to other medicine cats.

"You know what I found up on the moors?" Barkface went on, his voice growing more friendly as he changed the subject.

"Of course I don't, mouse-brain!" Cinderpelt flicked his ear gently with the tip of her tail. "But I can see you're dying to tell me."

"Goldenrod—huge tall clumps of it." The older cat let out a satisfied purr. "Very good for healing wounds."

"That's excellent news, Barkface," Cinderpelt meowed. "Let's hope you don't need to use it too soon."

The WindClan medicine cat agreed with a rumble deep in his throat. "But it's good to know where it is."

Leafpool felt a sudden chill. Even counting the fox and the badger, so far they hadn't encountered many enemies in their new home. They wouldn't need a supply of goldenrod unless the cats started fighting each other. *We all journeyed together not long ago*, she thought despairingly. *Why do we have to split into four again?*

Night had fallen by the time the four medicine cats reached the Moonpool. Ahead of them rose a cliff of black rock, hung with ferns and shaggy moss. A stream cascaded from a cleft about halfway up; stars glittered on its surface and on the bubbling water of the pool.

Leafpool felt calmer as she pushed through the barrier of bushes that guarded the hollow. Whatever the future would bring, they were all in the paws of StarClan now.

Barkface stood back to let Cinderpelt go first down the path that led around the sides of the hollow. Suddenly Leafpool heard gasping breaths behind her, and the bushes rustled as another cat thrust its way through.

"Mothwing!" she exclaimed, feeling weak with relief. "I thought you weren't coming. Is everything okay?"

"I'm fine," Mothwing panted. "Busy, that's all. Sorry I'm late."

Leafpool caught Cinderpelt giving Mothwing a look from narrowed eyes, as if she wondered what could be so important that it meant being late for a meeting at the Moonpool.

"You're not late," Littlecloud mewed, with a friendly wave of his tail. "We haven't started yet."

As Cinderpelt led the way down to the pool, Leafpool hung

back to whisper to Mothwing. "I thought maybe Feathertail's prophecy had come true."

"No, I've checked the territory over and over, and there's nothing." Mothwing's brilliant amber eyes gazed seriously into Leafpool's. "But I'll keep looking. I won't forget." She hurried after the other medicine cats.

Leafpool went down last, feeling her paws slip into the pawprints fixed into the hard earth of the path. No cat had been there for moons beyond counting until Spottedleaf had led Leafpool to the place, but the dimpled pawmarks proved that their ancestors had been there many times. Leafpool's paws tingled at the thought of being in a long line of medicine cats, all serving their Clans with the guidance of StarClan.

At the bottom of the hollow, all five cats crouched down by the edge of the pool and stretched their necks to lap the dancing, star-filled water. Leafpool felt its icy touch on her tongue, tasting of stars and night, and closed her eyes to receive the dreams StarClan wanted to send her.

She expected to see Feathertail, and perhaps receive more explanation of her warning to Mothwing, but the beautiful gray she-cat did not appear. Instead, Leafpool found herself walking through a windy darkness, where the outlined shapes of cats whisked into the corner of her eye and disappeared before she could confront them. She heard a distant wailing, the mingled lament of many cats rising into the night, with no words she could distinguish or voices she could recognize.

"Who are you?" she called aloud. "Where are you? What do you want?"

Only the eerie, distant caterwauling came back to her. Fear pulsed through her, throbbing to the rhythm of her heartbeat. It tugged at her paws, almost making her flee in blind terror through the shadows, but she made herself pace slowly forward, looking from side to side in an effort to find out where she was and what message StarClan had for her.

At last she saw a spot of pure white light, far ahead of her, like a star hovering on the horizon. She raced forward. The light swelled until it filled her vision; then she burst through it and found herself blinking awake on the edge of the Moonpool.

Shivers ran through her and she felt as if every hair on her pelt was on end. When she tried to stand up, she felt so shaky that she flopped down again and lay still, taking deep breaths to calm herself. Looking around, she saw Cinderpelt, Barkface, and Littlecloud still deep in their dreams. Mothwing, however, had curled up on a flattened stone and was obviously enjoying a peaceful sleep.

"Mothwing!" Leafpool whispered, reaching over to prod her with one paw. "Mothwing, wake up!"

The RiverClan medicine cat's eyes opened, blinking in confusion at Leafpool. Then she got up and extended her front paws in a graceful stretch. "Honestly, Leafpool," she complained. "Did you have to wake me? That was the best sleep I've had in moons."

"Sorry, but you wouldn't want the others to catch you, would you?"

Mothwing glanced at the other three medicine cats, who

were all beginning to stir. "No, I wouldn't. Sorry, Leafpool."

Leafpool sat up and began to groom her ruffled fur. She wanted to know if the others had received the same confusing dream, and to find out if they could make sense of it. She wasn't surprised when Cinderpelt, Barkface, and Littlecloud sat up looking solemn and a little puzzled.

"That was a much more confusing dream than usual," Littlecloud began, giving his chest fur a lick. "Maybe we should discuss it."

Good, Leafpool thought. *Perhaps one of them understands what it meant, because I certainly don't!*

"Claws," Cinderpelt put in. "I saw huge white claws, ready to tear fur and spill blood."

Barkface nodded. "And gaping jaws. But were they cats? I couldn't be sure."

"And then that voice." Littlecloud shuddered. "So loud, foretelling death and danger. What does it all mean?"

Leafpool froze. This wasn't her dream! Why had StarClan not shown these images to her as well? Was it because she was keeping Mothwing's secret? *But Feathertail came to me,* she thought confusedly. *If StarClan was angry about Mothwing, she would have told me.*

Maybe this had nothing to do with Mothwing. Perhaps StarClan had noticed Leafpool's feelings for Crowfeather. Was she becoming less of a medicine cat because she loved the gray warrior? *But that's not fair!* she wailed inwardly. *I haven't even spoken to him since that night by the hollow.*

"What do you think, Leafpool?" Cinderpelt broke in on her thoughts.

Leafpool started. "I . . . I'm not sure." *Does Mothwing feel like this when she's asked about StarClan?* she wondered. *Always needing to pretend?*

Mothwing stretched her jaws in an enormous yawn. "StarClan must be warning us about something," she meowed.

Leafpool glanced at her in surprise. But it wasn't difficult to guess that from what the others had said. Did Mothwing assume it was the same as Feathertail's warning? But that had been for RiverClan alone, whereas this prophecy had come to the three other Clans.

Cinderpelt bowed her head. "We must think about this," she mewed. "If there is danger ahead, StarClan will show us more."

"Let's talk about this again when we meet next time," Littlecloud suggested. "Maybe by then everything will be clearer."

"Good idea," Barkface grunted. "StarClan certainly wasn't giving much away tonight."

"Don't forget our warrior ancestors have to settle into a new home as much as we do," Cinderpelt added. "Maybe that makes it harder for them to reach us."

That was possible, Leafpool thought hopefully. But it didn't explain why she had dreamed something totally different from the others.

The medicine cats followed the spiral path out of the bowl and pushed through the barrier of bushes. As they made their way down the hill, Cinderpelt, Littlecloud, and Barkface drew ahead, murmuring anxiously as if it was too hard to keep to their agreement of waiting until next time to discuss the dream. Mothwing and Leafpool padded side by side behind them.

"Did you tell Leopardstar about my dream?" Leafpool asked her friend, quietly, so the other cats wouldn't hear.

Mothwing gave her a startled glance. "No, how could I? I couldn't admit that StarClan had sent me a message through another Clan's medicine cat."

"But you could have said it was your own dream." Leafpool touched the golden tabby's shoulder with her tail-tip. "I wouldn't mind. Leopardstar ought to know, so she can tell the warriors to keep a lookout for anything suspicious."

Mothwing's tail lashed once. "I *can't*, Leafpool. I've never told Leopardstar about a dream before this, and I probably never will again. It *wasn't* my dream. I just don't *have* prophetic dreams from StarClan." Her voice quieter and more troubled, she went on, "I have to find my own way of being a medicine cat, without StarClan. Trust me, Leafpool. I want nothing more than to care for my Clan, but it has to be on my own terms."

Leafpool eyed her friend doubtfully. Silverpelt blazed across the sky above them; how could Mothwing see the shining spirits of their ancestors and not believe in them? She knew Mothwing worked hard at her healing skills, and truly cared for her Clan, but without that belief she could not lap from the spring of strength and wisdom that came from StarClan.

Her own faith was so important to Leafpool that she couldn't imagine being a medicine cat without it.

"But if you don't believe—" she began, then stopped and struggled to figure out what she really wanted to say. "Mothwing, do you believe I had a dream where Feathertail warned me about trouble in your Clan?"

Mothwing gazed at Leafpool with eyes that gleamed pale in the moonlight. "Yes, I believe you had a dream."

That's no answer, Leafpool thought frustratedly. But then she realized that it might be the best answer her friend could give. And what right did she have to criticize, when she seemed to be losing her own connection to StarClan?

"It'll be okay," Mothwing reassured her. "I'm checking all the water sources regularly, and when I go out gathering herbs I keep my eyes open for anything to do with Twolegs." A flick of her tail told Leafpool she didn't want to talk about the warning anymore. "What about ThunderClan? Is everything okay with you?"

"Fine, thanks. We've just made a new apprentice—Birchpaw. You'll be seeing him at a Gathering before long, I expect."

"That's great. Who's his mentor?"

"Ashfur." Leafpool broke off as a hiss came out of the darkness. Her pelt pricked with the sense of danger.

"What was that?" Mothwing whispered.

They had reached the border of WindClan territory. The moorland stretched away from them on all sides, dotted with outcrops of rock and stunted thorn trees. Deep shadows lay in the hollows.

The hiss came again. "Leafpool!"

Leafpool relaxed as a lean gray shape slid out from behind the nearest rock and a familiar scent flooded over her. "Crowfeather!" she exclaimed. "You scared me out of my fur!"

"Sorry," the WindClan warrior muttered. He gave Mothwing a searching stare. "I want a word with Leafpool, if you don't mind."

Mothwing looked surprised, and hesitated as if she were about to object. Then she nodded and let out a faint, knowing *mrrow*. Leafpool felt her skin under her fur flush hot with embarrassment.

"Sure," Mothwing murmured. "See you soon, Leafpool." She turned and vanished downhill into the darkness.

Leafpool almost called her back. She wasn't sure she wanted to be alone with Crowfeather. "This isn't right," she began, taking a pace back.

"I knew you'd come this way," Crowfeather meowed urgently. "I followed Barkface's scent trail, and then I waited for you. Leafpool, we have to talk. I can't forget that night outside your camp."

"I know, but—"

Crowfeather interrupted. "At first I thought you felt the same way as I do. But then you avoided me at the Gathering, and I don't understand why." His claws raked the tough moorland turf. "I can't get you out of my head, Leafpool. The other day I missed a rabbit that practically leapt into my paws. I keep making mistakes—"

"I'm doing the same thing!" Leafpool exclaimed. "I tried

to give Firestar nettle seed instead of poppy, and I mixed up ointment of yarrow and mouse bile. That was so mouse-brained!"

The WindClan warrior twitched his whiskers. "Ashfoot said I was as daft as a new apprentice."

"Cinderpelt got cross with me, too."

"Leafpool, I *know* you feel the same as I do," Crowfeather meowed. "Somehow we have to be together."

His scent, his nearness was doing something to Leafpool's insides. She felt as if she were melting like ice in newleaf. "But I'm a medicine cat," she protested, struggling against the urge to press her muzzle into his fur. "And I'm from another Clan. There isn't any future for us, Crowfeather."

Amber eyes burnt into hers. "Leafpool, do you want to be with me as much as I want to be with you?"

Leafpool knew what her answer should have been, but she couldn't lie to him. "Yes, I do."

"Then there must be a way. Will you meet me again? Somewhere we can talk properly?"

Leafpool dug her claws into the ground. Surely this couldn't be wrong, this overwhelming need to be with Crowfeather? StarClan couldn't be so cruel as to deny her this. "Yes, I will," she whispered. "Where?"

"I'll think of something. I'll get a message to you."

Suddenly Leafpool heard Cinderpelt's voice, calling from farther down the hill. "Leafpool, are you there?"

"Coming, Cinderpelt!" More softly, she added to Crowfeather, "I must go."

Crowfeather's tongue rasped across her ear. "I'll let you know where we can meet. It won't be long."

Leafpool gazed at him until she knew her eyes would see nothing but his face all the way back to the ThunderClan camp. Then she spun around and pelted down the hillside as if a whole pack of foxes were behind her.

CHAPTER 9

❧

"Hey, Squirrelflight!"

Squirrelflight looked up from the mouse she was eating beside the fresh-kill pile. Her fur was ruffled uncomfortably by a cold wind. The weather had been gray and blustery for several days and the promise of early newleaf had vanished.

"Want to go for a hunt?" Cloudtail asked, strolling up to her. "Brackenfur and Spiderleg are coming."

"Great!" Squirrelflight replied.

Brackenfur was talking to Ashfur and the two apprentices near the thorn tunnel. He seemed to be giving them an order, waving his tail for emphasis. Then Ashfur led the two apprentices toward the elders' den, while Brackenfur strode over to join Squirrelflight and Cloudtail.

"Ashfur is going to supervise Whitepaw and Birchpaw while they do their duties for the elders," he explained. "They keep asking to work together."

Squirrelflight could understand why. Whitepaw had been the only apprentice since Spiderleg had been made a warrior more than a moon ago, while Birchpaw had been alone in the nursery since the Clan came to their new territory.

Squirrelflight remembered how much fun it had been to train with others when she had been an apprentice. Her best friend then had been Shrewpaw, who had died on their journey to the lake; she would have liked to train with Leafpool, but right from a tiny kit her sister had seemed to know that her path led to the medicine cat's den.

Swallowing the last gulp of mouse, Squirrelflight sprang to her paws. "Where are we going?" she asked, licking a paw and swiping it over her jaws to remove the traces of fresh-kill.

"I thought we might try the stream close to the lake," Brackenfur replied. "There's good cover there, plenty of places for prey to hide. Where's Spiderleg?" he added.

Before Cloudtail could answer, the long-legged black warrior pushed his way out through the branches of the warriors' den and bounded across the clearing. "What are we waiting for?" he demanded.

"You." Cloudtail flicked his tail over Spiderleg's ear. "Let's go."

Wind thrashed the branches above their heads and almost flattened the ferns as the four cats headed toward the stream. Squirrelflight shivered as it tugged her fur the wrong way, but there was something exhilarating about it too, as if it would make her senses keener and her paws run faster. Gradually she quickened her pace until she was racing through the woods with her tail streaming out behind her.

"Wait for us!" Brackenfur called.

Cloudtail was running alongside her, his white pelt almost brushing hers, and Brackenfur caught up on her other side.

With a yowl of triumph Spiderleg flashed past all three of them, his long legs eating up the ground.

"Don't go too far ahead!" Cloudtail panted. "You'll scare all the prey."

Squirrelflight slowed down; the run had stretched her muscles and made her feel she had enough energy for anything. They caught up with Spiderleg near the top of the bank that led down to the stream; he twitched his tail, warning them to keep silent, and Squirrelflight saw that he had spotted a starling. He dropped into the hunter's crouch, waggling his hindquarters as he crept up on the bird. He was ready to pounce when suddenly the wind changed, parting the grasses that had concealed Spiderleg from his prey. The starling let out a loud alarm call. Spiderleg leapt, but the bird fluttered away from his outstretched forepaws and vanished into a tree.

Spiderleg turned back to his Clanmates with his tail drooping. "Sorry."

"Nothing to be sorry for," Brackenfur meowed to the younger warrior. "It was just bad luck, the wind changing like that."

Squirrelflight stood on the bank, listening to the clatter of the branches and the stream bubbling below. Downstream, between the trees, she could see the surface of the lake, gray and ridged as the wind swept over it. For a moment she thought she heard another sound, the faint cry of a cat in distress, but it wasn't repeated, and Squirrelflight thought she must have imagined it.

Cloudtail came to stand beside her. "Can you scent anything?"

Squirrelflight shook her head.

The white warrior opened his jaws and tasted the air. Squirrelflight saw his ears prick up, and he exclaimed, "Intruders!"

"WindClan?" Brackenfur joined them and peered down at the stream that formed the border. Even now, at the end of leaf-bare, the slope was covered with grass and fern, where invaders could hide as easily as prey.

"No, not WindClan." Cloudtail drew in the scent again. "I don't know who it is."

Squirrelflight tasted the air. Cloudtail was right. There was definitely the scent of a cat—maybe more than one—but it wasn't from any of the Clans. It was a pungent scent, with a hint of grass, and it was coming from close by.

"Rogues, do you think?" Spiderleg began to creep down the bank.

"Stay where you are!" Cloudtail snapped. "Would you go sticking your nose into a bee's nest? We need to know what we're dealing with." He took a pace forward and called out, "Who's there? Show yourself!"

Squirrelflight scanned the ground that led down to the stream, muscles tensed for the first sign of danger. "If they're looking for trouble, they can have it," she muttered.

"We know you're there!" Cloudtail called again. "Come out!"

A tussock of long grass at the edge of the stream parted. To Squirrelflight's astonishment a she-cat with long, cream-colored fur padded out.

"It's Daisy from the horseplace!" Squirrelflight exclaimed. "What are you doing here? Are you lost?" Privately, she couldn't believe that even a kittypet could get lost here, when all she had to do was follow the lakeshore back to her home.

The she-cat cowered in the shelter of a bush and pressed herself to the ground as she looked up at the warriors. "Please don't hurt me," she mewed.

"I'll chase her out," Spiderleg offered, crouching down as if preparing to pounce on prey.

Cloudtail swished his tail. "Stand up, mouse-brain," he snapped. "Let's find out what's going on first."

He padded down the bank until he stood face to face with Daisy. Squirrelflight followed him. The kittypet was a pitiful sight: her long-furred pelt was muddy and tangled with burrs, and her blue eyes were blank with exhaustion.

"What's wrong? Has something happened at the horse-place?"

Daisy blinked up at her, but before she could reply a mewling cry rose from the other side of the bush.

"Kits!" exclaimed Cloudtail.

He pushed past Daisy and shouldered his way into the long grass. Daisy followed him, mewing desperately, "Don't hurt my kits!"

Dodging around the tussock of grass, Squirrelflight found three tiny kits huddled together, their tiny pink mouths stretched open in a wail of hunger and confusion. One was creamy-furred like Daisy, the others gray and white like the tomcat, Smoky, from the horseplace.

Daisy circled her kits with her body, drawing them close to her with her tail. "Please help us," she begged.

"Don't worry, we won't hurt any of you," Brackenfur reassured her.

"What are you doing here?" Squirrelflight asked. "Surely your kits are too young to travel all this way?"

Daisy bent down and licked the cream-colored kit. "When Floss had her kits, the Nofurs took them away."

Nofurs must be Twolegs, Squirrelflight thought. "Why would they do that?"

Daisy shook her head. "No cat knows. They were so young their eyes weren't even open."

Cloudtail let out a hiss of anger. "Fox dung! If I'd been there I'd have clawed their stupid faces."

"What good would that do?" Daisy asked, her eyes brimming with sorrow. "The kits would still be gone. Floss will never see them again. So when I had mine," she went on, lifting her head defiantly, "I decided to leave before the Nofurs found them. I saw lots of cats going past our fence in this direction, and I thought some of you would be friendly." She turned her huge, trusting blue eyes on Cloudtail.

The warrior bent his head to sniff the three little scraps of fur. The kits shrank away, shivering, and their mews grew shrill with panic.

"You will help us, won't you?" Daisy went on. "Back there"— she pointed with her tail toward WindClan territory—"some cats drove us off."

"That would be WindClan," Brackenfur meowed. "Don't worry, you're in ThunderClan territory now."

Daisy nodded. "That must be why they left us alone once we crossed the stream. But I don't think my kits can go any farther, and I won't take them back. The Nofurs will steal them if I do."

"We'll help you," Cloudtail promised. "You can bring your kits to our camp."

Daisy blinked warmly at him. "Oh, thank you! You're so kind!"

Brackenfur shot Cloudtail a look of surprise. "*Four* kitty-pets?" he murmured. "What's Firestar going to think about that?"

"Firestar will understand," Cloudtail replied. "He was a kittypet once, and so was I. Do you have a problem with that, Brackenfur?"

Brackenfur twitched his ears. "Of course not. But I wonder if this is the right time to take in more cats, when we haven't finished exploring our territory."

"Well, it's now or never for these kits," Squirrelflight pointed out. "We're not going to send them along the lake into ShadowClan. Come *on*!"

"Okay, let's get going," Cloudtail meowed. "Spiderleg!" he called to the younger warrior who had remained on watch at the top of the bank. "We need some help down here! You three can each carry a kit," he explained, "and I'll help Daisy."

Squirrelflight picked up one of the gray and white kits by the scruff; it let out a wail of terror and started wriggling.

"Shut up. I'm helping you," she muttered through a mouthful of fur.

Brackenfur and Spiderleg each took one of the other kits, and Cloudtail let Daisy lean on his shoulder as they struggled up the bank and made their way slowly back to camp.

When Squirrelflight pushed her way through the thorn tunnel the clearing was deserted, but as she headed toward the nursery Birchpaw bounded up to her, carrying a ball of dirty moss from the elders' den.

"What have you got there?" he asked, dropping the moss and peering curiously at the tiny bundle dangling from her mouth. "Oh, wow! Whitepaw, come and look at this!"

The older apprentice followed him out of the elders' den with more moss. "Kits!" she exclaimed. "Where did you get them?"

Squirrelflight couldn't explain with a mouthful of kit, so she padded on to the nursery, while the excited apprentices called the rest of the Clan to come and look. Ferncloud appeared from the warriors' den and stretched her eyes wide when she saw what Squirrelflight and the others were carrying.

"Poor little scraps!" she gasped. "Bring them into the nursery. Whitepaw, go and fetch Cinderpelt. And Birchpaw, let Firestar know. Are you their mother?" she meowed to Daisy, who had stumbled up with Cloudtail pressed close to her flank. "Don't worry. We'll look after all of you."

Ferncloud ducked into the nursery ahead of Squirrelflight

and began pulling moss and bracken together to make a warm, thick nest. Squirrelflight gently set her kit down in the middle of the nest; it had stopped wriggling long ago and lay very still, scarcely breathing. Brackenfur and Spiderleg set down the kits they carried and Daisy lay down beside them, nudging them anxiously.

"Whitepaw says there are kits here. Can I see?" Sorreltail stuck her head into the nursery. When she saw Daisy and her litter she pushed her way through the branches to crouch beside the nest. "Oh, they're beautiful!" she purred. "Here, let me help you." She began licking the nearest kit, rubbing its fur the wrong way to warm it up.

Squirrelflight was surprised to see how interested Sorreltail was in the kits, until she noticed how plump the tortoiseshell was looking, and how her scent had changed. *She must be expecting Brackenfur's kits*, she thought. *That's great! ThunderClan needs new kits.*

With Daisy, Sorreltail, and Ferncloud all busily licking, the kits soon started to stir, letting out faint, whimpering cries. But Daisy didn't look up until all three revived enough to nuzzle into her belly and start suckling.

"You saved their lives," she murmured. "I thought they were all going to die."

The nursery entrance rustled again as Cinderpelt padded in, followed by Leafpool with a mouthful of herbs. Squirrelflight slid across to her sister's side and whispered, "Do you think Sorreltail is expecting kits?"

Leafpool placed the herbs close to where Daisy was lying. "Of course she's expecting kits!" she snapped. "Any cat can see it. Where have you been for the last half moon?"

Squirrelflight twitched her ears. Leafpool wasn't usually so short-tempered. She felt strong emotion coming off her sister's fur in waves, but Squirrelflight couldn't make out what it was.

Cinderpelt edged past Spiderleg to reach Daisy and the kits. "What's this, a Gathering? Any cat who hasn't something to do here, out! Give us all room to breathe."

With a last glance at the new arrivals, Squirrelflight left, along with Spiderleg and Brackenfur. As they emerged into the clearing, Squirrelflight heard Cinderpelt meow, "Daisy, I've brought you some herbs to strengthen you and the kits. Don't worry. You're all going to be fine."

In the clearing, the apprentices were chattering excitedly, the soiled moss abandoned on the ground. Just outside the nursery, Cloudtail was reporting to Firestar, while several other cats crowded around to listen. Squirrelflight spotted Brambleclaw among them; the tabby tom looked disapproving—but then Brambleclaw *always* looked disapproving these days.

He wasn't the only cat to seem troubled by Daisy's arrival.

"How long are you going to let them stay?" Dustpelt asked the Clan leader.

Firestar twitched the tip of his tail. "That depends on a lot of things. How long do they want to stay?"

"I don't think Daisy ever wants to go back to the horseplace,"

Cloudtail meowed. "The Twolegs took Floss's kits away, so when her own kits were born she decided to leave in order to keep them safe."

"That's a good reason," Firestar commented.

"Does that mean you'd let them join the Clan? Permanently?" Brambleclaw's tone was clearly challenging. "Four kittypets?"

Squirrelflight felt a growl rising from the back of her throat. Had Brambleclaw forgotten that Firestar had been a kittypet, and she shared his kittypet blood?

"You only have to look at Daisy to tell she probably never killed a mouse in her life," Brambleclaw went on, before Squirrelflight could challenge him. "She'll need a lot of help to live out here."

"True," Firestar admitted. "But ThunderClan needs more young cats. We only have two apprentices, and although Sorreltail's kits will be very welcome, they won't begin their warrior training for moons."

Brackenfur and Sorreltail, who had emerged from the nursery to stand beside her mate, blinked proudly at each other.

"But these are *kittypets*," Brambleclaw objected. "How are they going to learn—"

"*What* did you say?" Cloudtail whirled around to face Brambleclaw, his blue eyes slitted with anger. "Have you forgotten that your Clan leader was a kittypet? That *I* was a kittypet? I'll show you that a kittypet can claw your ears off any time."

Brambleclaw took a step back, his eyes flaring. The rest

of the cats looked shocked too, including Cloudtail's mate, Brightheart. Squirrelflight hadn't realized the white warrior was still so sensitive about his kittypet origins; they were never mentioned by his Clanmates, and he had arrived in Thunder-Clan as a tiny kit, long before Squirrelflight was born.

"If Cloudtail doesn't claw you, I will," she hissed, padding forward to stand beside the white warrior and glaring furiously at Brambleclaw.

"That's enough." Firestar thrust between the bristling antagonists. "Sheathe your claws. There'll be no fighting here."

"Thank you for standing up for us." The quiet voice came from behind her. Squirrelflight turned to see that Daisy had appeared at the entrance to the nursery. "I couldn't help hearing what you were saying. I didn't intend to join anyone when I left home. I only wanted to save my kits from whatever happened to Floss's litter. If it's a problem having us here, we'll leave as soon as my kits are strong enough to travel."

"It's not a problem," Cloudtail assured her instantly.

"You can stay as long as you want," Firestar added, padding across to stand in front of Daisy. "But if you decide to leave you need to think very carefully about where you'll go. The life of a loner is tough. Are you used to catching your own food?"

"I bet she can," Squirrelflight put in, before Daisy could answer. "Barley and Ravenpaw catch mice in their barn, so why shouldn't Daisy and the others?"

Daisy shook her head, looking a bit embarrassed. "No, we—"

"No, she'd be too fat and lazy to run fast enough," Sootfur interrupted, loud enough to be heard. Squirrelflight was glad when Mousefur hissed at him and gave him a clout around the ear with a sheathed paw; she would have done the same if she'd been close enough.

"The Nofurs fed us," Daisy explained, blinking anxiously. "We did catch mice sometimes, in the barn. But there aren't very many mice there—and anyway, I expect it's harder out here."

"You're right. It is," Firestar meowed. "But we'll show you how, if you decide to stay. And we'll train your kits in our ways."

"You don't have to decide right now," Cloudtail put in. "Why don't you go back to your kits now? You need to rest."

"And we won't make any decisions without talking to you," Firestar added. He turned to the apprentices, who were hovering on the edge of the group with eyes like full moons. "Birchpaw, fetch Daisy a piece of fresh-kill from the pile, please."

The young apprentice bounded off.

"Come on, Daisy," Cloudtail meowed. "Everything will seem better when you're not hungry and tired."

Squirrelflight saw Brightheart looking a little disconcerted as her mate touched his nose to Daisy's flank. The ginger and white she-cat watched them walk back to the nursery, then murmured to Whitepaw, "Your father's doing exactly the right thing. Daisy's exhausted, and she must be scared out of her wits."

Brightheart hurried forward to catch up with Cloudtail and Daisy. "Do you need any help with the kits?" she offered.

Daisy glanced around and let out a little squeak of alarm. "What happened to your face?"

Squirrelflight was so used to seeing the injuries Brightheart had received from the dog pack that she didn't notice them anymore. But she could understand how Daisy, confronted by the bald pink scars and empty eye socket for the first time, might be frightened.

She doesn't have to show it like that, though, Squirrelflight thought crossly. *Poor Brightheart!*

"I was attacked by dogs." Brightheart lowered her head and turned the injured side of her face away from Daisy. She stepped back to let Cloudtail and Daisy go into the nursery alone, then she headed across the clearing to the warriors' den.

"Want to hunt?" Squirrelflight jumped at the sound of Ashfur's voice behind her. "It doesn't sound as if your patrol had much chance to bring back fresh-kill."

"No, we didn't," Squirrelflight admitted. "Let's go now."

"We'll need plenty of prey from now on," Ashfur remarked as they headed to the thorn tunnel. "Four more mouths to feed!"

Squirrelflight was pleased by the warmth in his tone. He was much more welcoming to the new arrivals than Brambleclaw had been, with his scathing comments about kittypets.

I'm half kittypet myself, she thought. *Do you think I shouldn't be a warrior either, Brambleclaw?*

Ducking her head to follow Ashfur through the brambles, Squirrelflight pushed thoughts of Brambleclaw out of her mind. It didn't make any difference where Daisy came from. ThunderClan was desperately short of young cats, after so many had died during the famine and the journey to the lake. Daisy's arrival could be exactly what they needed.

CHAPTER 10

Leafpool dropped the herbs she was carrying and looked down at the creamy-furred she-cat. "Cinderpelt says you need to eat these."

Daisy blinked up at her from sleepy blue eyes, lifting her head from where she lay among the thick moss in the nursery. In the two days since they came to the camp, she and her kits had almost recovered from their exhausting journey. Daisy had groomed her fur back into soft silkiness, while her three kits were curled up together in a purring heap. "You're all so kind," Daisy murmured. She chewed up the herbs obediently, wrinkling her nose against the pungent scent.

Careful not to disturb them, Leafpool bent to check the three kits. "They're beautiful," she mewed. "Have you given them names yet?"

"Yes. The one with cream fur like mine is Berry, the bigger gray one is Mouse, and the smallest one is Hazel." Daisy rested her tail softly on each kit as she named it.

"Those will work very well as Clan names," Leafpool told her. "Here they'll be Berrykit, Mousekit, and Hazelkit. I'll let Firestar know."

She thought Daisy looked a bit doubtful, as if she wasn't sure she wanted her kits to be part of the Clan, but before she could say any more Ferncloud crept in through the entrance with a mouse in her jaws.

"I've brought you some fresh-kill," she meowed to Daisy, placing the mouse next to her. Purring, she settled down in the moss beside the kits. "They look fine now. I'm sure you have enough milk."

Leaving them to discuss the kits, Leafpool said good-bye and emerged into the clearing. The weather was still gray and cold, and the trees above her head clashed in the wind.

More than a half moon had passed since their encounter on the hillside, but there had been no word from Crowfeather. Half the time, Leafpool drifted around in a haze of happiness, remembering the look in his eyes and the scent of his pelt.

But for the rest of the time she was clawed by guilt that she had agreed to meet him again. If she was a true medicine cat, she wouldn't even be thinking about him. She tried harder than ever to concentrate on her tasks, so that she could become the cat she had always longed to be. Besides, she didn't want Cinderpelt to scold her, or suspect that the WindClan warrior was occupying her thoughts.

Leafpool padded toward her den, but stopped short as a tortoiseshell cat hurtled through the thorn tunnel and skidded to a halt in the middle of the clearing. For an instant Leafpool thought it was Sorreltail, and her heart lurched at the thought of any harm coming to the kits she was carrying. Then she looked more closely and recognized Mosspelt, a warrior from RiverClan.

"Leafpool!" she gasped. "Thank StarClan you're here!"

"What's the matter?" Leafpool asked.

"Mothwing sent me." Mosspelt's chest heaved. "There's sickness in RiverClan. It's bad—very bad."

"And Mothwing wants me to come?"

Mosspelt nodded. "Mothwing said you would understand what the trouble is."

Leafpool swallowed, feeling as if a tough piece of fresh-kill were stuck in her throat. She understood too well. Feathertail's warning—that Twolegs would put RiverClan in great danger—had come true. Her dream, her long journey to tell Mothwing, had all been in vain.

More cats had begun to gather in the clearing. Firestar appeared on the Highledge with Sandstorm, while Brightheart and several other warriors emerged from the warriors' den. Daisy peered cautiously out of the nursery, then ran across to Cloudtail and began talking urgently to him, twitching her tail anxiously as she spoke.

Sootfur shot Mosspelt a hostile stare. "Why should we send our medicine cat all the way around the lake to help RiverClan? They should find help somewhere else."

"Oh, come on!" Thornclaw argued. "WindClan isn't likely to help, are they? And ShadowClan has never been exactly generous toward other Clans."

Leafpool was relieved to see Cinderpelt padding across to them.

"What's going on? Mosspelt, are you in trouble?"

"The whole of RiverClan is in trouble," the she-cat answered. More calmly, now that she had caught her breath, she repeated what she had told Leafpool. "Mothwing's den is full of sick cats," she mewed. "None have died yet, but they will die, if we don't have help."

"May I go?" Leafpool begged. She was racked with guilt that she hadn't tried to do anything else to find out what the trouble might be. Perhaps she really was losing her ability to speak with StarClan. "Please, Cinderpelt!"

Cinderpelt and Firestar exchanged a long glance. Then the medicine cat meowed, "If Firestar agrees."

The Clan leader nodded. "We can't refuse to help another Clan in trouble. Besides, this sickness, whatever it is, might come here. Leafpool, try to find out everything you can about it."

"I will," Leafpool promised. "Are you sure you can manage without me?" she asked Cinderpelt. Because of her lame leg, the medicine cat relied on Leafpool to collect most of the healing herbs they needed.

"Of course," Cinderpelt replied. "ThunderClan is lucky to have two medicine cats." A shadow flickered in her eyes.

Brightheart stepped forward. "I could help you, Cinderpelt," she offered. "I think I know what most of the herbs look like—the common ones, anyway."

"Thank you, Brightheart." Cinderpelt turned back to Leafpool. "There's no reason why you shouldn't go with Mosspelt. But come back as soon as you can. And may StarClan go with you."

Leafpool nodded and followed Mosspelt out of the camp. Already she had begun to run through a list of the herbs she might need: juniper, watermint, chervil root. . . . She shook her head. She couldn't tell what she needed until she'd had a chance to examine the sick cats. *StarClan, I need you now*, she prayed silently. *Show me what I have to do.*

A strong wind whisked across the surface of the lake as Leafpool and Mosspelt crossed WindClan's territory, buffeting the two cats' fur. After her frantic dash to ThunderClan, Mosspelt couldn't manage anything faster than a trot, and Leafpool kept pace with her. There was no point in racing on to the RiverClan camp if she arrived too exhausted to help.

They were drawing near the horseplace when Leafpool heard a yowl from somewhere above them. Glancing around, she spotted a patrol of four WindClan cats bounding down the hillside toward them. Her heart lurched as she saw Crowfeather's lean gray shape racing over the turf.

She and Mosspelt stopped and waited for the patrol to catch up. Tornear was leading it; behind him, flanking Crowfeather, came Owlwhisker and Webfoot.

"Greetings." Tornear dipped his head. "What are you doing on WindClan territory?"

His tone was formal, not aggressive, though Leafpool hardly registered his question. She was too conscious of Crowfeather's eyes scorching into her fur, though she dared not speak to him or even look at him with so many other cats around.

"We're on our way to RiverClan," Mosspelt meowed. She did not tell Tornear why; Leafpool guessed she was in no hurry to let WindClan know that RiverClan had been weakened by sickness.

"We're staying close to the lake," Leafpool pointed out, "just as the leaders decided at the Gathering."

"I can see you are," meowed Tornear. "Carry on, then, and—"

"What are you staring at *her* for?" Webfoot growled. "Aren't there enough cats in WindClan for you to be padding after?"

Leafpool froze. He was speaking to Crowfeather. She looked at the gray warrior and saw her own dismay reflected in his eyes.

"Great StarClan, Webfoot," Tornear meowed. "Don't be more mouse-brained than you can help. This is Squirrelflight's sister, remember? Squirrelflight who Crowfeather went on the journey with?"

Leafpool went limp with relief, breathing out silent thanks to Tornear.

"That's right," Crowfeather choked out. "Er . . . say hi to Squirrelflight for me, will you, Leafpool?"

"Sure." Leafpool dipped her head.

Mosspelt scraped her claws impatiently on the pebbles. "Can we keep going, please?"

Tornear nodded, waving Leafpool and Mosspelt away with a sweep of his tail.

Before Leafpool had taken a couple of paces she heard a hiss behind her and swung around to see Crowfeather following her.

"Meet me by the island at twilight," he whispered, adding in a louder meow, "Remember to tell Squirrelflight what I said."

"Yes, I will," Leafpool replied. Guilt and excitement thrilled through her until she felt that every hair on her pelt must be sparkling with it. This couldn't be wrong, could it? When it made her so happy?

"Crowfeather, are you coming?" Webfoot yowled.

The gray warrior darted away without another glance at Leafpool. She bounded along the lakeshore to catch up to Mosspelt, feeling as though her paws hardly touched the ground.

Long before she and Mosspelt reached the RiverClan camp, Leafpool could smell the sickness. It hung heavily in the air, a stench like rotting carrion. Then an eerie wailing rose above the gurgle of the stream that bordered the camp. Mosspelt shot Leafpool a terrified glance and bounded ahead, splashing through the stream and into the camp. Leafpool followed, hardly noticing the icy water that dragged at her paws and soaked her belly fur.

Leopardstar emerged from the ferns at the top of the bank and waited for Leafpool and Mosspelt to reach her. The terrible wailing went on and on.

"Ivytail is dead," Leopardstar announced. Her voice was calm, but Leafpool could see stark terror behind her eyes. "Do you think you can do anything to help us?"

"I don't know until I talk to Mothwing," Leafpool answered. "I'll go straight to her den—I know the way."

"I will send some of my warriors to help you," Leopardstar meowed.

Leafpool crossed the camp and picked her way down the bank to Mothwing's den under the thornbush. All thoughts of Crowfeather had vanished from her head. All that mattered was helping these sick cats.

On the way, she met Heavystep and Hawkfrost bearing the limp body of a brown tabby Leafpool didn't recognize. She stood aside to let them pass, her head respectfully bowed.

"Leafpool!" It was Mothwing's voice, high and panicky. The RiverClan medicine cat flung herself out of the den and pressed her muzzle into Leafpool's fur. "I knew you would come!"

Leafpool inhaled her friend's fear-scent, stronger even than the reek of sickness. "Tell me what the matter is," she mewed.

"They're all dying!" Mothwing's wide amber eyes were distraught. "I don't know what to do!"

"Mothwing, calm down," she ordered. "Your Clan will give up completely if they see their medicine cat panicking. You *must* be strong for their sake."

Mothwing took a couple of gulping breaths. "I'm sorry," she meowed after a moment. "You're right, Leafpool. I'm okay now."

"Tell me what's been happening," Leafpool repeated.

"Come and see."

Mothwing led Leafpool to her den. Close to the entrance, sheltered by the twisted branches of the thorn tree, a small black kit lay in a mossy nest. Its eyes were closed, and Leafpool had to watch closely for a few moments before she saw its shallow breathing.

Beside it were two other kits—another black one unconscious like the first but breathing more strongly, and a gray one thrashing back and forth, its jaws gaping in a feeble wail.

Farther along the bank, beyond the den, four warriors lay in rough nests of dried bracken, along with a younger cat who looked like an apprentice. Leafpool recognized Dawnflower's pale gray pelt, and Voletooth, who had recently been made a warrior.

She crouched down beside Dawnflower, who was nearest, and extended one paw to pat her belly gently. Dawnflower moaned and tried to pull away from her. Leafpool gave her a soothing lick, then sat back and looked up at Mothwing.

"It reminds me of the time the elders were ill from drinking poisoned water," she meowed. "But the scent isn't quite the same. I wonder—"

"But that was my fault!" Mothwing wailed. "I should have smelled there was a dead rabbit in that pool."

"Not when your paws were covered in mouse bile," Leafpool reminded her. "And this sickness isn't your fault either."

"It is!" Mothwing dug her claws into the earth. "If I were a true medicine cat, I would know what to do for my Clan."

"That's nonsense," Leafpool mewed sharply. "You *are* a true medicine cat. You've done nothing to cause this sickness, but we need to find out where it comes from."

"I haven't had time to check everywhere in the territory, not since the first cats fell ill," Mothwing admitted. "But all the streams are running clear, and there's no sign of Twoleg rubbish in the lake." She scraped the ground again with her claws. "I'm a useless medicine cat. Mudfur should never have chosen me."

"That's nonsense too, and you know it," Leafpool meowed more gently, brushing her tail against Mothwing's pelt. "What about the moth's wing that Mudfur found outside his den? It was a clear sign from StarClan that they wanted you to be his apprentice." Mothwing looked as if she was about to protest, but Leafpool went on rapidly, "Tell me what you've been doing for these sick cats."

"I gave them watermint for bellyache, and when that didn't work I tried juniper berries. That seemed to soothe the pain a bit, but the cats didn't get better."

"Hmm . . ." Leafpool ran her list of remedies through her mind. "If they've eaten something poisonous, then we should try to make them bring it up. Have you got any yarrow leaves?"

"A few," Mothwing replied. "Not enough for every cat, though."

"Then some cat will have to go and fetch more."

While she was speaking, Leafpool saw Mistyfoot and a young black warrior she didn't know padding down the slope toward her. Mistyfoot waved her tail in greeting. "Leopardstar sent us to help you," she meowed.

"Thanks," Leafpool replied. "We need yarrow leaves."

"I'll get some," the black tom offered immediately. Dipping his head to Leafpool, he added, "You don't remember me, do you?"

Scanning his slender figure and small, neat ears, Leafpool felt as if she should recognize him, but she couldn't remember his name. She shook her head. "Sorry."

"I'm Reedwhisker," the black warrior meowed. "You saved me when I nearly drowned, back in our old home."

"He was Reedpaw then," Mistyfoot added.

Surprise silenced Leafpool for a moment, as she remembered the cat Mistyfoot had dragged out of the flooded river. Mothwing hadn't known what to do to get the young cat breathing again, and Leafpool had been forced to take over. The spirit of Spottedleaf had been close beside her all the time, guiding her paws until it was clear that the apprentice would live.

"I'm glad to see you again," she mewed briefly, not wanting to remind Mothwing of another occasion when she had panicked. "We need as much yarrow as you can carry, and quickly.

Do you know where to find it?"

"There are some good clumps near the horseplace fence," Mothwing put in before he could reply.

Reedwhisker waved his tail. "I'm on my way. I've got an apprentice of my own now," he added. "Ripplepaw. I'll take her with me so we can carry more."

"Juniper berries too," Leafpool called after him as the slender black warrior whipped around and raced off. "There are bushes near the top of the slope above the marshes."

Reedwhisker flicked his tail to show he had heard and vanished over the top of the bank.

"Right, Mothwing," Leafpool meowed when he had gone. "Where's the yarrow you do have? We can get started while we wait for Reedwhisker to come back."

"Tell me what I can do first," Mistyfoot mewed. "Are there any other herbs you need?"

"Not right now," Leafpool answered. "But you could check the territory for anything that might have caused this."

Mistyfoot looked puzzled. "What kind of thing am I looking for?"

Leafpool shook her head, careful to say nothing that would reveal that the warning dream had come to her and not to RiverClan's own medicine cat. "I wish I could tell you. Anything unusual—especially anything that doesn't smell right. Look for something that Twolegs might have done or left behind."

"Twolegs? Around here?" Mistyfoot put her head on one

side. "Well, you know best, I suppose. I'll send out all the cats
we can spare."

She cast a sorrowful look at the row of sick cats lying along
the bank of the stream, then disappeared over the top of the
bank.

Meanwhile Mothwing had retreated into her den and
came back with a bunch of yarrow leaves, which she dropped
at Leafpool's paws. Leafpool blinked in dismay at how few
there were, but at least they looked reasonably fresh.

"Okay, let's treat the kits first," she meowed. "There's
enough here for all three of them, and with any luck Reedwhisker will be back soon." She nosed the gray kit, who was
still writhing in pain and letting out faint mewling sounds; a
chill crept over her as she realized he had weakened even in
the short time since she had first seen him. "Help me move
him over here," she directed Mothwing. "We don't want him
vomiting in the place where he's got to sleep."

As gently as they could, the two she-cats moved the kit
closer to the bank of the stream and laid him on a soft cushion
of moss. Leafpool chewed up a single yarrow leaf, being careful to spit out all the scraps. Then she stuffed the pulp into the
kit's wide-open mouth.

"Swallow it," she ordered, although she wasn't sure if the kit
could hear her.

The tiny throat convulsed as the kit tried to spit out the
scraps of bitter-tasting leaf. But some must have gone down,
because a moment later he vomited up several mouthfuls of

evil-smelling mucus. His cries died down, and he lay limp and shivering, blinking up at Leafpool.

"Well done." Leafpool stroked one paw over his head. "Now I want you to eat one juniper berry for me, and then you can go to sleep. Mothwing?"

The RiverClan medicine cat was already at her side with the juniper berry. She crushed it carefully and held it where the kit could lick it up, massaging his throat to make sure he swallowed it. Her soothing purr—so different from her earlier panic—quieted the tiny kit, and he was asleep by the time Leafpool and Mothwing moved him back to his nest.

"I think he'll be okay," murmured Leafpool, sending up a silent prayer to StarClan. "Let's treat the next one."

The next kit was still sleeping, but she stirred as the two medicine cats moved her to the edge of the bank.

"My belly hurts," she moaned.

"This will make it better," Leafpool promised, stuffing another yarrow leaf into the kit's mouth.

Instantly the kit spat it out. "Yuck, it's horrible!"

"Minnowkit, do as you're told and eat it," Mothwing mewed sharply.

"Don't want—" The kit's protest was interrupted by a feeble wail as her belly was seized by another cramp.

Mothwing took the chance to stuff the yarrow leaf back into her mouth, while Leafpool stroked her throat. Minnowkit wailed again, and like the first kit soon brought up the reeking mucus.

"Now you can have a juniper berry," Mothwing meowed, popping it in swiftly as Minnowkit opened her mouth to protest.

"Juniper's horrible," Minnowkit murmured, her voice fading as she drifted, still complaining, into sleep.

Leafpool and Mothwing dragged her back to the nest and examined the third kit, the one who seemed weakest.

Mothwing's eyes were huge with distress. "I think she's dead."

Leafpool bent over the tiny kit and felt her whiskers stirred by a faint breath. "No, she's still alive." She tried to sound hopeful, though privately she was afraid the kit was well on the way to joining the ranks of StarClan. *Not if I can help it*, she decided. "I don't think we should try moving her, though," she warned. "Fetch a dock leaf, and she can vomit onto that."

Mothwing hurried over to where docks grew at the edge of the stream and bit through the stem of a large leaf. Meanwhile Leafpool chewed up more yarrow. All her efforts to rouse the kit failed, so Mothwing had to part the kit's jaws while Leafpool forced the yarrow as far down her throat as she could.

The kit retched feebly and spat a few scraps of yarrow mixed with mucus onto the dock leaf before lying still.

"That's not enough," Mothwing mewed worriedly.

"No, but it's better than nothing. We'll let her rest for a while, then try again."

There were only two yarrow leaves left.

"We should treat Beechpaw next," Mothwing decided, pointing with her tail to where the young cat lay at the end of the row of sick warriors. "He's the weakest, except for the kits." She picked up the remaining yarrow in her jaws and padded off. Leafpool was about to go with her when Mistyfoot reappeared at the top of the bank, her sides heaving.

"Leafpool," she panted, "I've found something. Will you come and see?"

Leafpool glanced at Mothwing, who had also heard the deputy's arrival and turned to listen. "Go on, Leafpool," she urged. "I'll be fine here."

Leafpool made one last swift check of the sleeping kits, then climbed the bank to join Mistyfoot. To her relief, she spotted Reedwhisker and a silver-pelted apprentice padding across the camp, their jaws full of yarrow.

"That's great!" she exclaimed. "Take it straight to Mothwing, please."

"No problem," Reedwhisker mumbled around his mouthful of stems. "We'll fetch the juniper next."

The RiverClan deputy led Leafpool along the top of the bank as far as a barrier of thorns that stretched from stream to stream, blocking off the camp from intruders. When the two cats had pushed their way through a narrow tunnel, curved around many sleek bodies, Mistyfoot followed the smaller stream up a steep slope in the direction of the ShadowClan border.

Soon the slope became an almost sheer, sandy cliff, with jutting rocks that cats could climb, while the stream cascaded down beside them in a waterfall. Leafpool slowed down, careful not to slip on the wet stone. Mistyfoot waited for her at the top, where the stream gushed out of the hillside between moss-covered boulders.

"Not far now," she promised.

Leafpool paused to catch her breath and taste the air. She caught a faint hint of the Thunderpath that formed the border between RiverClan and ShadowClan, but the scent of monsters was faint and stale, as if none had been there for many days. Her ears pricked as she identified another scent—unfamiliar, but reminding her of the reek of sickness around Mothwing's den. She glanced at Mistyfoot.

"This way," the deputy mewed.

The stench grew stronger as they approached the border with ShadowClan. Leafpool was just starting to wonder if the problem lay in RiverClan's territory at all when Mistyfoot swerved around a hazel thicket and headed back into her own territory. Hawkfrost and Blackclaw were waiting a few fox-lengths away, in a small clearing enclosed by brambles. Hawkfrost swung to face them as they approached, neck fur bristling, then relaxed when he saw who they were.

"Nothing to report," he meowed. "Everything's been quiet since you left."

"No sign of ShadowClan," Blackclaw added.

Leafpool wondered why the RiverClan warrior was so worried about ShadowClan. They hadn't crossed the border between the territories. Perhaps he wanted to blame Shadow-Clan for the sickness.

"This has nothing to do with ShadowClan," Misty-foot mewed sharply. "It's a Twoleg thing, just like you said,

Leafpool. Come and see, but don't get too close."

Hawkfrost and Blackclaw stepped aside to reveal a smooth, round object about the size of a badger lying at the far side of the clearing, half hidden by brambles. It was hard and shiny, like the Twoleg monsters. As Leafpool crept toward it, she saw that in one place the smooth surface was crushed and broken. A sticky liquid oozed out of the crack, dripping down the side to form a silvery-green puddle. Traces of the liquid on the grass farther away suggested that cats or some other animal had trodden in the puddle and picked up some of the sticky stuff on their paws.

Leafpool opened her jaws to speak and coughed as the reek hit her throat. "This must be it!" she gasped. "That stuff could kill a cat; it even *looks* evil."

"And smells vile," Hawkfrost growled, his nose wrinkled in disgust.

"I don't get it," Blackclaw argued. "Surely no cat would be mouse-brained enough to drink that."

"Mouse-brain yourself," Mistyfoot retorted. "Can't you see cats must have picked it up on their pads? You tread in it accidentally, you lick yourself clean, and there you are."

"Other animals would tread in it too," Leafpool agreed. "Mice, for example. If cats killed them and ate them, they would pick up the poison that way."

Mistyfoot looked horrified. "That means it could be over the whole territory by now!"

"I don't think it's as bad as that," Leafpool told her. "You'll need to warn every cat to keep away from this area for a while, but any prey that picked it up would die before they had the chance to travel very far. I don't think there's much risk they'd be caught as fresh-kill anywhere else."

Mistyfoot nodded. "I'll tell Leopardstar right away."

"It's about time," Hawkfrost commented in a low voice to Blackclaw. "If the patrols had been properly organized, we would have found this long ago."

Leafpool froze. Patrols were the deputy's responsibility; Hawkfrost was criticizing Mistyfoot practically to her face. She remembered that back in the old forest Mistyfoot had been trapped by Twolegs, and while she was away Hawkfrost had been made RiverClan deputy in her place. Becoming an ordinary warrior again when Mistyfoot returned must have been hard for Hawkfrost, but that was no excuse for undermining Mistyfoot's authority to other cats. What he said wasn't even true; a Clan's territory was too big for patrols to find every single hazard right away.

Blackclaw was nodding agreement, with a hostile glance at the blue-furred she-cat; did he think Hawkfrost should still be deputy? Leafpool wondered. Was Hawkfrost trying to gain followers who were loyal to him alone, and not to the Clan?

Mistyfoot had begun to pad away, back to the camp. If she had noticed the exchange, she gave no sign of it.

"We'll find some thorns and build a barrier around the thing," Hawkfrost offered, calling after her. "Come on, Blackclaw," he added more softly. "We don't want any animals coming near it, cats or prey. *Some* cat has to look out for the Clan."

He bounded over to the nearest thicket and started clawing at a dead thorn branch. Blackclaw followed and helped to drag it back to the Twoleg thing with its stinking pool.

"Wash your paws when you've finished," Leafpool advised, trying to pretend she hadn't heard what Hawkfrost said. "*Don't* lick them."

"Good thinking," Hawkfrost replied, as he went off to find another branch.

Leafpool ran to catch up with Mistyfoot. "There's one thing I don't understand," she meowed, as the choking stench began to die away behind them. "How did those kits get ill? Surely they're too young to be this far from the nursery?"

Mistyfoot let out an exasperated sigh. "The other day they ran away from camp and went exploring on their own. It was Minnowkit's idea. She can think of more ways of getting into trouble than there are stars in Silverpelt. The sooner she has a mentor to keep an eye on her, the happier I'll be."

"They're too young to have caught any prey around here, so they must have found that Twoleg thing." Leafpool shivered at the thought of young kits sticking their paws into the vile green liquid. "They never told any cat what they had found?" When Mistyfoot shook her head, Leafpool went on, "The other cats must have gotten sick from poisoned prey, or *they* would have reported the Twoleg thing to Leopardstar."

"The kits never said a word," Mistyfoot agreed. "I was furious when I caught them trying to sneak back into camp. They probably thought they were in enough trouble already." She stopped suddenly. "Dawnflower's their mother. She gave them a good licking when they got back, and she was the first full-grown cat to fall ill."

"That makes sense," Leafpool meowed. "I'll have to have a word with those kits when they wake up."

"They *will* wake up?"

"I think so." Leafpool didn't mention the black kit who hadn't responded to the yarrow treatment. Mothwing needed more help than she alone could provide to save some of these fragile lives. "With the help of StarClan," she added quietly.

The day was nearly over when the two cats returned to the RiverClan camp. The setting sun was a sullen red glow behind bars of cloud. Leafpool had hardly noticed time passing; it seemed no more than a few heartbeats since Mosspelt had dashed into the stone hollow.

At least the camp was quiet; no eerie wailing signaled another death. Most cats were settling into their dens for the night, although two or three still crouched beside the fresh-kill pile.

"That reminds me," Leafpool meowed. "It would be a good idea to go through the fresh-kill pile and throw out anything with that scent on it."

Mistyfoot nodded. "I'll check the camp, too, in case any cat has brought that stuff in on their paws. And every cat should check themselves, and wash off the scent downstream if they have it."

She headed toward Leopardstar's den to report to her leader. Leafpool watched her go; then she slipped over the top of the bank and down to where Mothwing stooped over the sick cats.

"How's it going?" she asked, joining the RiverClan medicine cat, who was examining Dawnflower.

"Okay, I think. No cat has died, though Heavystep has fallen ill." She pointed with her tail to where the big tabby elder was curled up on the bank. "I've given him yarrow, and he doesn't seem as bad as some of the others."

Leafpool remembered that Heavystep was one of the cats who had been carrying out the dead cat when she arrived. Perhaps he had picked up the poison that way. Hawkfrost had been with him, but he seemed fine, and he knew now that he had to be careful not to get the sticky Twoleg stuff on his fur.

"We found what the problem is," Leafpool told Mothwing. She described the shiny Twoleg thing and the greenish liquid that was seeping out from it.

Mothwing shuddered. "So it *was* Twolegs who brought the trouble!" Her blue gaze locked with Leafpool's. Then she flicked her tail. "Come and check the cats."

Leafpool had hardly begun to sniff Dawnflower when she glimpsed movement out of the corner of her eye. A kit was standing at the other end of the line of sick cats; in the twilight Leafpool could only just make out her dark gray pelt. At first she thought she must be one of Dawnflower's litter making a spectacular recovery, but this kit was older, and she didn't look ill at all.

"Mothwing, over here!" the kit called urgently.

"Who's that?" Leafpool asked, following Mothwing as she began to pick her way around the sleeping bodies.

"Willowkit," Mothwing replied; her eyes glowed with affection as she reached the dark gray kit and looked down at her. "Mosspelt's daughter. She often comes to help me, and she already knows nearly all the herbs. Willowkit, this is Leafpool from ThunderClan."

Willowkit dipped her head. "Mothwing, I think you ought to look at Beechpaw," she urged.

The apprentice was lying on his side, his limbs splayed out, his claws scraping feebly at the ground. His chest heaved and he was struggling to breathe. His wide-open eyes were glazed.

"What's the matter with him?" Willowkit asked, her eyes huge with anxiety. "None of the others are like this."

Mothwing hesitated, and it was Leafpool who spoke first. "Did you give him juniper?"

"Yes, for the bellyache," Mothwing replied. "It ought to help his breathing as well. I wish we had coltsfoot," she added with a frustrated lash of her tail. "The flowers are up, but it's the leaves we need, and they won't appear for another moon."

Leafpool couldn't see the point of wishing for a herb that wasn't in season. Beechpaw's efforts to breathe were already growing weaker; if they didn't think of something soon he would die in front of them.

Suppose this wasn't caused by the Twoleg stuff at all? It might be a completely new problem, and Beechpaw didn't have much time for them to find the answer.

"Could there be something stuck in his throat?" she suggested. This didn't look like ordinary choking, but with Beechpaw weakened already by the poison he might not be able to cough up an obstruction.

Mothwing prized open the apprentice's jaws, holding him firmly as he writhed to free himself. Leafpool peered down his throat. "There's something there, but so far down . . ."

"Let me try." Instantly Willowkit poked a slender paw down Beechpaw's throat, let out a faint sound of satisfaction, and withdrew it to show a wad of half-chewed yarrow leaves hooked into her claws.

"Well done!" meowed Leafpool.

As Mothwing released him, Beechpaw collapsed, trembling and drawing in great gasping breaths.

"Willowkit, fetch him some water," Mothwing directed.

The kit darted to the edge of the stream, tore off a clump of hanging moss, and dipped it in the water. Within heartbeats she was back, squeezing a few drops into Beechpaw's mouth. Gradually his sides stopped heaving, his trembling died away, and he shifted into a more comfortable curled position with his eyes closed.

Mothwing touched Willowkit on the shoulder with the tip of her tail. "You saved Beechpaw's life," she mewed. "I'll make sure he knows it when he wakes up."

Willowkit's eyes blazed with happiness. "Is this what it feels like to be a medicine cat?" she asked. "It's the best thing ever!"

"I know." Leafpool let out a sympathetic purr. "I remember the first time I put burdock root on a rat bite. I could hardly believe it when the wound started healing!"

"And don't forget how you saved Reedwhisker when he nearly drowned," Mothwing meowed. "You were only an apprentice then."

Leafpool blinked warmly at her friend, grateful that Mothwing was generous enough to remind her. "There's no feeling like being able to help your Clanmates," she told Willowkit. "I can't think of any other way I'd rather live my life."

"But you can't save lives every day," Mothwing teased, with an affectionate glance at Willowkit. "There are routine jobs to do too."

"But those jobs are important, aren't they?" Willowkit mewed.

"Of course they are," Mothwing assured her. "And I want you to do an important job for me now. Stay here with Beechpaw, and call me right away if there's any change in his breathing."

"Yes, Mothwing." Willowkit sat beside the apprentice, her tail wrapped around her paws and her eyes fixed intently on him.

Mothwing and Leafpool left her while they checked the other cats. Leafpool couldn't help wondering whether Mothwing had already found the perfect apprentice, and then she asked herself how Mothwing could train an apprentice at all, when she couldn't pass on any knowledge of StarClan.

She forced the problem to the back of her mind as she and Mothwing examined the sick cats. All of them were sleeping. Leafpool started to believe that they would all recover, though Dawnflower was still very weak.

Last they came to the three kits in the mossy nest by Mothwing's den. The little gray tom was sleeping, but Minnowkit had her eyes open. "I'm hungry!" she wailed.

"That's a good sign," Leafpool commented to Mothwing. "It means the poison's gone."

"Your mother can't feed you now," Mothwing meowed, with a glance at Dawnflower's unmoving shape. "You can have a drink of water if you want one."

Minnowkit looked ready to complain again, then staggered to her paws and tottered the few pawsteps to the stream, where she crouched down to lap. Leafpool kept an eye on her in case she lost her balance and fell into the water.

"Leafpool." Mothwing's voice was tight and quiet.

Leafpool glanced around. Mothwing had bent to sniff the weakest kit. She looked up, grief dulling her amber eyes. "We must have been too late with the yarrow. She's dead."

Leafpool nosed the tiny body, but Mothwing was right. The kit had gone to join the ranks of StarClan. *Take care of her*, Leafpool prayed. *She's so little.*

Minnowkit had finished drinking and was staggering up the bank again.

"Don't say anything," Leafpool whispered urgently to Mothwing, pulling up a covering of moss to hide the motionless scrap of fur. "They'll be stronger in the morning, and maybe Dawnflower will be awake to comfort them. Minnowkit," she went on, as the tiny black she-cat settled herself again in the soft moss, "did you and your littermates find something unusual, that day you ran away from camp? Something Twolegs left behind?"

Minnowkit's eyes stretched wide. "You know about that?"

Leafpool nodded. "I've seen it too. Did you touch the sticky stuff?" When Minnowkit hesitated, she added, "Don't worry, you won't get into trouble."

The black kit hesitated for a heartbeat longer. "Okay, we did touch it," she admitted. "We played at running through it and making pawmarks on the grass. Then I dared Pebblekit to drink some."

Mothwing drew in a shocked breath. "How *could* you be so mouse-brained?"

"And did he drink it?" Leafpool prompted, silencing Mothwing with a swift glance.

"We all did." Minnowkit's nose wrinkled in disgust. "It was yucky."

"You know that's what made you ill, don't you?" Mothwing mewed.

Minnowkit stared at her in dismay. "We didn't know!"

"That's why you must never touch anything strange," Leafpool told her. "When you're an apprentice and you're allowed out of camp on your own, you must report anything you find to your mentor. Even in your territory, not everything is safe. Promise?"

"Okay," Minnowkit mewed. Her eyes closed and then blinked open again. "Is this all my fault?"

Leafpool shook her head. There would be time enough for Minnowkit to blame herself when she discovered her sister was dead. "No, little one. Go to sleep now."

"I don't know how you can be so kind to them!" Mothwing hissed when the kit was asleep again. "I'd like to claw their ears off. All this trouble, and cats dead!"

"You know you wouldn't really hurt them," Leafpool replied. "They're only kits. They didn't know what they were doing. And anyway, it's not all their fault. Dawnflower probably got the poison from them, but the rest of the cats must have picked it up by themselves, or eaten prey that was tainted with it."

"I know." Mothwing sighed. "But you'd think they'd have more *sense*!" Her jaws parted in an enormous yawn.

"You're worn out," Leafpool meowed. "Why don't you get some sleep too? I'll keep watch and wake you at moonhigh."

Mothwing yawned again. "Okay. Thanks, Leafpool— thanks for everything."

She padded into her den under the roots of the bush. Leafpool took one last look at the sick cats; all of them were sleeping quietly, even Beechpaw.

"He's doing fine," she murmured to Willowkit. "I'll look after him now. You can go back to the nursery to your mother. Make sure you tell her how well you did."

Willowkit dipped her head, eyes shining, and dashed off up the bank. Leafpool settled down beside the sleeping apprentice, tucking her paws under her. Above her head the stars of Silverpelt blazed down, scattered around the bulging shape of the moon, which was almost full. Leafpool sent up a wordless prayer to StarClan, a surge of thankfulness that at last RiverClan's sickness seemed to be under control.

Only then did she realize that she had completely forgotten to meet Crowfeather at twilight.

CHAPTER 11

❧

Squirrelflight stopped underneath a tree and listened. The woods were silent except for the wind rustling in the trees. When she tasted the air, the scents were faint; the cold weather must have sent all the prey deep into their holes. Shrugging, she padded on, letting her paws decide where to take her.

She hadn't left the camp intending to hunt. She had set out with Ashfur and Birchpaw on the way to the mossy clearing Brightheart had discovered. But when they emerged from the thorn tunnel they met Brambleclaw on his way back from a training session with Spiderleg and Rainwhisker.

"Where are you going?" he asked Squirrelflight, gesturing for the two younger warriors to go on without him.

"Ashfur's going to teach Birchpaw some fighting moves," Squirrelflight meowed, ignoring the tabby warrior's aggressive tone. "I thought I'd go along and help."

"Well, you thought wrong," Brambleclaw snapped. "*Ashfur* is Birchpaw's mentor, not you. If you're looking for something to do, the elders need their pelts checked for ticks."

Squirrelflight drew her lips back in the beginning of a snarl. "Don't order me around!"

"Then stop being so irresponsible," Brambleclaw retorted. "There's still a lot to do." He flicked his tail angrily and vanished into the tunnel.

"We'd better go by ourselves," Ashfur meowed. He glanced at Birchpaw, who had listened to the exchange with wide, scared eyes. "There's no point making trouble."

"It's Brambleclaw who's making all the trouble," Squirrelflight pointed out, although she had to admit that Ashfur might be right. Back in their old home, mentors and apprentices had usually trained alone. "I'll see you later. But I'm not checking the elders for ticks," she added, as Ashfur and Birchpaw headed for the clearing. "I'm not letting Brambleclaw think he can tell me what to do."

As she bounded away from the camp, Brambleclaw's actions started to make more sense. He must be jealous of Ashfur because he had been chosen to mentor Birchpaw. *And maybe because I'm spending time with Ashfur instead of him*, she realized. *But he made it perfectly clear how he felt about me, so he has no right to act like a bee-stung badger!*

She had decided to hunt for a while and take back a decent contribution to the fresh-kill pile. She wouldn't give Brambleclaw the satisfaction of telling her off yet again for neglecting her warrior duties.

Suddenly she was flooded with the reek of ShadowClan. Her wanderings had taken her close to the border, not far from the dead tree. A heartbeat later she heard a fierce snarling, followed by the screech of a fighting cat. She froze. Had she crossed the border by mistake?

In front of her, a few tail-lengths on the ShadowClan side, a clump of bracken started waving madly, and two cats locked in a yowling knot of fur crashed into the open. One was Tawnypelt; the other was the huge black and white tomcat from the Twoleg nest in ShadowClan's territory.

Squirrelflight heard a shriek of pain from Tawnypelt as the kittypet fastened his teeth in her throat. She couldn't stand by and watch her friend and former Clanmate get killed. She streaked across the border and flung herself on top of the tomcat.

"Let her go!"

She raked her claws down his side and as he tried to writhe away she bit down hard on his tail. He let out a yowl of mingled pain and fury, and Tawnypelt pulled free from him, whirling around to aim her claws at his ear. The kittypet rolled over, battering at both she-cats with his powerful hind legs, then leapt to his paws and raced off into the trees.

Squirrelflight scrambled up and watched him until he was out of sight; a moment later Tawnypelt joined her and stood panting hard.

"Thanks," she gasped. "He jumped me when I wasn't expecting it."

"You're welcome. Any time."

There was a haunted look in Tawnypelt's eyes and her gaze darted warily from side to side as if she expected to find an enemy behind every tree. Squirrelflight was close enough to catch the fear-scent coming from her friend. She couldn't understand it; Tawnypelt was a brave warrior, and in her own territory. "Is there something wrong?" she asked.

Alarm flared briefly in Tawnypelt's eyes, then she shook her head. "Nothing we can't deal with."

"Yeah, and hedgehogs can fly," Squirrelflight retorted. "Come on, Tawnypelt, I can see something's upsetting you. It can't surely be that mangy brute."

"Leave it, will you, Squirrelflight?" Tawnypelt snarled. "You shouldn't even be here. Consider yourself lucky a patrol hasn't caught you already." She spun around and bounded away, deeper into ShadowClan territory.

Her pelt prickling with anxiety, Squirrelflight checked that no cats were in sight, then she ran after her friend. "Tawnypelt, wait!"

Tawnypelt skidded to a halt in the shadow of a pine tree. "Squirrelflight, you mouse-brain!" she hissed. "Go back! If a patrol catches you here they'll claw your ears off, and I'll be in just as much trouble for letting you get this far."

Squirrelflight ignored her. Scanning her closely, she saw how thin her friend looked, her ribs showing like branches and her pelt rough. She looked exhausted from more than the recent fight. "I'm not going back," Squirrelflight mewed stubbornly. "Not until you tell me what's going on."

Tawnypelt sighed. "You never give up, do you?" She crept backward into the shelter of the pine tree until its low-growing branches screened them from passing patrols.

Squirrelflight gave her a comforting lick around the ears. "Come on, you can tell me."

"You know where that black and white tom comes from?"

Tawnypelt began. "The Twoleg nest in our territory? There's another kittypet there too—a tabby."

Squirrelflight's tail curled up. "Did you think I'd forgotten? They nearly clawed my fur off!" *And I wouldn't have got away if Brambleclaw hadn't helped me*, she added to herself.

"Well, ShadowClan is having some trouble with them," Tawnypelt explained reluctantly.

"Trouble with kittypets? ShadowClan?" Squirrelflight echoed. "You're telling me a whole Clan of warriors can't deal with a couple of kittypets?"

"It's not funny," Tawnypelt snapped. "Yesterday they caught Talonpaw out on his own. They attacked him and left him wounded. He managed to drag himself back to camp, but he died." She stared down at her paws.

"Oh, Tawnypelt, I'm sorry!"

Tawnypelt went on, her voice dull as if she was too exhausted to share Squirrelflight's horror. "Rowanclaw, who was Talonpaw's mentor, led a patrol to take revenge. But as soon as the kittypets saw them they fled back into the nest. Their Twolegs threw hard things at the patrol, and Cedarheart's leg was badly injured." Tawnypelt curled her lip. "Those kittypets are cowards. They only come after cats who are weak, or alone."

Squirrelflight pressed her muzzle against Tawnypelt's side. "ThunderClan will help," she promised. "I'll go and tell Firestar right away."

Tawnypelt stared at her. "Don't be a mouse-brain. This is ShadowClan's problem."

"So? We can't let you be picked off one by one without doing something."

Tawnypelt lifted her head, grief giving way to defiance. "Are you saying that my Clan isn't strong enough to solve our own problems?"

"Oh, you'll sort them out in the end," Squirrelflight agreed. "But how many more cats will die or be injured in the meantime? What's wrong with both Clans putting our heads together and coming up with a plan to teach the mangy brutes a lesson once and for all? You're worse than stupid if you turn down help when it's offered."

For a heartbeat Tawnypelt's eyes blazed and Squirrelflight only just stopped herself from flinching away as she remembered what a formidable fighter her friend was. Then the tortoiseshell warrior let her fur lie flat again. "That's for Blackstar to decide," she meowed.

Squirrelflight gave her ear a last reassuring lick. "I'll come straight back," she promised.

Not caring if any cat from either Clan saw her, she raced for the border and back toward the ThunderClan camp. ThunderClan had to help! They hadn't come this far to watch another Clan be driven out by a couple of kittypets.

When she came in sight of the barrier of thorns she slowed down, getting her breath back so she could tell Firestar exactly what was going on. To her relief her father was one of the first cats she saw when she pushed her way through the tunnel. He was crouched near the fresh-kill pile, sharing a vole with Sandstorm. Dustpelt and Ashfur sat close by, talking with their heads close together. A few tail-lengths away, Bramble-claw was eating alone, devouring a wood pigeon with swift, hungry bites.

Squirrelflight raced over. "I've just seen Tawnypelt." She reported what the ShadowClan warrior had told her. "They're being terrorized by those two bits of fox dung," she finished breathlessly. "I told Tawnypelt we'd come and help."

"You'd no business telling her any such thing," Dustpelt growled.

Squirrelflight bristled, but Firestar gestured with his tail for her to keep silent. "It's true each Clan should fend for themselves," he agreed. "That's part of the warrior code. But how far would we have gotten if we'd tried to follow the code when the Twolegs were tearing up the forest? Their monsters would have killed us all."

"Then you'll let us help?" Squirrelflight asked eagerly. "Don't forget I spotted that tabby brute on *our* territory first. We could have trouble with them ourselves if we don't do something to stop them."

"I'll go."

Squirrelflight jumped when Brambleclaw spoke behind her. She hadn't noticed that he had come over to listen.

Firestar twitched his ears at the tabby warrior. "I haven't said yet that any cat is going."

"I'm not sure we should," Dustpelt meowed. "We're still recovering from the journey, one of our medicine cats is already away helping another Clan . . . You can't take every cat's troubles on your shoulders, Firestar."

"No, but we can try," Sandstorm pointed out, giving him a long gaze from her pale green eyes. "An apprentice was killed, Squirrelflight says. What if that had been Birchpaw?"

The question silenced Dustpelt.

"Then you'll send a patrol?" Brambleclaw prompted. "Tawnypelt's my sister. I'd fight StarClan for her, never mind a couple of kittypets."

"So would I," Squirrelflight added. "We journeyed with Tawnypelt. We can't just ignore this!"

Brambleclaw's eyes narrowed as he focused on something behind her, and she turned to see Ashfur coming over, looking troubled. He padded up to her and touched her muzzle with his nose.

"We have to help ShadowClan," she meowed, worried that he would disapprove. "You do see that, don't you?"

"I understand why you feel like this," he replied. "You're loyal to your friends. I wouldn't want you to be anything else."

Squirrelflight felt a purr rise in her throat. She pressed herself against Ashfur's shoulder, aware of Brambleclaw standing rigid on her other side.

"Very well," Firestar meowed. "We'll send a patrol. Brambleclaw, you can lead it, but you're to speak to Blackstar before you do anything. And come straight back if he doesn't want you on his territory. Understood?"

"Yes, Firestar."

"Squirrelflight, you'd better join him. You'll go anyway, so you may as well have permission."

Squirrelflight's tail curled up. "Thanks, Firestar!"

"Pick a few more cats to go with you, Brambleclaw," the Clan leader went on, "then you can leave at once."

Brambleclaw nodded and ran across the clearing to the warriors' den, vanishing between the branches.

"I'll go too," Ashfur volunteered.

"No, I don't think so," Firestar meowed, and as the gray warrior looked crestfallen, he added, "I heard you promise to take Birchpaw hunting. You don't want to disappoint him, do you?"

Ashfur sighed and murmured, "Of course not, Firestar."

Squirrelflight figured Brambleclaw wasn't likely to choose him to be a part of his patrol anyway. Her claws scraped the ground impatiently as she waited for the tabby warrior to come back.

"I suppose it's no good telling you to be careful," Ashfur meowed despondently.

Squirrelflight touched his shoulder with the tip of her tail. "Don't worry about me," she mewed. She remembered her first fight with the kittypets—she should have known they would cause more trouble! The fur on her shoulders rose at the prospect of revenge. "We'll be fine," she promised Ashfur. "We're going to make those kittypets wish they'd never heard of the Clans!"

CHAPTER 12

Brambleclaw reappeared from the den with Brackenfur, Thorn-claw, Cloudtail, and Rainwhisker behind him. Squirrelflight dashed across to join them.

"Good luck!" Ashfur called.

Squirrelflight waved her tail in farewell. Once through the thorn tunnel, she joined Brambleclaw at the head of the patrol.

"Tawnypelt should be waiting where I left her," she meowed. "She can take us to Blackstar."

Brambleclaw nodded. "Okay. You lead the way, then."

He kept pace with her as she trotted through the trees, not racing at top speed because they had a long way to go and had to be fit to fight when they got there.

"What's the plan?" Thornclaw asked.

"There isn't one," Brambleclaw replied. "We'll tell Black-star that we've come to help and are willing to do whatever he wants. If he wants us to stay, we'll work out a plan with him and his warriors."

Tawnypelt was sitting close to the border, crouched under a brittle clump of bracken that hid her pale fur. She sprang to her paws, relief showing in her eyes when she saw her brother and the strong force of cats he had brought with him.

"See?" Squirrelflight meowed. "I told you Firestar would send help."

Brambleclaw and Tawnypelt touched noses. "Take us to Blackstar," Brambleclaw meowed.

Tawnypelt turned and led the way swiftly through the undergrowth, deeper into ShadowClan territory. Soon the leafless trees gave way to dark pines, shutting out most of the light, and the ground underpaw grew soft with a covering of fallen needles. They splashed through a stream, the water running cold and shallow over a stony bed, and up a gentle slope on the other side. Gradually the scent of ShadowClan grew stronger, and Squirrelflight realized they were approaching the camp.

The ground sloped more steeply here, with rocks jutting out of the covering of fallen pine needles. At the top of the rise the trees grew more thickly, guarding the edge of a wide, shallow dip almost filled with bushes. Squirrelflight recognized the place she and her friends had discovered when they first explored the territory. Back then, no cat had expected that the kittypets would be a problem, but now she wondered whether ShadowClan had made their camp too close to the Twoleg nest.

Although the scent of fear and injury wafting from the camp almost took her breath away, Squirrelflight couldn't spot any cats at first. But as they waited at the edge of the hollow, branches rustled beneath them and Blackstar appeared.

He climbed up in a couple of bounds, his fur bristling.

"What's going on?" he demanded. "ThunderClan cats in my territory? Tawnypelt, what do you know about this?"

Tawnypelt dipped her head to her Clan leader. "Squirrelflight helped me fight off one of the kittypets. I told her about the trouble they're causing, and she brought a ThunderClan patrol to help us."

A growl rose in Blackstar's throat. "You told a warrior from another Clan about our Clan's problems?"

Tawnypelt stared at him without flinching. "I told *Squirrelflight*. She's a friend."

"And Tawnypelt's my sister," Brambleclaw added, stepping forward to stand beside her.

Blackstar gave a contemptuous sniff. "Tawnypelt's first loyalty is to her Clan—or it should be."

The tortoiseshell warrior began to bristle. "Blackstar, I've never given you any reason to doubt my loyalty."

The ShadowClan leader's gaze swept over the six Thunder-Clan cats. "You expect me to believe that, when you bring these warriors right into our camp?"

"We'll turn right around and go home again if that's what you want," Thornclaw meowed. "Just say the word."

"Don't be a fool, Blackstar." The voice was Cedarheart's. The gray tom heaved himself out of the cover of the bushes and scrambled up the slope to stand beside his leader. Squirrelflight saw that he was limping, and she remembered Tawnypelt telling her that the Twolegs had injured him when he went to fight the kittypets. "We can't deal with this by ourselves."

"Cedarheart is right." Rowanclaw came to stand at his Clanmate's shoulder. "Those kittypets killed my apprentice. I'd welcome any cat who'd help me rip out their entrails."

Blackstar hesitated for a moment, looking from one of his warriors to the other, taking in their burning gazes and bristling fur. At last he bowed his head. "Very well. Cedarheart, fetch Russetfur. We'll send a patrol with these Thunder-Clan warriors to the Twoleg nest. But you're not going," he added as Cedarheart retreated into the bushes. "You're not battle-fit."

Cedarheart shot him a furious look, but vanished without a protest.

"Blackstar, I don't think we ought to kill these kittypets," Brambleclaw meowed when he had gone.

"*What?*" Rowanclaw spat, before his Clan leader could reply. "They killed my apprentice. I want revenge!"

"And if we kill the kittypets, the Twolegs will want revenge," Brambleclaw pointed out. "They must know you're here."

"That's right." Cloudtail lashed his tail. "Twolegs have little Clans of their own." He shuddered as he added, "I was trapped in one once. If their kittypets are hurt or killed, they won't rest until they've killed you or driven you out. You saw what they did to us in the old forest. Do you want that to happen here?"

"Then how do we stop their kittypets from bothering us?"

Rowanclaw challenged. "Just ask them nicely?" He gave a disgusted snort.

"If we could trap them, we could make them promise to stay away," Squirrelflight suggested. "Seeing all of us together should scare them out of their fur."

"It's an idea," murmured Brambleclaw.

Squirrelflight glanced at him, startled and pleased by his support.

"It's worth a try," Blackstar decided, as his deputy Russetfur slid out of the cover of the bushes and came to join her Clanmates. Oakfur, a smaller ShadowClan tom, followed her.

"Right, this is the plan," Blackstar meowed. "Go to the Twoleg nest, trap the kittypets, and make them promise to leave us alone. Tell them we will kill them if they lay a claw on any of our cats again." He caught Brambleclaw's gaze and added, "I mean that. I will do whatever it takes to protect my Clan. But for now, don't hurt them any more than you have to. Is that clear, Rowanclaw?"

The ginger tom dipped his head, muttering something inaudible.

"Then go," Blackstar continued. "Russetfur, you will lead. I'll stay here and guard the camp."

They must be really scared of the kittypets, Squirrelflight thought, *if the Clan leader has to stay behind to protect the camp!* Then she saw Blackstar's gaze slide sideways to give Brambleclaw a suspicious look. She guessed he was afraid the ThunderClan cats were trying to trick him and meant to attack his camp while his senior warriors were safely out of the way. *Typical ShadowClan!*

She sniffed crossly. *They think every cat is as untrustworthy as they are.*

"May StarClan be with you," Blackstar added, before he slipped back into the shelter of the bushes.

The ShadowClan deputy gathered the patrol together with a wave of her tail and led them around the edge of the hollow and down the slope on the other side. Brambleclaw nodded to his Clanmates and waved his tail for them to follow.

Russetfur brought them to a halt a few fox-lengths away from the Twoleg nest, in the shelter of a bank covered with ferns. The nest was surrounded by a rough stone wall. Both the kittypets were sitting on it, gazing out into the forest. Squirrelflight recognized the big black and white tom with the torn ear who had been fighting with Tawnypelt, and the smaller light brown tabby she had chased out of ThunderClan territory a few days before.

"There they are!" she meowed.

Russetfur irritably flicked one ear. *"Quiet!"*

Both cats looked full-fed and sleepy; after a moment the big tom started to wash himself, drawing his tongue lazily over his shoulder.

"They don't know we're here," Rowanclaw hissed. "Let's attack!"

"No!" Russetfur snapped. "As soon as they see us they'll run into their nest and fetch their Twolegs. We're no match for those creatures. Even I know that."

"We'll have to get them to come out here to us," Thornclaw put in.

"Listen." It was Brambleclaw who spoke, pushing forward

to stand beside Russetfur. "Suppose one of us goes over there"—he nodded toward the space between the ferns where they were hiding and the wall of the nest—"and pretends to be hurt, or ill. If what you say about them is true, they won't miss a chance to attack an easy victim. Meanwhile, some of us should get between them and the wall, so they can't flee back into the nest."

"Good idea!" Brackenfur meowed enthusiastically. "Then we can jump on them and tell them exactly what we'll do if they cause any more trouble."

"What do you think?" Brambleclaw asked Russetfur.

The deputy's ears twitched. "Great StarClan," she muttered, "a ThunderClan cat with brains." Squirrelflight bounced with impatience while she made up her mind. "Okay, we'll go with Brambleclaw's plan," she decided. "We need a cat to go out there as bait."

"I'll do it." Squirrelflight and Tawnypelt spoke at the same time.

"Tawnypelt," meowed Russetfur. Waving her tail at Squirrelflight, she added, "If they pick up a different scent, they might guess it's a trick."

True enough, Squirrelflight thought.

Brambleclaw pushed his nose into his sister's fur. "Don't worry," he meowed. "We won't let them hurt you."

Tawnypelt gave him a long look. "I know."

Squirrelflight watched as Tawnypelt limped out into the clearing and collapsed on her side as if she were too exhausted to go any farther. Maybe the black and white tom would think he'd hurt her badly when they had fought earlier, by the ThunderClan border.

Russetfur chose Rowanclaw, Oakfur, Thornclaw, and Cloudtail to creep in opposite directions and cut off the kittypets from the nest as soon as they made a move. The rest of the cats stayed where they were.

"Keep as quiet as you can, even in the battle," Russetfur ordered. "We don't want the Twolegs to hear what's going on."

Squirrelflight crouched in the bracken with her gaze fixed on the kittypets. As soon as Tawnypelt appeared, they both sat up, ears pricked. The black and white tom mewed something to his companion. Then both cats flowed down from the wall and stalked across the open ground toward Tawnypelt.

At once Russetfur signaled with her tail, and the warriors split into two groups and slid away, their bellies pressed close to the ground as they crept in a wide circle. Neither kittypet noticed; Squirrelflight guessed they weren't used to picking up unexpected scents, and besides, they were too intent on their prey.

Tawnypelt lay on her side, her chest heaving with painful, panting breaths. As the kittypets drew closer she raised her head and gasped out, "Don't hurt me, please!"

The big tomcat thrust his muzzle into her face. "We won't hurt you, roadkill," he sneered. "We'll just take off a few pawfuls of your fur."

"That'll teach you to come into our place," the tabby hissed, slashing a paw toward Tawnypelt's eyes.

Tawnypelt flinched. Squirrelflight heard Brambleclaw

gasp and saw the huge warrior dig his claws into the ground as if he had forgotten that his sister wasn't as helpless as she looked.

At the same moment Russetfur leapt out of the bracken. "Now!"

Squirrelflight pelted across the open ground, Brambleclaw and the rest of the patrol keeping pace with her. The two kittypets took one appalled look at the tide of cats rising to engulf them and turned tail and fled back toward the nest. But the other warriors were already in place behind them, advancing shoulder to shoulder. The small tabby kittypet let out a terrified wail, but the big tom leapt into battle, charging straight for Cloudtail and carrying the white warrior off his paws. Rowanclaw leapt on top of them as they writhed on the ground in a whirl of teeth and claws.

Tawnypelt scrambled up and sprang at the tabby. Rainwhisker and Russetfur piled in to help her, so Squirrelflight launched herself at the big tom as he tore himself away from his opponents' claws and tried to flee across the clearing. Hissing in fury, she raked one paw across his face; his blood spattered onto her fur, warm and sticky. She ducked as he swung a paw at her, slamming her head into his chest so that he staggered back and collided with Brambleclaw coming up behind. Squirrelflight scrambled on top of him, avoiding his battering hind paws; a heartbeat later Brambleclaw had him pinned by the haunches while Rowanclaw came up and sank his teeth into the thrashing black and white tail.

"Don't mess with our warriors, you hear me?" Squirrelflight

hissed into his ear. At that moment, she was speaking for all four Clans, ready to kill if a hair was harmed on the pelt of a cat from any one of them.

Glancing over her shoulder, she saw that Tawnypelt and Rainwhisker had pinned down the tabby cat. Russetfur spoke to him in a low growl, then turned and stalked over to the big tom. She looked down at him in silence for a moment, while he glared back with yellow eyes full of hatred.

"You are a kittypet, and you belong with your Twolegs," she snarled, her voice full of contempt. "The forest is ours now. Cause any more trouble for us, and you know what will happen to you."

Squirrelflight jabbed her claws into the tom's pelt. "Understand?"

The black and white cat spat at her.

"Understand?" Squirrelflight repeated. "Or would you rather I bit your throat open now?"

"I understand," the cat growled.

"Let him go," Russetfur ordered, adding to the big tom, "Go back to your Twolegs and stay there."

Reluctantly Squirrelflight and the other warriors released the kittypet. He staggered to his paws, shaking drops of blood from his pelt. The tabby slunk over to his side and stood with head lowered and tail drooping to the ground.

"Go!" Russetfur bared her teeth. "Now!"

Both kittypets backed away a couple of paces, then turned and fled for the nest. They scrambled over the wall and vanished into the garden. Squirrelflight heard the door of the nest open and a Twoleg voice raised in alarm.

Russetfur twitched her tail and the combined patrol of ShadowClan and ThunderClan cats bounded back into the shadow of the pine trees, not stopping until they were within sight of the camp.

"I'll fetch Blackstar," Russetfur meowed, slipping over the edge of the hollow.

Tawnypelt padded over to Brambleclaw and pushed her nose into his fur. "Thanks. You were great—all of you," she added, lifting her head.

"It was a pleasure," Brambleclaw purred. "Any time."

"Wasn't that great?" Squirrelflight meowed. "I'll never forget the look on those kittypets' faces when they saw us coming. And Brambleclaw, you were in just the right place when I attacked that big brute. You were terrific!"

The warmth welling up inside her turned to ice as Brambleclaw's gaze swept over her from ears to tail-tip. "You fought well too," he replied stiffly, as though he were paying a compliment to another cat's apprentice.

Squirrelflight sank her claws into the leaf mold and bit back an angry retort. She wasn't going to quarrel with her Clanmate in front of the ShadowClan cats. But his coldness hurt more than any wound she had received in the battle.

The bushes rustled in the hollow and Blackstar appeared. "Russetfur tells me you made the kittypets promise to leave us alone."

"You shouldn't have any more trouble," Brambleclaw meowed, "but if you do, let us know. We'll be glad to help."

"Thank you." Blackstar's voice was cool. "But I think we'll be able to manage for ourselves now."

His words were a dismissal. Brambleclaw didn't try to change his mind. He gathered his cats together with a sweep of his tail and briefly touched noses with Tawnypelt. "Goodbye," he mewed to Blackstar. "I expect we'll meet at the next Gathering." He turned and headed back toward Thunder-Clan territory, following the scent trail they had left on their way.

Padding behind him, Squirrelflight felt dull anger slow her paws. The excitement was over; the brief feeling of closeness to Brambleclaw was over too. Why couldn't they just be friends? This antagonism was such a *waste*, when the two of them fought so well together. Her belly twisted with pain that Brambleclaw could put aside old rivalry for the sake of ShadowClan, but not for her.

"Fine. If that's the way he wants it," she muttered, too low for any cat to hear. "See if I care."

But her shoulders ached and her drooping tail brushed the pine needles as she followed her Clanmates back to the stone hollow.

CHAPTER 13

❧

"*I'll be glad when newleaf comes,*" Mothwing remarked, turning over her store of juniper berries with one paw. "We're very short of herbs."

"It's just as bad in ThunderClan," Leafpool told her, touching her shoulder sympathetically with the tip of her tail. "This has been a long leaf-bare, and we don't know the best places yet to find supplies. At least your cats are getting well now."

"Yes, thanks to you." Mothwing let out a purr, then turned to Willowkit, who was standing just outside the medicine cat's den, shifting from paw to paw. "Give two juniper berries to each cat—except for Minnowkit and Pebblekit. They can have one each. Can you remember what juniper is for?"

The small gray kit paused with one paw raised, ready to snag a couple of berries on her claws. "Bellyache," she began, eyes narrowed with the effort of remembering, "but they're getting better, and their bellies aren't aching anymore." She hesitated, puzzled; then her eyes brightened. "Strength!" she mewed triumphantly. "You're giving them juniper so they'll get strong again."

"Very good!" Mothwing purred. She watched the young kit

as she tottered away to give the juniper to Dawnflower. "She's been such a help—and so have you, Leafpool. My Clanmates would have died without you."

"I don't think so," Leafpool meowed, embarrassed by her friend's praise. "You knew what to treat them with all along."

Her third night in the RiverClan camp was drawing to an end. Dew glittered on every leaf and blade of grass in the slanting rays of the sun, and Leafpool was convinced it felt warmer than before. Newleaf could not be far off.

No more RiverClan cats had fallen ill. Mistyfoot had organized the fittest warriors to clean up any traces of the silver-green liquid they found in and around the camp, while Hawkfrost had finished the barrier around the Twoleg thing and made sure every cat knew they had to avoid it.

Meanwhile, all the remaining cats who had been poisoned by the sticky stuff were recovering. Heavystep had already returned to the elders' den, while Minnowkit and Pebblekit were feeling well enough to get into mischief. They were down by the stream now, dabbing a paw into the water as if they were pretending to fish.

"Stay away from the edge!" Mothwing called out. "I don't have time to rescue you if you fall in."

The two kits glanced at each other and drew back a couple of pawsteps, then started to chase each other in a circle.

"They'll have to go back to the nursery," Mothwing sighed. "Dawnflower isn't really strong enough to look after them yet, but I'll get Mosspelt to help her. They'll only get into trouble if they stay here. I caught Minnowkit sniffing around my herb store yesterday."

Leafpool let out a *mrrow* of amusement. "You'd think they'd had enough bellyache without stuffing themselves with the wrong sort of herbs."

She stood up and gave herself a good long stretch. Along the bank of the stream the sick cats were stirring: Dawnflower had rolled onto her side to wash her belly fur, while Beechpaw was sitting up with his jaws parted in an enormous yawn. No cat looked uncomfortable or in pain.

"It's time I was leaving," Leafpool meowed. "You don't need me anymore."

Mothwing nodded, although there was a flash of regret in her eyes. "It's been great, having another medicine cat to work with. But I know you have to go home to your Clan."

"You're leaving?" Willowkit bounced up to them to collect another dose of juniper berries. "We'll miss you, Leafpool." Hesitantly she added to Mothwing, "Will you still need me to help?"

"Of course I will," Mothwing reassured her.

Willowkit's tail pointed straight up and her eyes shone.

Leafpool padded along the bank to say good-bye to those cats who were awake. When she returned to Mothwing's den she saw that Leopardstar had appeared.

"Mothwing tells me you're leaving," the RiverClan leader meowed. "The thanks of all RiverClan go with you, Leafpool."

Leafpool bowed her head. "Any medicine cat would have done the same."

"We won't forget in a hurry," Leopardstar told her. "Have a safe journey, and give my thanks to Firestar, too."

With a last good-bye to Mothwing, Leafpool followed the stream down to the lake, splashing through at a shallow spot and heading along the shore, past the tree-bridge. She hoped Crowfeather hadn't been too angry when she had broken her promise to meet him. She had forgotten about him on the first night in her desperate rush to help the sick cats, and on the next two nights she had been too exhausted. Besides, she hadn't known if he would wait for her again, since she'd let him down the first time.

When she reached WindClan territory she kept one eye on the moorland, half-hoping to see his lean, gray-black shape racing toward her, yet half-dreading it too. Maybe it was better to end it this way, letting him think she wasn't interested.

But the only WindClan cats she spotted were a patrol high up on the hillside; they were too far away for her to identify them, except to be sure none of them was Crowfeather. She felt as if she would recognize his sleek dark shape from the other side of the lake.

As she approached the stone hollow, the warm scent of ThunderClan cats surrounded her. A purr rose in her throat and she pushed her way eagerly through the thorn tunnel, glad to be home.

Firestar was talking to Cloudtail close to the nursery entrance. "I can't see Daisy ever becoming a warrior," Leafpool heard him meow as she approached. "But sure, you can teach her some fighting moves. She needs to be able to defend herself and her kits if she's going to live in the wild."

Cloudtail's blue eyes gleamed. "She'll be fine," he promised, before vanishing into the brambles to tell her.

Firestar shook his head doubtfully, then straightened up as he spotted Leafpool. "Welcome back," he purred, touching her ear with his nose. "How are things in RiverClan?"

"They were very bad when I first arrived. Twolegs left some sticky poisonous stuff on their territory." Leafpool described what she had discovered, and how she had helped Mothwing care for the sick cats. "But they'll be fine now," she finished.

"You've done well. I always knew you would be a brilliant medicine cat." Her father dipped his head and licked her ears. "I'm very proud of you."

Leafpool's pelt tingled with pleasure. "I'd better go and find Cinderpelt," she mewed. "She must have been rushed off her paws without me to help her."

She bounded across the clearing and slipped behind the screen of brambles to Cinderpelt's den. "Cinderpelt, I'm—"

She skidded to a halt at the mouth of the den. Rainwhisker was lying on the sandy floor with one paw held out, while Brightheart vigorously licked his pad. "That's better," she meowed. "I should be able to get it out now."

There was a thorn sticking out of Rainwhisker's pad. Carefully Brightheart gripped it in her teeth and pulled; it came away easily, followed by a spurt of bright blood.

"That looks fine," Brightheart murmured, nosing the thorn to make sure no scraps of it were left in the paw. "Give your paw a good lick, and you should be able to walk on it soon."

"Thanks, Brightheart," Rainwhisker meowed.

Every hair on Leafpool's pelt bristled from shock. How many medicine cats did ThunderClan need? She knew Brightheart had offered to help Cinderpelt collect herbs while Leafpool was away, but Leafpool had never imagined she would start doing any of the other medicine cat tasks.

Brightheart looked up. "Oh, Leafpool, you're back."

Before Leafpool could reply, Cinderpelt emerged from her den with a mouthful of borage leaves. "Here you are, Brightheart," she mewed, setting them down. "This should help Mousefur's fever."

Brightheart sprang to her paws. "Thanks. I'll take them to her right away." Grabbing them in her jaws, she hurried across the camp to the elders' den.

Leafpool struggled with a pang of envy as sharp as a thorn. It looked like she wasn't needed anymore! Then she told herself to stop overreacting. She should have been grateful that Brightheart had made it possible for her to help RiverClan.

A warm tongue rasped across her ear. "Welcome back," Cinderpelt meowed. "Tell me all about what happened."

As Leafpool sat down, tail wrapped neatly over her paws, she tried to put Brightheart out of her mind. Helping with one thorn and a few herbs didn't make a medicine cat.

I'm home now, and everything will soon be back to normal.

When she had finished reporting to Cinderpelt, she padded off to the fresh-kill pile for something to eat; her belly was yowling, because she hadn't had so much as a sniff of food since she left RiverClan. She was about to sink her teeth into a plump vole when Squirrelflight and Ashfur appeared, their jaws full of fresh-kill.

"Hi," Squirrelflight meowed, dropping her load on the pile. "It's great to see you again. You'll never guess what happened while you were away!"

"What?" Squirrelflight's eyes were gleaming with satisfaction, so it couldn't be anything bad.

Ashfur brushed his nose against Squirrelflight's fur. "You tell Leafpool all about it," he mewed. "I'll go back and collect that last squirrel you caught."

"Thanks." Squirrelflight flicked her ears at him. "See you later."

While she listened with half an ear to Squirrelflight telling her about the kittypets in ShadowClan territory, another pang of envy sank its claws into Leafpool. Her sister and Ashfur were getting along so well together, working as a team, sleeping side by side in the warriors' den. Why couldn't she share anything like that with Crowfeather? *Because you're a medicine cat*, she reminded herself. She had no right to be in love, even if Crowfeather had been a ThunderClan cat. There was no hope that they could be together.

"Are you okay?" Squirrelflight broke off what she was saying to look at Leafpool with concern. "Everything's all right in RiverClan, isn't it?"

"Yes, everything's fine now." Leafpool longed to pour out her problems to her sister, but she couldn't take any cat into her confidence. Instead, she forced herself to sit and eat her vole, and make all the right admiring comments about the raid on the kittypets.

Oh StarClan, she sighed, *why does your way have to be so difficult?*

Leafpool was still feeling confused as the sun went down, but when she curled up in her nest outside Cinderpelt's den, she fell asleep almost at once. She found herself padding through deep woods, the kind of place where she had often walked with warriors of StarClan.

"Spottedleaf?" she called. She was desperate to speak with her, to make sure her warrior ancestors weren't punishing her for thinking about Crowfeather. "Are you there?"

But there was no trace of the medicine cat's sweet scent. Clumps of fern arched above her, and when she looked up for a glimpse of the starry warriors overhead, massive branches blocked her view of the sky. They shifted with a desolate creaking sound; the wind that stirred them probed her pelt with icy claws.

"Where are you?" Panic surged through her. "Spottedleaf, Feathertail, don't leave me alone!"

She remembered her dream at the Moonpool, when she had been unable to work out what her warrior ancestors were saying. She knew instinctively that they were not here now. Perhaps she had lost them forever. She began to run, scrambling over gnarled roots and forcing her way through thorn thickets.

At last Leafpool spotted a faint light through the trees. She veered toward it until she halted, gasping for breath, at the edge of a clearing. Light filtered down, but it seemed gray and sickly, not like the silver blaze of the stars she was used to. It lay heavily on a thick covering of dead leaves and clumps of fungus that glowed with a light of their own.

In the center of the clearing a gray rock pushed up at an angle out of the leaf-mold. A massive tabby tom crouched there, his paws tucked under him and his gaze fixed intently on two cats who sat at the base of the rock, their faces turned toward him.

Leafpool let out a gasp, so loud she was sure the three cats must have heard her, and shrank back fearfully against the nearest tree trunk. She recognized the two cats on the ground instantly: one was her Clanmate Brambleclaw, the other his half brother, Hawkfrost. And that meant she could put a name to the huge tabby on the rock, who looked so much like both of them.

He must be their father, Tigerstar!

CHAPTER 14

Shivering, Leafpool peered out into the clearing. If Tigerstar looked up, she felt as if his amber gaze could have burned away the tree trunk to reveal her cowering behind it. Instead, his eyes were fixed on his sons. But this was a dream! Had Tigerstar called them to him as they slept, in the same way that medicine cats walked in dreams with StarClan? He had brought them somewhere Leafpool had never been before, a place of endless night where living cats never set paw. Even StarClan, she guessed, had never breathed the dank airs of this forest, or padded through its sickly light.

"Courage matters more than anything," Tigerstar was saying. "Remember that, when you are leaders."

Hawkfrost meowed something that Leafpool didn't catch; Tigerstar twitched his tail impatiently.

"Of course courage in battle is important," he rasped, "but I'm talking about courage in the way you deal with your own Clan. They must accept your orders, and if they question you, back up your decisions with tooth and claw."

Leafpool's eyes stretched wide in disbelief. Firestar had

never attacked a member of his Clan, even if they disagreed with him.

"Weakness is dangerous," the huge tabby continued. "You must hide your doubts—or better still, don't have doubts at all. You must always be certain that what you are doing is right."

Was that how Tigerstar had felt, Leafpool wondered, when he had murdered Redtail and plotted the murder of Bluestar so that he could be Clan leader? When he led the dog pack to the ThunderClan camp to gain revenge, and brought Blood-Clan into the forest to help him force the other Clans into submission—had he been completely sure that he was right?

Hawkfrost's ice-blue eyes were fixed on his father; he was obviously drinking in every word. Brambleclaw had his back to Leafpool so she couldn't see his expression, but his ears were pricked. Icy claws gripped her heart. Tigerstar was train-ing his sons, like a warrior preparing an apprentice for battle! He was trying to turn them into the kind of murderous tyrant he had been.

"But how do we become leaders?" Brambleclaw asked. "I don't think Firestar will ever make me his deputy. I haven't even had an apprentice yet."

The fur on Tigerstar's shoulders bristled. "When you hunt, do you expect the mice to leap into your jaws?" he hissed. "No. You scent your prey, you stalk it, and then you pounce. It's the same with power. It won't come to you unless you seek it."

Brambleclaw muttered something, and Leafpool saw Tigerstar's neck fur lie flat again.

"Don't worry," he meowed. "Both of you have the true

spirit of warriors. I know you will succeed if you follow my pawsteps closely."

"We will!" Hawkfrost leapt to his paws. "We'll do whatever you tell us."

His enthusiasm chilled Leafpool. What could this blood-thirsty cat command his sons to do? She shrank back, shivering, and although she didn't think she had made a sound, the huge tabby's head swung around and he peered into the shadows where she was hiding.

Terrified, Leafpool turned and fled, blundering among roots and trailing stems of bramble, bracing herself to hear sounds of pursuit and to feel a massive paw grabbing her by the throat. There were no paths out of the dark forest. Trees stretched endlessly on every side, and there was no birdsong or rustle of prey, no sign that any living creature had ever trod-den among these dark thickets.

Where am I? There was no reply to Leafpool's silent wail. What had brought her to this place where StarClan had never set paw, where the spirit of a murderous cat could call his sons to him in dreams?

In her panic-stricken flight Leafpool didn't look where she was going. Suddenly the ground gave way under her paws. She let out a shocked yowl as she plunged into darkness; her body hit the ground with a thump that drove the breath out of her.

Her eyes flew open and she let out a gasp of terror. A tabby head was a mouse-length away from hers, amber eyes staring down at her.

"Are you okay?" Brambleclaw meowed.

Leafpool scrambled into a sitting position, scattering scraps of moss. She was in her nest outside Cinderpelt's den. The creamy light of dawn was seeping into the sky above the trees.

"Leafpool?" Brambleclaw sounded concerned. His pelt was ruffled, with bits of bracken sticking to it, as if he had only recently roused from his own nest in the warriors' den. "Is something the matter? I heard you cry out."

"What? No—no, I'm fine." Leafpool stared uncertainly up at Brambleclaw. Had he come to tell her that he'd seen her in his dream?

"Firestar is choosing cats to go to the Gathering tonight," he meowed, yawning. "Are you fit to come? I know you had a long journey yesterday."

Relief swept through Leafpool from ears to tail-tip. If Brambleclaw had really had the same dream, he hadn't noticed her in the shadows. But her relief faded as she wondered if he had *chosen* to visit his father in the dark forest. What was Tigerstar going to make him do to become Clan leader?

She got up, still feeling shaky but determined to hide it. "I'm fine," she repeated. "Tell Firestar I'd like to come."

Brambleclaw dipped his head and backed away. Leafpool took a few deep breaths before giving her pelt a quick grooming. She had completely forgotten that this was the night of the full moon. Even though her pelt prickled with fear, she wanted to watch Hawkfrost and Brambleclaw together. Would they give away what was happening as they slept? How often had Tigerstar called them to him in dreams before now?

Leafpool knew there was no cat she could ask for advice.

Firestar and Cinderpelt both took her dreams from StarClan very seriously, but this dream was different. She didn't dare tell them about it; she was terrified of what the dream might mean, for she had never heard of any other medicine cat walking where she had walked. In that forest, she had felt farther than ever from her warrior ancestors. If she lost touch with them altogether, would she be condemned to wander forever in that dark place, and never find her way back to the light?

Even though it was very early, she knew she wouldn't be able to go back to sleep now. Cinderpelt was still in her den, so Leafpool decided to go out and look for herbs. They could do with more borage leaves, especially if Mousefur was feverish.

She knew a patch of borage grew close to the abandoned Twoleg nest. Leafpool slipped out of the camp and padded along the disused path. The gray, cloudy weather had given way to sunlight that shone warmly on her fur. Green shoots were thrusting up through the ground. Buds were swelling on the trees and birds sang above Leafpool's head, promising plentiful fresh-kill as newleaf approached. The forest couldn't have been more different from the dark place of her dream, yet Leafpool could not shake off the terror, and found herself glancing over her shoulder at every pawstep.

Her pelt crawled when she came in sight of the tumbledown nest, with shadowy holes in its sides like eyes staring at her. Then she braced herself and padded more boldly through the trees, sniffing for the borage she had come to collect. What was there to be frightened of here, for a cat who had walked in Tigerstar's forest?

She was on her way back, carrying a satisfying clump of fragrant borage leaves, when she spotted a flash of pale fur behind a clump of bracken. Curious, she circled the bracken and found herself on the edge of the mossy clearing where the cats went for battle training. Cloudtail was there with Daisy, standing over her with his ears pricked.

"No," he meowed. "You've got to *hit* me. Hard."

Daisy blinked at him with limpid blue eyes. "But I don't want to hurt you."

Cloudtail's tail curled up. "Don't worry, you won't. Come on, try again."

The horseplace cat gave him a doubtful look, then ran at him, flashing out a paw as she went past. Cloudtail dodged aside and hooked out Daisy's paws from under her so that she sprawled on the grass in a tangle of legs and fluffy tail.

"That's not *fair!*" she wailed. "You never said you were going to do that."

"Oh, right." Cloudtail couldn't keep the amusement out of his voice. "Do you think in the thick of a battle an enemy warrior will come up and say, 'Be careful, I'm going to push you over now?'"

Daisy lashed her tail. "It's not like I'll ever need to fight."

"You might." Cloudtail's gaze was serious now. "If another Clan attacked us—or other creatures like foxes or dogs—you need to know how to defend yourself. If you don't, you could get *really* hurt."

"Oh, all right." Daisy gave her creamy chest fur a couple of licks. "Show me again what I've got to do."

Leafpool thought Cloudtail had a tough task ahead of him if he was going to turn this kittypet into a competent warrior. Daisy didn't seem to have any fighting instinct at all. But the white warrior seemed willing to teach her. Leafpool remembered how he had shown infinite patience with Brightheart after the she-cat had been attacked by the dogs, and needed to learn a whole new way of fighting and hunting. Perhaps he would be able to teach Daisy to be a warrior too.

Thinking about Brightheart made Leafpool want to get back to camp. She still didn't like the way the ginger and white she-cat was taking over all her duties.

She waved her tail in greeting as she padded past Cloudtail and Daisy; as she left the clearing she heard Cloudtail meowing, "This time try to pretend I'm a badger and I'm going to eat your kits."

"But my kits really like you," Daisy protested.

More warriors were up and about by the time Leafpool reached the stone hollow. She nodded to Sandstorm, who was leading Spiderleg and Thornclaw out on a hunting patrol; then she went to find Cinderpelt in her den. But it was Brightheart, not Cinderpelt, who came out to meet her.

"Borage!" the ginger and white she-cat exclaimed. "Thanks, Leafpool. We have hardly any left, and Mousefur's fever isn't down yet." As soon as Leafpool put down the borage at the mouth of the den, she grabbed up a couple of the stalks and hurried toward the clump of fern and bramble where the elders slept beneath the twisted branches of a hazel bush.

Leafpool let out a hiss of annoyance and slashed at the

nearest bramble with her paw. Brightheart was behaving as if she were the medicine cat, and Leafpool just her helper.

"What's the matter?" Cinderpelt emerged from the mouth of her den, gave the remaining borage an appreciative sniff, then limped across to join Leafpool.

Leafpool shrugged. "Just too many medicine cats around here," she muttered.

Cinderpelt's blue gaze rested on her. Leafpool looked up and saw wisdom and compassion there, and something deeper she could not name. "Be patient with Brightheart," the medicine cat mewed. "Everything has changed for her." More quietly she added, "The greatest gift we could ask for is the courage to accept what StarClan sends us, however hard it seems."

Leafpool was surprised to see a flash of sadness in her mentor's face. She wanted to ask Cinderpelt what she was talking about, but she was afraid of the answer. Was she just talking about Brightheart, and the courage she had shown in accepting her disfigured face? Or was she trying to tell Leafpool that she wasn't needed anymore, now that Brightheart had begun to take on the role of medicine cat?

Before she could summon the courage to say anything, Cinderpelt disappeared back inside her den. Leafpool was about to follow her when she saw Cloudtail push his way through the thorn tunnel with Daisy just behind him. Daisy's kits, who were tumbling together at the entrance to the nursery, sprang up and scampered across the clearing to fling themselves on Cloudtail. The white warrior toppled onto his side and wrestled with the kits in a play fight, his claws carefully sheathed.

"Hey, Berrykit, get off!" he panted, giving the creamy-white kit a gentle cuff around the ear. "Mousekit, that *tickles*. And who's got their teeth in my tail?" He rolled over, taking the smallest kit with him. "Hazelkit, show a bit of respect for a warrior!"

"He's really good with them." Brightheart had returned and stood gazing at her mate with a wistful look. "He'll be a fantastic mentor," she went on. "He was so patient with me when I was injured. He worked out all kinds of fighting moves for me so I could be a warrior again."

Leafpool felt an unexpected stab of sympathy for her. Maybe Cinderpelt was right, and Brightheart had more changes to get used to than any of them. It couldn't be easy for her to watch Cloudtail spending so much time with Daisy and her kits. But her sympathy dissolved when Mousefur padded up and spoke to Brightheart.

"I forgot to ask you," the brown-furred elder meowed. "Can I have some poppy seed? This fever has kept me awake for two nights now."

"I'm not sure," Brightheart replied. "I don't think you should have poppy seed on top of all that borage. Let's ask Cinderpelt if she has anything better."

She led the elder behind the brambles that screened Cinderpelt's den, leaving Leafpool to stare after them in frustrated disbelief. *Who's the medicine cat around here?* If Mousefur or Brightheart had bothered to ask her, she would have suggested chewing a dandelion leaf instead of poppy seeds. But they'd acted as if Leafpool wasn't even there.

Maybe Cinderpelt would make Brightheart a medicine cat apprentice. *But I'm still her apprentice*, Leafpool thought miserably. Even though she had her proper name now, she would continue to learn from Cinderpelt for many more seasons. She had never heard of a medicine cat having two apprentices at the same time. *Besides*, she added to herself, *Brightheart has a mate, and a kit. She can't be a medicine cat. Right?*

She felt as if a huge stone hung in her belly, weighing her down. *Maybe this is a sign from StarClan after all*, she thought. *A sign that I'm not needed in ThunderClan anymore.*

CHAPTER 15

A few wisps of cloud drifted across the sky, but the full moon floated clear of them as the ThunderClan cats crossed the tree-bridge to the island. Leaping down onto the pebbly shore, Leafpool scanned the cats who were already there and spotted Ashfoot and Barkface making their way toward the line of bushes that guarded the center of the island.

WindClan is here, so where's Crowfeather? She told herself to stop looking for him, but when she couldn't spot him her belly clenched with disappointment. She paused in the shadow of the tree roots, tasting the air for his scent, but it was impossible to pick one out among so many mingled scents.

Tail drooping, she trudged up the slope toward the barrier of bushes. She saw Brambleclaw and Hawkfrost padding up to touch noses; amber eyes gazed into ice blue. Some unspoken message passed between them; then both cats turned and disappeared beneath the thick branches.

Leafpool felt chilled to the depths of her fur. For a moment the island vanished, and she was back in that dark forest where Tigerstar was advising his sons how to seize power. What

215

were Hawkfrost and Brambleclaw planning?

She heard the bushes rustle as the two tabby toms pushed their way into the clearing, and she waited for the leaves to stop quivering before she followed them. Her paws tingled with the sense of danger. Was Brambleclaw plotting to take over ThunderClan, just as his bloodthirsty father had plotted so many seasons ago?

She emerged from the bushes, blinking in the shining wash of moonlight that outlined every leaf and stem. Brambleclaw and Hawkfrost were sitting side by side in front of her, not far from the roots of the Great Oak. Leafpool was just in time to see Squirrelflight glare at them before she settled down beside Ashfur. Tawnypelt and Russetfur joined them and the four warriors greeted one another in a friendly way, as if they were remembering how they had recently fought side by side against the kittypets.

Mothwing was comfortably crouched near the edge of the clearing with her paws tucked under her, beside Cinderpelt and the other medicine cats. Leafpool padded over to her.

"Is everything okay? Have you had any more trouble with that Twoleg stuff?"

Mothwing shook her head. "Everything's fine, thanks. Dawnflower and her kits have gone back to the nursery, with Mosspelt to keep an eye on them. And Beechpaw is training with Blackclaw again."

"That's great news," Leafpool purred, at the same moment as Littlecloud asked, "What Twoleg stuff?"

Mothwing began to tell him about the leaking green and silver liquid, while Leafpool glanced around the clearing. She flinched as she made out the lean gray-black shape of Crowfeather, sitting in a group of other WindClan cats. She had been so sure he wasn't there! She stared at him for a few heartbeats, only tearing her gaze away when his ears twitched as if he knew he was being watched.

A yowl sounded from the branches of the Great Oak. She looked up to see Blackstar standing on a branch that jutted out over the clearing. Firestar was sitting on a branch just above him, with Leopardstar beside him. Onestar was a couple of tail lengths away, crouched in the fork between a thick bough and the tree trunk. Ashfoot and Mistyfoot were already sitting on the roots; Russetfur bounded up to join them as Blackstar stepped forward.

"Cats of all Clans," he began, "StarClan has brought us here again to gather in the light of the full moon. Firestar, will you begin?"

The ThunderClan leader stood up and dipped his head to Blackstar. "ThunderClan has a new apprentice," he reported. "Ashfur is now mentor to Birchpaw."

Not far away, Leafpool saw Ashfur give his chest fur a couple of self-conscious licks, while Squirrelflight, beside him, gazed around proudly. Birchpaw himself hadn't come to this Gathering.

"Daisy, one of the cats from the horseplace, has brought her kits to ThunderClan," Firestar went on as soon as the meows of congratulation had died away. "I have given them permission to stay as long as they like."

A murmur of surprise rose up in the clearing, along with one or two yowls of protest. Rowanclaw of ShadowClan sprang to his paws. "Is that wise?" he demanded. "What good will kittypets be?"

Leafpool saw her father's neck fur bristle, then relax again as if he were trying hard to keep his temper. "Daisy isn't exactly a kittypet," he replied evenly. "She lived with the horses, not in the Twoleg nest. And she did a brave thing in bringing her kits to us so the Twolegs couldn't take them away."

Rowanclaw flicked his tail. "They'll never be warriors."

"You don't know that," Firestar meowed, with a glance at Cloudtail, who was sitting near the roots of the Great Oak. "A good warrior doesn't have to be forestborn, just as being forestborn doesn't guarantee being a good warrior. Daisy is settling in well, and her three kits will be apprenticed as soon as they're old enough. They'll soon learn the warrior code."

"Maybe," grunted Rowanclaw, sitting down again. Leafpool was close enough to hear him mutter to Oakfur, "Why do we expect him to understand the importance of being Clanborn? Firestar would fill the forest with kittypets if he could."

Oakfur twitched his ears. "You've got to admire him," he mewed. "You think Blackstar would turn down the chance to have three extra warriors for the Clan?"

Rowanclaw just snorted.

While Leafpool was listening to the ShadowClan warriors she had missed the end of her father's report. When she started paying attention again, Leopardstar was on her paws.

"Twolegs left poison in our territory," she meowed. "Ivytail and one of our kits died, but all our other cats are recovering, thanks to Mothwing—and Leafpool, who came to help us from ThunderClan."

Her gaze swept the clearing and fixed on Leafpool; the RiverClan leader dipped her head in a gesture of thanks before she sat down again. Embarrassed to be praised in front of every cat, Leafpool studied her paws.

"ShadowClan has reason to thank ThunderClan too," Blackstar began, going on to recount what had happened. Leafpool knew how hard it must be for him to admit that his Clan hadn't been able to deal with the trouble without ThunderClan's help, but at least he didn't try to hide the debt he owed. "Since then the kittypets have stayed inside the Twoleg garden," he finished.

Onestar jumped to his paws. "What sort of a Clan leader are you?" he growled. "Aren't you ashamed that you needed help from another Clan? You too," he added, rounding on Leopardstar. "RiverClan has its own medicine cat. Why do you have to go crawling to ThunderClan?" He ignored the muttering that broke out below him as he glared at Firestar. "It's time ThunderClan stopped paying so much attention to what's happening in the other Clans. Your warriors ignore our boundaries and think they can tell every cat what to do. We all made the journey here together, and ThunderClan is no stronger than any other."

Before Firestar could reply, Cloudtail leapt up. His white

pelt was bristling, his tail fluffed out to twice its size. "You were glad enough for ThunderClan's help when WindClan were starving," he snarled.

"That was different," Onestar retorted.

"Exactly." Firestar's voice was quiet, but full of authority. "Back then, we had to join together to survive what the Twolegs were doing to the forest. I don't believe StarClan would want us to stop helping each other now."

"They would, if it meant keeping the Clans separate," Onestar insisted. "There have always been four Clans. Every kit knows that."

More protests broke out. "WindClan would have been destroyed without us!" Dustpelt yowled.

Onestar took a pace forward, his claws scraping on the bark. "Look up at the moon!" he rasped. "Do you see clouds covering it? No, it's shining brightly—and that means StarClan agrees with what I'm saying."

"No cat has ever claimed there shouldn't be four Clans," Firestar defended himself. "But that doesn't mean StarClan wants us to turn our backs on each other when trouble comes."

"I can see why you would say that," Onestar hissed. "You think your Clan is the strongest and make sure to prove it to the rest of us whenever you get a chance."

"Mouse dung!" Blackstar growled. "ThunderClan helped us *once*. If they set paw on our territory without an invitation, they'll find out just how strong we are."

Leafpool dug her claws into the ground. Why couldn't the

other leaders see that Firestar was right? Even if there were four Clans, that didn't mean they couldn't help each other in a crisis. She turned to Cinderpelt, but before she could ask her mentor what she thought, she felt a light touch on her shoulder. Drawing in her breath sharply, she looked around to see Crowfeather crouching in the shadows at the edge of the clearing.

"I have to talk to you!" he whispered, jerking his head in the direction of the bushes.

Cinderpelt was staring up at the Clan leaders. Cautiously Leafpool slid backward until the shadows engulfed her, too. An overhanging branch screened them from the cats in the clearing as they pushed their way through the encircling bushes. Together they retreated a few pawsteps toward the shore of the island until they could put a jutting rock between themselves and the Gathering place.

"What happened to you?" Crowfeather's eyes looked hurt. "Why didn't you meet me that night?"

Leafpool swallowed nervously. "Don't be angry with me," she pleaded. "I *couldn't* come. I had to help Mothwing."

Crowfeather lashed his tail. "It's no good, stealing moments together like this," he murmured. "I never get to see you."

"I know. I feel the same. But Crowfeather, I'm a medicine cat . . ." Leafpool knew this was her chance to tell Crowfeather that there was no point in loving her. But here, standing beside him, her pelt brushing his, his scent flooding over her, she couldn't begin to find the right words.

For a moment her guilt and anxiety faded. She felt as though nothing mattered except being close to him, gazing into his burning amber eyes.

"I know there are problems," Crowfeather went on, scraping the earth with his claws. "You're a medicine cat, and we're in different Clans. The whole of the warrior code is against us. But there *must* be a way."

Leafpool blinked at him. "How?" All their difficulties came rushing back until she felt trapped by them.

The gray-black warrior was so tense she could almost see lightning playing around his fur. "I wish we could just escape everything!" he burst out. "Clans, traditions, all the rules and boundaries . . . I want to get away from all of it!"

"Escape?" Leafpool echoed. "Do you mean—go away?"

Was Crowfeather really suggesting they could leave their Clans and the lives they had known ever since they were kits? She would have to say good-bye to her mother and father, to Squirrelflight and Sorreltail, and to her mentor, Cinderpelt. More than that, she would have to give up her life as a medicine cat. Pain twisted in her belly. How could she face never again walking in dreams with StarClan, never seeing Spottedleaf, never healing her Clanmates with the help of her warrior ancestors?

Crowfeather nudged her. "Leafpool?"

Unhappily she shook her head. "We can't leave our Clans. That's not the answer."

"I don't know what the answer is, either." He broke off with a hiss.

Leafpool realized that the sounds of argument from the clearing had died away; they could just hear Blackstar drawing the meeting to a close.

"It's time to go," Crowfeather muttered. "Tomorrow, at sunhigh, go and collect herbs by the stream near the stepping-stones. I'll come and talk to you there. Please."

Without waiting for her reply he whipped around and skirted the bushes until he reached his Clanmates as they made for the tree-bridge.

Leafpool waited for a few heartbeats before creeping back through the branches into the clearing. It didn't look as if any cat had noticed her leaving to talk to Crowfeather. The medicine cats were still huddled together on the edge of the bushes. Leafpool padded over to join them.

"I've had the same dream again and again," Littlecloud was meowing anxiously. "Warnings of danger to come . . . yet StarClan never tells me what the danger is." He glanced anxiously from cat to cat. "Have any of you had a clearer sign?"

Leafpool didn't look at Mothwing. There were now two medicine cats whose dreams were closed off to StarClan. Her warrior ancestors certainly hadn't sent her the dream of the dark forest where she had seen Tigerstar and his sons. She couldn't let any cat know she hadn't received the dreams Littlecloud was describing, and she hoped that Cinderpelt wouldn't ask her directly.

Mothwing broke the silence. "I don't know what any of these dreams mean," she mewed. Leafpool realized how careful she was being not to reveal her lack of faith in StarClan.

"But we should warn our Clan leaders to be alert for danger."

Cinderpelt dipped her head approvingly. "Good idea."

"But what *sort* of danger?" Barkface asked with a twitch of his whiskers. "WindClan hasn't seen much that could threaten us since we moved in, unless you count the fox, and that was quickly dealt with."

"We had the problem with the Twoleg poison," meowed Mothwing. Glancing at Leafpool, she added, "But StarClan sent a special warning about that."

"And we had trouble with the kittypets." Littlecloud nodded to Cinderpelt. "ThunderClan helped us sort that out, so StarClan wouldn't still be sending dreams about it."

"There must be another danger," Cinderpelt decided. "Something that hasn't come yet, and something that could affect every Clan."

"All of us must keep watch for signs," Barkface rumbled. "Maybe by the time of the half moon StarClan will have shown us something more."

His words were the signal for them to leave. The clearing was almost empty as the last of the cats made their way out through the bushes. Leafpool emerged to find the stretch of shore beside the tree-bridge crowded with cats milling around the roots, waiting for their turn to cross.

Leafpool let her gaze travel over them; when she spotted Crowfeather, she felt as if a bolt of lightning had ripped through her fur.

The WindClan warrior sprang nimbly onto the tree trunk and began making his way to the shore, balancing easily with his tail straight up in the air. Leafpool hardly knew how she stopped her paws from dashing after him, even though they were surrounded by cats from every Clan.

StarClan, help me! she begged. *I don't know what to do!*

CHAPTER 16

"Daisy! Daisy, where are you?"

Squirrelflight stopped and looked around when she heard the furious yowl that came from the medicine cats' den. A moment later Brightheart appeared, carrying one of Daisy's kits by the scruff. The tiny creature was wailing miserably, his paws thrashing the air. His littermates crept out after them, heads down and tails drooping, and huddled together beside the brambles that shielded the den.

The horseplace cat had been in camp long enough for her kits to grow stronger and more confident, and to begin exploring the camp. And that was likely to mean trouble; Squirrelflight's whiskers twitched as she remembered some of the things she and Leafpool had got up to before they were apprenticed.

Brightheart dropped the kit she was carrying—it was Mousekit, Squirrelflight realized, taking a closer look. The ginger and white she-cat's good eye was blazing with anger. "Daisy! Come here!"

There was no response from the nursery, but a heartbeat later Daisy appeared from the thorn tunnel and raced across the camp to confront Brightheart. Cloudtail followed her more slowly.

"What's the matter? What are you doing to my kits?" Daisy demanded.

"Ask your kits what they've been doing in Cinderpelt's den," Brightheart retorted. "And stop making that noise," she added to the kit she had dropped, who was still wailing, his tiny pink jaws gaping wide. "I haven't hurt you."

"What happened?" Daisy's blue eyes were just as furious, and her long, creamy fur couldn't hide the tension in her muscles. For a moment Squirrelflight thought she might fly at Brightheart with one of the fighting moves Cloudtail had been teaching her. Squirrelflight knew Brightheart could look after herself, but Daisy might not get away unscratched. She padded over in case some cat was needed to stop the fur flying.

"Your kits came into Cinderpelt's den and started messing with the herbs," Brightheart explained. "Did you eat anything?" she hissed, rounding on Berrykit and Hazelkit. "Any of you?"

Mute with terror, the kits shook their heads. Squirrelflight knew that part of Brightheart's anger was fueled by fear that the kits might have eaten something dangerous. Cinderpelt wouldn't keep anything like deathberries among her supplies, but there were plenty of remedies that could give a cat a nasty bellyache if they ate too much.

Brightheart's fur began to lie flat again, but annoyance still crackled off her like lightning in greenleaf. "Just go and *look* at the mess they've made," she meowed to Daisy. "Why weren't you keeping an eye on them?"

"She was with me," Cloudtail meowed.

"And that makes it okay for her kits to spoil Cinderpelt's supplies?" Brightheart challenged him.

"They didn't know any better."

"Then they should!" Brightheart snarled back at her mate. "Do you think we have nothing better to do than clean up after them? I spent all day yesterday collecting berries."

"Look, I'm sorry," Daisy mewed, glancing uneasily from Cloudtail to Brightheart and back again. She nudged Mousekit to his paws and collected the others with a sweep of her tail. "I'll make sure it doesn't happen again."

"You do that," Brightheart snapped.

The horseplace cat headed back to the nursery, herding her kits in front of her. Squirrelflight heard Mousekit complain, "That ugly cat frightened me!"

"Then you shouldn't get into trouble," Daisy replied.

Squirrelflight saw Brightheart flinch at what Mousekit said. She and Cloudtail were nose to nose, their tail-tips twitching back and forth.

"I'll help clean up," Squirrelflight offered, backing around the brambles. She didn't want to get involved in a quarrel between Brightheart and her mate.

When she turned around she saw why Brightheart had been so angry. Berries were scattered all over the ground at the mouth of the den, and herbs lay in untidy clumps. Some of the leaves had been torn off their stems and were covered in dirt; they would probably have to be thrown out.

Squirrelflight began to roll the berries that could be salvaged into a pile. She wondered where Leafpool and Cinderpelt had gone. After a few moments she heard another cat padding up behind her.

"There you are!" meowed Ashfur, touching his nose to her shoulder. "I thought we were going hunting. Why are Cloudtail and Brightheart glaring at each other like a couple of badgers?"

Squirrelflight went on sorting berries as she explained.

"Clanborn kits would know not to do this sort of thing," Ashfur commented. "Maybe these kittypets will never settle here properly."

"*What* did you say?" Squirrelflight spun around to face him. "Have you forgotten that my father was a kittypet?"

Ashfur blinked. "I'm sorry. But Firestar's pretty special. Most kittypets couldn't live our sort of life. They need their Twolegs to look after them."

Squirrelflight let out a furious hiss, and her claws slid out; it took a massive effort to shield them again and go on sorting berries. *How dare Ashfur make judgments based on a cat's birth?* she fumed. Did that mean he thought less of her because she was half kittypet? Couldn't he see that she and Leafpool, Cloudtail, and his kit Whitepaw were as important to the Clan as any warrior who was forestborn through and through?

Before Ashfur could say anything else, the bramble screen shook as Leafpool and Cinderpelt brushed past. Both medicine cats carried large bunches of chickweed.

"What's going on here?" Cinderpelt asked, dropping her mouthful.

Squirrelflight explained what had happened for the second time, while Leafpool began examining the scattered leaves and piling up the ones that would have to be thrown out.

"Kits!" Cinderpelt grunted, nosing a muddy and crumpled stack of yarrow leaves. "Still, if they didn't eat anything there's no real harm done."

"A lot of extra work, though," Ashfur pointed out.

"We can manage," Leafpool meowed sharply, and Squirrelflight glanced at her in surprise. "I'll throw out these damaged herbs and go collect some more."

A bolt of strong emotion made Squirrelflight's fur stand on end. She stared at her sister. Was that *guilt* Leafpool was feeling? Why should she feel guilty about collecting herbs? Even more mysteriously, mixed with the guilt there seemed to be a thrill of anticipation, and beneath it all a layer of piercing unhappiness.

Squirrelflight told herself her sister was just tired; the night before had been the half moon, when Leafpool and the other medicine cats paid their regular visit to the Moonpool. But deep down she knew Leafpool was suffering from more than the long journey and lack of sleep. Perhaps the medicine cats had received a sign from StarClan of trouble ahead. Yet Leafpool hadn't been her normal self for some time. In fact, she'd been as jumpy as a grasshopper since the Gathering.

"I'll help you," Squirrelflight offered. "Ashfur, you'd better hunt without me. I'll join you later if I can."

Ashfur gave her a long look. "Okay." With a nod to Cinderpelt he left.

Squirrelflight opened her mouth to call him back, wishing she hadn't spoken so sharply to him, but her need to talk to Leafpool was greater. Besides, perhaps it was best for them both to have some space after their quarrel.

"Which herbs do we need to throw out?" she asked her sister.

"These." Leafpool pointed with her tail. "The rest are okay, I think."

Squirrelflight divided the heap of bruised and dirty leaves into two bunches and picked up one of them. Cinderpelt had begun to carry the herbs and berries worth keeping back into her den. Leafpool picked up the remaining herbs and followed Squirrelflight out of the camp. They carried the leaves to the rough ground a few fox-lengths from the entrance where the cats went to make their dirt.

"It's good to get out of there," Squirrelflight remarked when she had finished spitting out scraps of sharp-tasting leaf. She wanted to tell Leafpool about Ashfur's hurtful comments, but now she could see how tense and miserable Leafpool was, her quarrel didn't seem important. "Is everything okay with you?" she asked.

"Why shouldn't it be?" Leafpool scraped the ground in front of her and sniffed at an unfurling frond of bracken.

"When Cinderpelt suggested collecting more herbs, I just thought you seemed . . . well, weird, sort of." A thought struck her and she added, "You're not worried about Brightheart, are you? I mean, you're Cinderpelt's *real* apprentice. Brightheart is just helping out."

Leafpool blinked. "No, of course I'm not worried about Brightheart. Look, Squirrelflight," she went on, "we'd better split up if we're going to collect herbs, otherwise it will take all day. I know Cinderpelt wants more catmint. Do you think you could fetch some from the abandoned Twoleg nest?"

Squirrelflight stared at her. It couldn't be more obvious that Leafpool was trying to get rid of her. "Where are you going to go?"

"Oh . . . near the ShadowClan border, maybe."

Another bolt of guilt and impatience flashed from her, making every hair on Squirrelflight's pelt tingle. She was sure Leafpool was lying, and she clamped her teeth shut on a yowl of outrage. *We never lie to each other!*

"You know," she mewed, trying to sound calm, "you *are* weird these days. It feels like something's changed."

She had meant the words as a joke, an attempt to recover the closeness to her sister that somehow seemed to have vanished. But instead of being amused, Leafpool flinched as if a bee had stung her. Her eyes narrowed.

"I'm going to collect herbs," she meowed coldly. "I'm a medicine cat. You can't expect to share every part of my life." Turning her back on her sister, she stalked off into the undergrowth.

For a few heartbeats Squirrelflight was tempted to follow her, but if Leafpool found out she would be even more furious. But Squirrelflight couldn't just ignore her sister's unhappiness, not when they had always meant so much to each other. She would just have to keep her eyes open and wait for the chance to discover what was wrong.

The hooting of an owl woke Squirrelflight. Faint moonlight filtered through the branches of the warriors' den, outlining the curled-up bodies of her Clanmates. The den was filled with the warmth of their breath.

Squirrelflight's jaws gaped in a yawn, but she didn't feel like going back to sleep. She was wide awake now and restless. Sliding out of her nest, being careful not to wake Ashfur, who was sleeping a tail-length away, she crept between the overhanging branches and into the clearing.

The moon, waning now to the thinnest crescent like a claw scratch in the indigo sky, shed just enough light to see the boundaries of the hollow. Clumps of bramble and fern cast dark shadows around the edges. Opposite her, beside the entrance to the thorn tunnel, Squirrelflight could just make out the pale pelt of Cloudtail, sitting on guard.

She flexed her claws, wondering whether to tell the white warrior that she felt like some night hunting. Suddenly a movement flickered in the corner of her eye, and she turned to see Leafpool emerging from the medicine cats' den.

Squirrelflight almost called out to her. Then she realized how strangely her sister was behaving. Leafpool glanced around carefully before she crept out of the shelter of the brambles, although she clearly failed to spot her sister's dark ginger pelt in the shadows by the warriors' den. Then she headed around the edge of the clearing, hugging the darkness as if she were being hunted like a mouse. Her tension shivered through Squirrelflight from ears to tail-tip.

All Squirrelflight's earlier uneasiness returned as she padded into the shadows after her sister, placing each paw silently onto the ground. She didn't want to disturb Cloudtail or any of the other warriors until she knew what Leafpool was trying to do. Leafpool was in some kind of trouble, and this could be the chance Squirrelflight needed to find out more.

Before she reached the thorn barrier across the entrance to the hollow, and risked being seen by Cloudtail, the young medicine cat veered sharply into a clump of brambles. Squirrelflight heard a brief thrashing and froze as Cloudtail's head swung around, but after listening for a few moments the white warrior twitched the tip of his tail and turned back to watch the tunnel again.

Her heart pounding, Squirrelflight slipped into the brambles behind Leafpool. This was a corner of the hollow that was still too overgrown to be used for sleeping or storing fresh-kill. To her surprise, Squirrelflight saw that part of the rock wall had crumbled away here, and it wouldn't be too difficult for an agile cat to climb right to the top of the cliff. Leafpool had found a secret way out of the camp! It occurred to Squirrelflight that her sister must know the way very well, to have vanished already. How many times had she used this exit before?

Squirrelflight launched herself upward, fighting her way through the tendrils of bramble and sinking her claws into a straggling bush that had rooted itself in a crack. At last she scrambled over the edge of the hollow and dived for cover into the nearest clump of ferns, her ears pricked for any sound in the hollow below that might mean some cat had spotted her.

But everything was quiet, except for the rustle of wind in the branches. Gradually Squirrelflight's racing heartbeat slowed, and she dared to poke her head out of the ferns to look around.

Leafpool was nowhere to be seen, but it didn't take long for Squirrelflight to pick up her scent. The trail skirted the top of the hollow, then set off into the forest.

Squirrelflight followed, pausing every now and then to taste the air. She wanted to believe that Leafpool had left the hollow on medicine cat business, but as far as she knew, there were no herbs that had to be gathered by moonlight. Besides, the way Leafpool had sneaked out of camp, and the mingled guilt and excitement Squirrelflight picked up from her, meant that she must be doing something she shouldn't.

You could have told me, Squirrelflight thought crossly. *Maybe I could have helped.*

Leafpool's scent trail wound around hazel thickets and clumps of fern. After a while Squirrelflight realized she could hear the gurgling of the stream that marked the border with WindClan. She stopped and thought for a moment. Could Leafpool be going to the Moonpool? If she were, she would be furious that Squirrelflight was intruding on a medicine cat ritual. But if that were the case, why sneak out of the camp? Leafpool wouldn't mind if every cat in the Clan knew she was going to share tongues with StarClan.

Squirrelflight went on, doing her best to follow the trail, but the woodland was full of the smell of newly bursting leaves and rising sap. Mouthwatering hints of prey crossed and recrossed Leafpool's scent, until Squirrelflight could hardly distinguish it from all the others that flooded her senses. Several times she had to stop and take deep, gulping breaths before she could go on. Once she thought she had lost the trail on a bare patch of ground where rock pushed up close to the surface, but she picked it up again on the other side. Then the scent vanished completely in a patch of marshy ground, and though Squirrelflight padded all over it with her nose to the ground she couldn't find it again.

"Huh!" she grunted. "Call yourself a hunter?"

She could still hear the sound of running water, and she slid silently through the trees until she came in sight of the stream. The breeze brought WindClan scent to her; could Leafpool have crossed the border into WindClan territory? For a heartbeat Squirrelflight thought of crossing to see if she could pick up her sister's scent on the other side. But there was always the chance that some WindClan cat might have felt like hunting at night. If she were spotted on their territory there would be big trouble, with Onestar feeling the way he did about ThunderClan. Squirrelflight decided she would have a better chance of finding out what Leafpool was up to if she went back and waited outside the hollow until she returned.

She crouched among the ferns above the place where the cliff had crumbled away, guessing Leafpool would return the same way she had left. Her belly growled with hunger, but she didn't want to hunt in case she missed her sister.

The sky was growing milky with the first sign of dawn when she heard a cat approaching through the undergrowth. Squirrelflight drew in her sister's scent; rising to her paws, she saw Leafpool coming toward her, her head lowered and her tail brushing the grass.

"Where have you been?" she demanded.

Leafpool's head shot up and she stared at her sister in dismay. "What are you doing out here? Have you been spying on me?"

"No, you daft furball." Squirrelflight padded up to her sister, wanting to brush against her fur and reassure her, but Leafpool drew back a pace, and her eyes were wary. "I saw you leave last night, that's all, and I'm worried about you. I know something's wrong. Can't you tell me what it is?"

The strength of Leafpool's emotions almost swept Squirrelflight off her paws. She could tell her sister longed to confide in her, but a barrier stronger than thorns blocked her way. Squirrelflight's belly clenched. Leafpool's problem must be even more serious than she had thought.

Leafpool shook her head. "Nothing's wrong. Leave me alone."

"I'm hardly going to do that now," Squirrelflight scoffed. "Leafpool, this isn't like you, sneaking off—"

"Sneaking!" Leafpool hissed, her tail fluffing out in fury. "You're a fine one to talk! Why is it okay for you to sneak out and follow me?"

"I didn't!" Squirrelflight protested. "I only wanted to know what was wrong."

"It's none of your business! If you trusted me, you wouldn't ask all these questions."

"Fine!" Squirrelflight snapped. "My sister's in trouble and I'm supposed to ignore that?"

"If I wanted your help I would ask for it!" Leafpool flashed back at her.

"You know you need help." Squirrelflight made a huge effort to control her fury. "If it's medicine cat stuff, why don't you talk to Cinderpelt?"

"Cinderpelt never listens to me." Leafpool's voice was sad. "She's got Brightheart to help her. She doesn't need me."

"That's the most mouse-brained thing I've ever heard!"

Leafpool let out a hiss. "And you're so wise and clever all of a sudden? I suppose you're going to tell Firestar about this, too."

Squirrelflight's anger died away. Her sister seemed so desperate, it was impossible to go on challenging her. Wherever she had been, whatever she had been doing, it hadn't made her happy.

"I won't tell any cat," she mewed quietly. "You'd better get back to your den before you're missed."

Leafpool nodded and brushed past, then turned and gave her such a sorrowful look that Squirrelflight felt a pang pierce her heart, as sharp as a thorn.

"I'm sorry," she murmured, her voice so low that Squirrel-flight could scarcely hear her. "I'd tell you if I could, I promise."

Without waiting for a reply, she disappeared over the edge of the hollow.

Squirrelflight stayed where she was, shaking like a leaf in the wind. She knew there was no point in going back to her den and trying to sleep. Her belly growled again, reminding her how long it had been since she had eaten. She would hunt for a while: a vole for herself, maybe, and then as much prey as she could catch for the fresh-kill pile. She turned to plunge back into the forest, and jumped as the undergrowth rustled and Brambleclaw stepped out.

"Was that Leafpool I saw just now? Where had she been?"

"I've no idea," Squirrelflight replied, her pelt prickling. "She doesn't need permission to leave the camp."

Brambleclaw's eyes narrowed; he clearly guessed Squirrel-flight was hiding something from him. "It's not safe for cats to wander around alone at night," he commented.

"I think it was medicine cat stuff." Squirrelflight automati-cally lied to protect her sister. "You know, looking for herbs."

Brambleclaw blinked; Squirrelflight wasn't sure she'd con-vinced him. He might have noticed that Leafpool hadn't been carrying any herbs when she vanished into camp. And why would she have climbed down the cliff instead of using the tunnel? Squirrelflight's tail twitched in her eagerness to get away before the tabby warrior could go on questioning her.

"I'm going hunting," she mewed briskly.

"So am I." Brambleclaw hesitated as if he were about to suggest they hunt together.

That was the last thing Squirrelflight wanted. "Well, I'm going this way." She swung around and headed in the direction of the ShadowClan border, glancing over her shoulder to add, "See you later."

She could feel the tabby warrior's gaze following her as she plunged into the undergrowth, and she couldn't stifle a pang of regret, deep within her belly. Once, she would have told him everything about Leafpool, trusting him to do everything he could to help. Now she didn't trust him at all—especially not to keep her sister's secret, whatever it was. Squirrelflight couldn't imagine what it could be, but fear for Leafpool hung over her like a heavy black cloud that would soon unleash a storm.

CHAPTER 17

Leafpool picked her way through the undergrowth, ears pricked for the sound of pursuit. Ever since she had returned from meeting Crowfeather to find her sister waiting for her, she had been terrified of being followed. Her belly clenched with pangs as sharp as hunger when she imagined the rest of her Clan finding out what she was doing. *They'll find out sooner or later*, a voice inside her mewed.

The quarrel with Squirrelflight still haunted her. Without the closeness she had shared with her sister since they were kits, Leafpool felt utterly alone in her Clan. But she couldn't tell Squirrelflight the truth, and she couldn't give up her meetings with Crowfeather. He was the only cat she could talk to now.

She'd tried to work up enough courage to tell Cinderpelt, but the medicine cat seemed obsessed with restocking her supplies, hunting through the territory for the tiniest signs of new growth. Besides, Leafpool was afraid Cinderpelt had already guessed her secret and was showing her disapproval in an uncharacteristic quickness of temper. She missed the afternoons they had spent talking back in the forest, when their paws had been busy sorting berries and leaves. Now her mentor seemed distant and more judgmental, less of a friend than she had always been.

In desperation, Leafpool had considered telling her mother, approaching her one evening by the fresh-kill pile. But Sandstorm had been discussing the best hunting grounds with Dustpelt, only giving her daughter a friendly nod before returning to the debate. And as for Sorreltail, Leafpool's friend was so close to having her kits that she spent all her time with Daisy and Ferncloud in the nursery. Apart from when Cinderpelt asked her to take strength-building herbs to the queens, Leafpool kept away.

She paused when she heard a twig snap, freezing with one paw in midair. But it was only a squirrel, jumping down from an oak tree and racing in the opposite direction. Leafpool took a deep breath and carried on. A little earlier, at sunset, heavy rain had fallen from thundery black clouds. The skies were clearer now, but every fern and grass stem was loaded with drops of water, reflecting the pale glow of moonlight. Leafpool's pelt had soaked through long ago, the cold seeping into her skin. Stopping to shake herself, she gazed up at the waning moon. It would have to wax again before her next visit to the Moonpool, yet she longed to lie down beside the water and share tongues with StarClan in her dreams. But what if StarClan refused to speak to her again?

"Oh, Spottedleaf," she whispered, "I wish you'd tell me what to do."

Leafpool's head spun with weariness. She had been meeting

up with Crowfeather every few nights, leaving her short of sleep and restless whenever she was away from him. During the day she had to pretend to Cinderpelt and the rest of the Clan that she was as committed as ever to being a medicine cat, that the only important thing was where to find juniper berries or easing the stiffness from the elders' leaf-bare-damp joints.

You can't go on like this, the small voice warned her.

Crowfeather had said the same thing: "We can't go on like this, Leafpool. We'll never be together unless we leave our Clans."

Leafpool had stared at him in horror. Through all their difficulties, her fear and guilt warring with her love, she had never really imagined that they would have to leave their Clans. "Crowfeather, we can't!"

Crowfeather shook his head. "It's the only way. Will you think about it, please?"

Reluctantly, Leafpool had nodded. "All right. I will."

But how could she give up her life as a medicine cat, give up her Clan, her family, her friends? Whatever decision she made, she was afraid she would not survive the loss.

Close to the border stream, she tasted the air for the first traces of Crowfeather's scent; every hair on her pelt prickled with excitement as she detected it, and a heartbeat later she made out the lean gray-black warrior waiting for her in the shadow of a bush on the WindClan side of the stream. "Crowfeather!" she called, bounding forward.

"Leafpool!" Crowfeather sprang to his paws and his tail

shot straight up as he spotted her.

She halted on the brink of the stream. Crowfeather climbed down the bank and splashed through the water as if he hardly realized it was there. Hauling himself out on the Thunder-Clan side, he padded up to Leafpool, droplets spinning from his pelt as he shook himself. His scent wreathed around her and she shut her eyes blissfully.

"I'm so glad you could come," Leafpool purred. "Did you have any trouble getting away from camp?"

Crowfeather was about to reply when he froze, ears standing up. At the same moment, Leafpool heard a rustling in the bushes behind her. ThunderClan scent flooded her senses. She spun around.

"All right, Squirrelflight, come out!" she snapped. "I know you're there."

There was a brief silence. Then the bracken in front of her parted and out stepped not Squirrelflight, but Cinderpelt.

"What . . . what are you doing here?" Leafpool stammered, casting an anguished glance over her shoulder at Crowfeather.

The medicine cat limped forward and faced her calmly. "You know what I'm doing, Leafpool. I'm here to tell you that this has to stop."

Leafpool stiffened. "I don't know what you mean."

"Don't lie to me, Leafpool. Not with that WindClan warrior standing there, on *our* territory."

There was no anger in her blue eyes, only concern. Her steady gaze pinned Leafpool like a claw, until the younger cat had to look away. "I suppose Squirrelflight told you to follow me," she muttered.

"Squirrelflight? No. I was collecting herbs when I picked up your scent, and a WindClan cat's close by. I came to see what was going on. Besides, do you think I didn't suspect you've been sneaking out at night?"

Terror flashed through Leafpool. "You've been spying on me!"

"I didn't need to," Cinderpelt meowed. "You're obviously so exhausted that you can't do your job properly. Only yesterday you tried to give Sootfur borage leaves instead of watermint for his bellyache. As for Crowfeather, I can't say I'm surprised. Do you think I haven't noticed the two of you at Gatherings? I'm not blind, Leafpool."

"Wait," Crowfeather began, stepping forward to Leafpool's side. "This is between me and Leafpool. She's not betraying her Clan, if that's what you think."

Cinderpelt fixed him with a stern gaze. "I never imagined she would. But she shouldn't be here with you, and you know that as well as I do."

Crowfeather bristled. Leafpool's belly lurched, terrified that the aggressive young warrior might launch himself at the medicine cat with claws unsheathed.

"It's okay, Crowfeather," she mewed. "I can handle this." Reluctantly she added, "You'd better go back to your camp."

"And leave you alone to get your ears clawed?"

"Cinderpelt won't do that. Please," Leafpool begged.

Crowfeather hesitated a moment longer, limbs stiff with anger. Then he swung around and bounded back across the stream; Leafpool's gaze followed him until he vanished into the undergrowth on the other side.

Turning back to her mentor, Leafpool sank her claws into the ground. "We aren't doing any harm," she mewed.

"Leafpool!" Cinderpelt's tone hardened and she lashed her tail. "Crowfeather belongs to a different Clan, but that's only the beginning. You're a medicine cat. You can't fall in love. Not with Crowfeather, not any cat. You have always known that."

I knew it, Leafpool wailed inwardly, *but I never knew what it would mean!*

"It's not fair!" she meowed. "I've got feelings too, just like any other cat."

"Of course you have. But a medicine cat has to control those feelings for the good of her Clan. The path we follow has its own rewards. I've never felt cheated by the destiny StarClan sent me."

Every word she spoke tore into Leafpool like a badger's fangs. Fury surged inside her. "You can't possibly understand!" she spat. "You've never been in love!"

Cinderpelt's blue gaze rested on her, unspoken thoughts flickering like minnows in her eyes.

"It's easy for you," Leafpool went on bitterly. "You've never wanted anything else."

The medicine cat flexed her claws, and her neck fur began to rise. "How do you know what I want?" There was the hint of a snarl in her voice. "How do you know what hopes I gave up to follow the path StarClan laid down for me?"

Leafpool flinched. She had never seen Cinderpelt this angry.

"You'll come back to camp with me—now!" Cinderpelt growled. "And stop this nonsense for good. It's for your own sake, Leafpool. Meeting Crowfeather can't be right if you have to lie and sneak around in the shadows. I haven't spent all this time training you to be a good medicine cat for you to throw it away like this. Your Clan needs you!"

"No! I won't come!" A gale of guilt and anger swept through Leafpool. "I'll go on seeing Crowfeather whenever I want to, and there's nothing you can do to stop me!"

Cinderpelt's eyes flashed and she launched herself at Leafpool, claws out. Leafpool turned tail and ran. As she fled, all she knew was that she must escape from that accusing stare, those lashing claws. The forest whirled past her as if she were caught up in the wind, and when exhaustion finally forced her to stop she wasn't sure where she was.

She was standing on the edge of a narrow valley with gorse and bracken growing on each side. In the distance it grew deeper, and very faintly Leafpool could hear the sound of running water. Suddenly relief flooded her heart. She had left ThunderClan territory behind, and was halfway to the Moonpool!

She could be completely alone there, without Crowfeather pleading with her to leave, or the fear that her secret would be discovered. The shining spirits of her ancestors would come to her and tell her what to do.

She padded on, more slowly now, until she reached the starlit stream that tumbled down from the hollow where the Moonpool lay. By the time she reached the barrier of bushes around the top she was staggering from weariness, but the sight of the glimmering water below gave her strength. As she followed the spiral path down to the water's edge, her paws slipping easily into the marks left by generations of cats so long ago, her churning emotions grew calmer. She crouched down by the pool, lapped once from the water, and closed her eyes.

"Leafpool! Leafpool!" The gentle voice spoke in her ear, and soft fur brushed against her pelt. Leafpool opened her eyes to see the beautiful tortoiseshell, Spottedleaf, sitting beside her, wreathed in starlight.

"Oh, Spottedleaf!" she purred. "I've missed you so much. I thought you had abandoned me."

"Never think that, dear one," Spottedleaf mewed. Her sweet scent flowed over Leafpool as she bent her head to draw her tongue over the younger cat's ears. "How could I leave you to struggle with your feelings alone?"

Leafpool felt her fur crawl with guilt. "You know about Crowfeather?"

Spottedleaf nodded.

"I love him so much. I can't be a medicine cat anymore!" Leafpool blurted out helplessly.

Spottedleaf pressed her muzzle against Leafpool's shoulder. Then she murmured, "I know what it is to love, although my path was different from yours. Who knows   if I had lived, I might have suffered what you are suffering now."

"Please tell me what to do!" Leafpool begged. "I can't bear this! I don't feel like I'm needed in ThunderClan anymore. Cinderpelt doesn't want me; she has Brightheart to help her."

"Brightheart needs a purpose just now." Wisdom shone like moonlight in Spottedleaf's eyes. "She has found it in helping Cinderpelt. Be generous to her."

"But she's always *there*," Leafpool muttered. She knew she was being unreasonable. "I'll try to understand," she promised with a sigh. "But Brightheart isn't the only reason I don't think my Clan wants me. I've quarreled with Squirrelflight, and we *never* quarrel."

Spottedleaf gave her a gentle lick between the ears. "Your sister loves you. One quarrel will not change that."

"And Crowfeather?" Leafpool mewed, feeling her heart beat faster as it always did when she thought of the WindClan warrior. "He wants us to go away together. I want to be with him so much, but should I really leave my Clan for him?"

"No cat can make this choice for you," Spottedleaf replied, letting the tip of her tail brush against Leafpool's shoulder. "Deep inside, you know what is right, and you must follow your heart."

Leafpool sat up, feeling as if a bright light had shone straight into her mind. Surely her heart was where her feelings for Crowfeather came from? Spottedleaf *did* understand. "You mean it's all right for me to love Crowfeather? Oh, Spottedleaf, thank you!"

The beautiful tortoiseshell began to fade, dissolving into stars. Her scent remained, hanging in the air with a few last words that died away into silence. "Remember, you know what is right."

Leafpool blinked. Her nose was almost touching the shining water of the Moonpool, and her legs were cramped from lying on the cold stones, but when she sprang up, she felt as if she could run forever.

You must follow your heart.

Spottedleaf had told her she could do what her love demanded and leave the Clans with Crowfeather. It didn't matter if she gave up being a medicine cat, because Brightheart was helping out. Besides, Cinderpelt was young and healthy; she had many seasons to train another apprentice. It didn't matter that Leafpool felt as if her Clan didn't need her anymore. Her destiny lay elsewhere, far beyond this territory, with Crowfeather beside her.

Her heart light as a leaf, she bounded up the spiral path, thrust her way through the bushes, and raced down the hill to find Crowfeather. The long journey between the Moonpool and the lake seemed to skim by in a few heartbeats, although by the time she reached the stream that divided ThunderClan from WindClan the sky was growing paler and one by one the stars were fading.

At first she was afraid she would have to wait for the next Gathering before she saw Crowfeather again. After all, she had sent him back to his camp to avoid a quarrel between him and Cinderpelt. Maybe he had been so angry that he wouldn't even want to see her again.

Then she spotted him sitting in the shelter of a gorse bush a few tail-lengths inside WindClan territory. He looked so lonely, staring down at the lake with his tail curled over his paws. Leafpool's heart flipped over. They were both loners in their own Clans, but now they could be together forever.

"Crowfeather!"

He spun around. Leafpool splashed through the stream toward him, and he met her on the far bank, his eyes shining as he pressed his muzzle into her shoulder and wound his tail with hers.

"I've thought about what you said," she mewed. "About leaving."

"You have?"

"I've been so scared, Crowfeather—scared about leaving my Clan and my kin. But I went to the Moonpool, and Spottedleaf came to speak to me." Seeing Crowfeather look puzzled, she added, "She was ThunderClan's medicine cat once, but now she walks with StarClan. She often visits me in dreams."

Crowfeather still seemed bewildered; Leafpool wasn't sure if he believed her, or if he thought that her encounters with Spottedleaf were nothing more than dreams.

"What did she say?" he asked.

"She told me to follow my heart."

Crowfeather's eyes widened. "You're a medicine cat, Leafpool. Isn't that where your heart has led you?"

"Once it was." Leafpool's heart thumped as she realized

that Crowfeather thought she was about to reject him. "But ThunderClan has a medicine cat. Cinderpelt is young and strong, and she'll serve the Clan for seasons yet. And Brightheart will help out for now. Cinderpelt can train another apprentice when I've gone."

Crowfeather drew in a painful breath. "When you've gone? Leafpool, does that mean . . . ?"

"Yes. I'll come with you."

Leafpool could hardly bear to look at the blaze of happiness in Crowfeather's eyes. Did he really love her this much? Her belly twisted with fear. She couldn't let him down now. She had to go through with this.

"I've been scared too," Crowfeather admitted. "I don't want to leave my Clan or my friends. I even hoped I might be leader one day. But more than that, I don't want to lose *you*, Leafpool. And there's no way for us to be together if we stay here."

Leafpool pressed her side against his, the warmth of his pelt comforting her as she stared into a future that was suddenly dark and terrifying. "Where should we go?"

"Not back toward the forest," Crowfeather decided. "We'd end up in the mountains, or places where there are too many Twolegs. There are hills beyond WindClan where we can look for a place to live. I'll take care of you, Leafpool." For a moment his gaze darkened and drifted away from her, filled with memories. "I promise I'll take care of you," he repeated more strongly. "Are you ready?"

"You mean, we're leaving now?" Leafpool gasped.

"Don't you think we should?"

But I want to say good-bye! Leafpool almost wailed out loud, but she knew that it would be impossible. Saying good-bye would cause anger and pain and confusion, and maybe their Clans would prevent them from going at all.

"You're right." She tried to sound brave and optimistic. "I'm ready."

Crowfeather touched his nose to the top of her head. "Thank you. I promise I'll do everything I can to make sure you won't regret this."

They turned their backs on the lake and padded side by side up the hill. Ahead of them the rising sun filled the sky with streaks of flame, as they left their Clans and everything they had ever known.

CHAPTER 18

Squirrelflight was on the dawn patrol with Ashfur and Thornclaw, checking the ShadowClan border. Everything was quiet. The ShadowClan scent markings at the foot of the dead tree were strong and fresh.

"Have you scented either of those kittypets?" she asked Ashfur as he came up to join her.

"Not a thing." Ashfur's blue eyes gleamed with satisfaction. "You must have scared them off for good."

Squirrelflight twitched her ears. "I hope so. If I never see them again, it'll be too soon."

Ashfur waved his tail to summon Rainwhisker, who had been renewing the ThunderClan scent markers farther up the border, and the patrol set off back to camp. The sun was rising as they emerged from the thorn tunnel. Golden rays slanted down into the stone hollow and the ground was dappled with shadows of fresh leaves. Stopping just inside the entrance, Squirrelflight arched her back in a long stretch and let the warmth soak into her pelt.

"Squirrelflight!" Cinderpelt called to her from across the camp; the medicine cat was limping rapidly toward her.

"Have you seen Leafpool this morning?"

Alarm flared in Squirrelflight's belly. "No," she replied. "We were over by the ShadowClan border." She almost added, *and Leafpool only ever goes toward WindClan*, but stopped herself in time.

Cinderpelt nodded, and Squirrelflight realized the medicine cat already knew what she had not put into words. "I saw her last night—" Cinderpelt broke off, twitching her ears. Squirrelflight stared at her. What was the medicine cat not telling her?

"When I woke up, her nest was cold," Cinderpelt went on, "and her scent was stale. She hasn't been here all night."

"But she always comes back before dawn!" Squirrelflight blurted out.

Cinderpelt's eyes narrowed and Squirrelflight flinched. Would the medicine cat be angry that Squirrelflight had known her sister's secret all along? "I'm sorry, Cinderpelt," she began.

Cinderpelt stopped her with a dismissive flick of her tail. "It's all right. I know she's been visiting Crowfeather."

"Crowfeather?" Squirrelflight felt every hair on her pelt bristle. All she had known was that Leafpool had had some reason to sneak out of the camp at night. "That can't be true! Crowfeather is in love with Feathertail."

"Feathertail is dead. And it's possible to love more than one cat in a lifetime. Squirrelflight, have you never noticed how they look at each other at Gatherings? Where did you think she was going all these nights?"

Squirrelflight stared at her, speechless with shock. Leafpool was a *medicine cat*! Then she remembered sensing her sister's chaotic feelings of guilt and excitement, and she knew Cinderpelt must be right. Guilt flooded over her; she had been so distracted by her new friendship with Ashfur that she hadn't tried hard enough to find out what was troubling her sister.

"Do you think she's gone to WindClan to be with Crowfeather?" she asked, her voice hoarse.

Cinderpelt's whiskers twitched. "Perhaps."

"Would WindClan accept her?"

"What do you think?" The medicine cat's tone was dry. "Leafpool is a valuable cat for any Clan. But we can't be sure," she added. "Last night, when Leafpool left the camp, I followed her. She saw me, and we quarreled. We both said things that should have been left unsaid. Perhaps she's somewhere in ThunderClan territory, waiting until her temper has cooled before she comes back to camp."

Cinderpelt spoke briskly, without betraying much feeling. Squirrelflight wondered if her coldness came from anger and disappointment at Leafpool's betrayal. But as Cinderpelt turned away, Squirrelflight heard her mutter, "StarClan be with her, and bring her back safe!" The anguish in her voice revealed how much she had been torn apart by Leafpool's disappearance.

The camp was stirring around them. Daisy appeared at the entrance to the nursery, blinked lazily in the sunlight, then called her kits out. The three little scraps tumbled happily on the ground in front of her, squealing and batting each other with soft paws. On the other side of the clearing, Sandstorm slid out of the warriors' den, calling to Cloudtail and Dustpelt for a hunting patrol; the three cats loped across the clearing and out through the tunnel, waving their tails at Squirrelflight and Cinderpelt as they passed. A few moments later Whitepaw and Birchpaw emerged from the apprentices' den, arguing about whose turn it was to fetch mouse bile for the elders' ticks.

Squirrelflight knew it wouldn't be long before some cat noticed Leafpool's absence and started asking questions.

"I'm going to tell Firestar." Suddenly Cinderpelt sounded exhausted.

Squirrelflight ran after her. "No, don't tell him or any other cat just yet. I'll go out and look for Leafpool. Maybe I can bring her home before any cat notices she's gone."

Cinderpelt hesitated. Then her eyes seemed to focus again and she nodded. "Thank you, Squirrelflight. It's *very* important to find her. She'll lose so much—her Clan, her kin, her life as a medicine cat—if she doesn't come back." She looked away and added more quietly, "I don't think she understands how much her Clan needs her."

"I'm on my way." Squirrelflight whipped around and plunged back into the thorn tunnel.

She headed straight for the WindClan border. In spite of what Cinderpelt had said, she didn't believe Leafpool was sulking somewhere in ThunderClan territory. Leafpool never sulked . . . but maybe Squirrelflight didn't know her sister as well as she thought.

She paused to taste the air, searching for a trace of Leafpool's scent. "If I don't find her on the border, I'll have to go into WindClan territory," she decided out loud.

"Go to WindClan? Why?"

Squirrelflight jumped. "Brambleclaw! You nearly frightened me out of my fur," she gulped, spinning around to see the tabby warrior stepping out from the shelter of a hazel thicket.

"What were you saying about WindClan?" Brambleclaw persisted. "We don't want to stir up trouble with them. Onestar's prickly enough as it is."

"I'm not looking for trouble!" Squirrelflight retorted. She was too shaken to lie about where she was going. "I've got to find Leafpool. Cinderpelt thinks she's gone to WindClan so she can be with Crowfeather."

Brambleclaw's ears twitched. "But she's a medicine cat."

Squirrelflight glared at him. "Tell me something I don't know."

Brambleclaw still remained infuriatingly calm. "You're right, we have to go after her," he meowed. "We don't want Onestar to think we're driving our cats away." As Squirrelflight let out a furious hiss, he added, "And we want Leafpool back. She's making a big mistake, leaving her own Clan."

"She's lost her mind!" Squirrelflight tore at the ground with her claws. "I've got to find her before Firestar finds out."

"Do you think she'll come back?" Brambleclaw's amber gaze was serious. "We can't force her."

"She *has* to!"

"If she has really gone to join WindClan, it must have been

a hard decision for her," Brambleclaw pointed out. "It won't be easy to change her mind."

"But I have to try," Squirrelflight protested. "And even if I can't convince her, I need to know where she is."

"Can you sense anything?" Brambleclaw asked. "You know, like when we were on our journey?"

Squirrelflight reached out with that strange sense she had always shared with her sister. She tried to picture Leafpool, and for a heartbeat she thought she picked up a trace of wind on the moorland, but then it was gone, leaving nothing but emptiness.

"I can't see her anywhere," she mewed wretchedly.

Brambleclaw straightened up. "Well, standing here won't solve anything. Let's go."

"You'll come with me?" Squirrelflight stared at him in surprise.

"If you're going to WindClan, you'll need some cat with you," Brambleclaw replied. "ThunderClan cats aren't exactly Onestar's favorite guests these days."

Gratitude flooded over Squirrelflight like a warm wash of sunlight. Whatever she felt about Brambleclaw's private ambitions, or his willingness to trust Hawkfrost, she couldn't think of any other cat she'd rather have beside her right now.

They padded toward the border in silence; Squirrelflight was still feeling too stunned to speak. How could Leafpool think of giving up her life in ThunderClan? Didn't her kin, her friends, her work as a medicine cat mean anything to her? What about StarClan? Did Leafpool have a *choice* not to be a medicine cat? And what about Firestar? Squirrelflight's pelt prickled as she wondered what she could possibly say to her father to explain where Leafpool had gone.

The sun shone down from a blue sky dotted with tiny puffs of cloud. Dew glittered on the grass and on strands of cobweb stretched precariously across thickets of bramble. New fronds of bracken were beginning to uncurl and everywhere Squirrelflight could smell the sharp, green scent of growing things. But even the rustle of prey in the undergrowth couldn't distract Squirrelflight from her troubled thoughts.

Glancing sideways, she met Brambleclaw's eyes and saw nothing but calm sympathy in his face. She realized he must understand part of what she was feeling because he too had lost a sister to another Clan.

"Did you feel like this when Tawnypelt left? As if nothing would ever be all right again?"

Brambleclaw waited until they had ducked beneath some low-hanging ferns before replying. "At first I felt so lonely I thought I wouldn't be able to bear it," he meowed. "But I knew I had to respect her decision. And we're still friends, even though she is in a different Clan."

But it's not the same, Squirrelflight thought. *And Tawnypelt wasn't a medicine cat, chosen by StarClan to serve her Clanmates.*

They followed the stream upward on the ThunderClan side, tasting the air every few paces for any sign of Leafpool. When the trees gave way to bare moorland Squirrelflight picked up a faint trace, but it was stale, at least from the night before, and it stopped at the edge of the stream. "She crossed here," she meowed to Brambleclaw.

The tabby warrior nosed the grasses that overhung the water, then nodded. "It looks like it." He raised his head and gazed across the moorland. "Okay, WindClan it is."

He led the way across the stream and Squirrelflight followed, splashing through brown peaty water that ran ice cold over pebbles. On the other side they found more of Leafpool's scent, mingled with a second cat's.

"WindClan," Brambleclaw meowed. "Crowfeather, I think."

"He must have been waiting for her." Squirrelflight's last hope vanished, and for the first time she realized she might have lost her sister forever.

CHAPTER 19

"We'd better go straight to the camp," Brambleclaw decided. "And hope that Onestar is in a welcoming mood."

"I'm not going home without talking to Leafpool," Squirrel-flight mewed determinedly.

She hoped Onestar wouldn't try to stop them from seeing her sister. The WindClan leader had been so hostile at the last Gathering that she felt very vulnerable crossing the open moorland where they could be spotted so easily. She kept scanning the bare slopes for approaching cats, but it was still a shock when a patrol leaped out from behind a jutting rock and raced across the turf toward them.

She let out a hiss. "Look—it's Webfoot and Weaselfur."

They stopped and waited for the WindClan cats to reach them. As well as the two warriors, there was an apprentice Squirrelflight didn't recognize. Her belly clenched when she saw the hostility in Webfoot's eyes and the way his neck fur bristled as he skidded to a halt in front of them.

"What are you doing on our territory?" he snarled.

"We need to speak to Onestar," Brambleclaw told him.

Webfoot's tail lashed from side to side. "More ThunderClan

interference? What does Firestar want this time?"

"We'll tell that to Onestar."

Webfoot and Weaselfur exchanged a glance. Squirrelflight wondered if they were going to have to fight their way past.

Then Webfoot let out a faint snort of disgust. "We don't need you to tell us why you're here. We already know. And I guess Onestar will want to hear what you have to say."

He and Weaselfur fell back to let Brambleclaw and Squirrel-flight keep going, while the apprentice watched them with hot, accusing eyes. Squirrelflight shot a questioning glance at Brambleclaw, but the tabby warrior looked as bewildered as she felt. Webfoot must have been talking about Leafpool, but it didn't make sense that they'd be so angry about a cat wanting to join their Clan.

The two WindClan warriors flanked them all the way to the camp, one on each side. As they climbed toward the hollow, the apprentice ran ahead to warn Onestar. By the time Squirrelflight and Brambleclaw reached the edge of the hollow, Onestar was waiting for them beside the pile of rocks in the center. His deputy, Ashfoot, and a couple of other warriors stood beside him, all looking up expectantly as Squirrelflight and Brambleclaw started to climb down into the hollow. There was no sign of Leafpool and Crowfeather, and Squirrel-flight gulped. Surely Onestar wasn't keeping them under guard?

"Here they are," Webfoot mewed.

Onestar stepped forward, his ears flattened. "Well, I presume Firestar sent you. Have you come to explain why

ThunderClan has stolen one of our warriors?"

"*What?*" Fury raced through Squirrelflight like flame through dry grass. She stepped forward until she was nose to nose with Onestar. "How dare you call us thieves? It's Wind-Clan who—"

She broke off when Brambleclaw slapped his tail across her mouth; she glared at him but his amber eyes clearly signaled a warning. Flexing her claws, she reluctantly took a pace back.

The tabby warrior dipped his head to Onestar. "Thunder-Clan hasn't stolen any WindClan warriors," he meowed. "Why? Has one gone missing?"

"It's Crowfeather, isn't it?" Squirrelflight's heart started pounding hard.

Onestar's eyes narrowed, but before he could speak, Ashfoot interrupted. "Yes—do you know where he is?" She sounded desperate, and Squirrelflight remembered she was Crowfeather's mother.

"Keep quiet!" Onestar snarled, glaring at Ashfoot, but the gray she-cat didn't flinch.

"When did you last see him?" Brambleclaw asked, breaking the tension between the WindClan leader and his deputy. "We might be able to help."

"We don't want help from ThunderClan!" Webfoot spat.

Onestar silenced him with a wave of his tail. "Crowfeather did not sleep in the warriors' den last night," he meowed. "This morning we followed his scent trail as far as the border with ThunderClan. There his scent mingled with a Thunder-Clan cat's. They obviously met there."

Weaselfur pushed forward to stand beside his leader. "Wait a moment," he mewed to Brambleclaw. "If you knew nothing about Crowfeather, why are you here? Do you know which ThunderClan cat he met with?"

Squirrelflight nodded. There was no use hiding the truth now. "My sister, Leafpool. She's vanished too. We followed *her* scent trail to the border. "

"But she's a medicine cat!" Ashfoot exclaimed.

"Medicine cats have feelings just like any other cat," Squirrelflight said, defending her sister.

Onestar let out an angry hiss. "She has broken the laws of StarClan."

"Crowfeather must have persuaded her to go!" Squirrelflight flashed back at him.

Brambleclaw shot her a warning glance. "Onestar, you're making a big mistake if you try to turn Firestar and Thunder-Clan into enemies. We have to work together and find both our missing cats."

"How?" Onestar was clearly making a massive effort to control his anger; as it ebbed away, he just sounded bewildered. "If Crowfeather isn't with you, then where have they gone?"

"Where *could* they go?" Ashfoot asked despairingly, as if she didn't expect an answer.

"We can try to find out," Brambleclaw meowed. "Maybe we can follow their scent trail."

"I'll go and look," Ashfoot offered.

Onestar nodded. "Take another warrior with you."

"We'll come too," Squirrelflight mewed. To her relief, Onestar didn't object.

Ashfoot beckoned to Tornear; the four cats left the camp and headed for the place close to the border where they had last scented their Clanmates. Squirrelflight felt more anxious with every step. Would Leafpool be safe, traveling into unknown territory with only one other cat? How could they live a normal life, without the support of their Clans? *We* must *find them*, she vowed. *They're making a huge mistake!*

Ashfoot was first to pick up the scent trail again. "This way!" she meowed, gesturing with her tail.

The four cats spread out with a few tail-lengths between them, noses to the ground in case the cats they were following split up again. But the two trails went on side by side, across the WindClan scent markers and on into the hills. Squirrelflight's heart sank. Until then she had clung to a faint hope they would find Leafpool and Crowfeather hiding on the edge of the territory. Now she had to admit they were truly gone.

The lake soon vanished behind a fold of moorland. The hills grew steeper and bleaker, with rocks jutting through the scratchy grass. Squirrelflight started to feel tired and cold. She couldn't imagine how Leafpool had found the strength to set out into this hostile country. *She must have been so desperate . . .*

At last Brambleclaw came to a halt at the top of a rise. Beyond, the ground fell away into restless gray scree, with only a few stunted thornbushes poking out of it.

"I can't scent them anymore," he announced.

All four cats exchanged worried glances. Unwilling to

give up yet, they padded along the crest of the hill, trying to pick up the scent again. But there was nothing. Squirrelflight launched herself down the slope, splinters of rock sharp beneath her paws. But there was no scent there either, nothing to tell her which way her sister and the WindClan cat had gone.

"This is hopeless," Tornear was mewing as Squirrelflight scrambled up to join the others. "We're never going to find them."

"We'd better go back," mewed Brambleclaw.

"No!" Squirrelflight protested. "We can't let them go like this."

Brambleclaw waved his tail to take in the harsh rock stretching in front of them, the barren moorland, and the sky. "They could be anywhere."

"He's right." Ashfoot's eyes were dark with pain. "There's nothing more we can do."

Brambleclaw padded up to Squirrelflight and rested his tail on her shoulder. "We can't track them down if they don't want to be found," he meowed gently.

Squirrelflight wanted to insist that they could, but deep within her fur she knew Leafpool and Crowfeather had gone. *I'll never see my sister again.* She turned her head to press her cheek against Brambleclaw, letting his familiar scent comfort her. They had been through so much together to lead the Clans to their new home. She was glad he was here, helping her with this new agony.

The sun was close to sinking below the horizon when they

reached the WindClan border again. Squirrelflight said good-bye to Ashfoot and Tornear and splashed wearily through the stream behind Brambleclaw. What were they going to say to Firestar?

"We're losing all the cats who made the journey to find Midnight," she mewed to Brambleclaw. "Feathertail, Storm-fur, and now Crowfeather." A chill rippled across her fur. "Do you think that means StarClan doesn't want us to settle here after all?"

Brambleclaw shook his head. "I'm sure this is where they wanted the Clans to be. Don't start doubting them, Squir-relflight. We never thought settling into our new homes would be easy."

"No, but I never thought it would be this difficult," Squir-relflight murmured as she followed him back through the shadowed forest.

Though it was dark under the trees, a few rays of sun still reached into the stone hollow, staining the clearing with blood-red light. Squirrelflight suppressed a shiver and wondered if a medicine cat would think that was a sign from StarClan.

As soon as she entered the camp, she could tell the whole Clan had noticed Leafpool's disappearance. Ferncloud and Dustpelt were crouched beside the fresh-kill pile, their heads close together. Brackenfur, Ashfur, and their two apprentices were in an anxious huddle outside the apprentices' den. The elders had emerged from their den underneath a twisted hazel bush, and just below the Highledge Firestar was speaking to

Sandstorm, Cinderpelt, and Brightheart. Only Daisy's kits hadn't seemed to notice anything was wrong, scuffling happily together on the dusty ground outside the nursery.

Squirrelflight was aware of cats turning to look at her, their eyes burning into her fur as she crossed the clearing with Brambleclaw. She felt a ripple of hope go through her Clanmates like wind across grass, only to die away when they saw Leafpool wasn't with them.

Firestar began to pad toward them, but it was Brightheart who reached them first. "I'm sorry, I'm sorry!" she meowed. Her voice cracked with distress and her good eye was filled with guilt. "I wasn't trying to take her place. *Leafpool* is our medicine cat, just like Cinderpelt."

"I'm sure she didn't leave because of you," Squirrelflight replied awkwardly. She knew quite well that Leafpool had been unhappy about the way Brightheart was taking over her medicine cat duties.

"What happened?" Firestar demanded, halting in front of his daughter. "What did you find out?"

"Did you find Leafpool?" Sandstorm added.

Other cats gathered around, echoing Sandstorm's question. Some of them mentioned Crowfeather. Leafpool's secret wasn't a secret any longer. Cinderpelt must have been forced to tell her Clanmates everything she knew.

It was Brambleclaw who explained. "Her scent trail led into WindClan territory, so we went to visit their camp."

Cinderpelt limped up just then, in time to hear Brambleclaw's words. "Did you speak to her?"

Brambleclaw shook his head. "She wasn't there. She and Crowfeather had already left the territory. We followed their trail with a couple of the WindClan cats, but we lost it in the hills. They've gone."

"No!" Cinderpelt's voice was a rough whisper; terrible fear dulled her eyes.

Firestar and Sandstorm moved closer together until their pelts brushed. "We've lost her," Sandstorm mewed softly.

"The whole Clan has lost her," Firestar meowed.

Squirrelflight wanted to wail out loud. Leafpool had lost so much too. She must have loved Crowfeather very much to give up everything for him.

Would I do that for Ashfur? Squirrelflight wondered. Somehow, she didn't think she would.

For Brambleclaw?

She blinked, realizing that that was a question she couldn't answer.

CHAPTER 20

❧

Leafpool paused at the top of a ridge, trying to ignore the ache in her paws as she turned to look back. The lake and the trees were long gone; all around her stretched fold after fold of unfamiliar hills. She opened her mouth, picking up the sharp scent of moorland grass and a hint of rabbit. The sun was going down, but there was no sign of any trees or bushes where she and Crowfeather could shelter for the night.

The WindClan warrior followed her up the slope and stood close beside her. Warmth crept back into Leafpool's tired legs as she felt his pelt brush hers. This cat could still give her courage and hope when everything else seemed strange and frightening.

And what about everything you've left behind? a small voice mewed inside her.

Leafpool tried to imagine what was happening in her Clan. Firestar would be furious that she'd abandoned them without saying a word. Cinderpelt would have to find a new apprentice. Squirrelflight would miss her so much. . . . A jolt of pain shook Leafpool, almost enough to make her turn her paws back toward the lake. But how could she go back now, when every cat knew what she had done, and that Crowfeather was with her?

Nothing mattered as long as she had Crowfeather. Her love for him tingled through her from ears to tail-tip; she had to keep on believing that her decision was the right one.

"Just a bit farther." Crowfeather nosed her ear. "We need to find somewhere to sleep before it gets dark."

"Okay." Leafpool forced her paws to follow him along the ridge. They had been traveling all day, even though neither of them had gotten any sleep the previous night, and she felt more exhausted than she had ever been in her life.

Suddenly Crowfeather stopped and pointed down with his tail. "Look!"

When she caught up, Leafpool saw that just ahead the ground fell away into a rocky hollow. A tiny pool lay at the bottom, shaded by a couple of wind-scorched thorn trees.

"Thank StarClan!" she exclaimed. "Shelter and water."

Summoning up her last scrap of energy, she bounded down the slope, paws slipping on the loose stones, until she could crouch beside the pool and lap from it. The memory of her last visit to the Moonpool flooded her mind.

Never again, the inner voice told her. *You're not a medicine cat anymore.*

But that didn't matter either, Leafpool reminded herself. Spottedleaf had told her to follow her heart. She must be doing the right thing.

The gray-black warrior joined her beside the pool, peering into the water. "I can't see any fish," he commented.

His words reminded Leafpool how hungry she was. The only fresh-kill they'd had all day was a scrawny vole they had shared beside the stream not long after setting out. It seemed like moons ago now.

"You can catch us a rabbit in the morning," she mewed, trying to ignore how faint the scent of rabbit had been. "You're good at hunting on moorland like this. You can teach me how too."

"Sure. You'll soon learn," Crowfeather replied. "But I don't think we need to wait till morning. There must be some sort of prey around here."

He stood with his jaws wide, tasting the air. Leafpool stood beside him, ears standing straight, until she heard the sound of a tiny creature scuffling under the thorn trees. A heartbeat later she spotted a mouse and dropped into the hunter's crouch. With a purr of satisfaction she pounced.

At the same moment a second mouse shot out of some dead leaves. Crowfeather grabbed it with one paw.

"There, what did I tell you?" he mewed, padding over to Leafpool so they could eat together.

They found a patch of sand between the roots of one of the stunted trees, sheltered from the wind by its twisting branches, and devoured the mice in a few famished gulps.

"You were right about the prey," Leafpool murmured, swiping her tongue around her mouth. "I'm glad you're here. I would be so scared without you."

"I'll always look after you," Crowfeather promised, resting his nose in her fur. "Tomorrow we're bound to find somewhere better to live. After all, the Clans found the lake, and we don't need such a big territory when it's just the two of us."

Leafpool nodded. "These hills can't go on forever." *Can they?*

"We'll be fine. You'll see," Crowfeather assured her.

"I know." Leafpool's voice faded as she sank exhaustedly into sleep.

She was standing in a dark place, her paws cold on dew-drenched grass. She was surrounded by fearful snarling, but she couldn't see where it came from, even though she wrenched her head frantically from side to side. Then she realized that the darkness that surrounded her was a rolling cloud of black fog. It drifted apart for an instant to show her waves lapping the lakeshore. Her dream had taken her home. But the reek of blood engulfed her, and she saw that the water in the lake was a blood-red tide sucking hungrily at the land.

"No!" she gasped.

Before all is peaceful, blood will spill blood, and the lake will run red.

Every hair on her pelt stood on end. She had left her Clan far behind. Why couldn't she escape StarClan's terrible prophecy?

The snarling died away, only to break out again behind her, louder than before. Leafpool spun around. The black fog still billowed around her, but she could see huge lumbering shapes moving within it. They were too blurred for Leafpool to make out, although she caught glimpses of blunt claws, snapping jaws, and small, malicious eyes. A huge dark mass loomed over her, and a claw slashed across her face, ruffling her whiskers and barely missing her eye. She leapt back and felt sticky liquid washing around her paws. The stench of blood filled her nose and mouth.

"StarClan help me!" she yowled.

Her eyes flew open. She was lying in the moorland hollow with thorn branches above her head and Crowfeather at her side. She drew a long breath of relief. Then she realized that the WindClan warrior was rising to his paws, his body rigid with tension as he stared into the darkness.

"Who's there?" he called sharply.

Leafpool heard shuffling pawsteps coming closer. Crowfeather moved protectively in front of her; peering past him, Leafpool could just make out a dark, slowly moving shape like the ones in her dream.

Am I really awake?

Then a cloud moved away from the moon. Silver light washed down into the hollow, revealing a large, thick-furred creature with a broad white stripe down its pointed muzzle. A badger!

Leafpool sprang to her paws. "Keep back!" she growled.

Crowfeather waved his tail. "It's all right, Leafpool," he meowed. "It's Midnight."

Still trembling, Leafpool gazed up at the old she-badger. Midnight lived beside the sun-drown-place; what was she doing here on the moor? Leafpool padded forward curiously. She had always wanted to meet the badger who had warned her sister and Brambleclaw that the forest was being destroyed by Twolegs, and all the Clans would have to leave. Without her, they would never have discovered the new place StarClan had chosen for them.

"Greetings, Crowpaw." Midnight's eyes were bright with surprise. "Even I not foresee meeting you here."

"Greetings, Midnight," Crowfeather meowed. "We didn't expect to see you, either. And I'm not Crowpaw anymore," he added. "My warrior name is Crowfeather . . . in memory of Feathertail."

"Yes, she watches you still," Midnight told him.

Leafpool winced. Crowfeather seemed to sense she was feeling awkward, and he brought her forward with a gesture of his tail. "This is Leafpool," he meowed. "Squirrelflight's sister."

Leafpool dipped her head. "It's good to meet you at last, Midnight. I've heard a lot about you."

"Your sister speak of you," Midnight replied. "StarClan show you much of future also?"

"Yes, I'm a medicine cat." Leafpool blinked. *Not anymore.*

The old badger glanced from her to Crowfeather and back again. "You flee, yes?" she demanded.

Leafpool stiffened. Did Midnight know she and Crowfeather were running away from their Clans? Is that why she came to find them?

"How do you know?" she asked warily.

Before Midnight could reply, Crowfeather took a pace forward. "We *had* to leave," he explained. "We're from different Clans, and there's no way we could stay together if—"

"Wait." Midnight raised a massive paw. "You mean here alone you are? Where rest of cats?"

"In their territories, by the lake." Crowfeather pointed with his tail.

"Then you not know?"

"Know what?" Leafpool's claws slid out in sudden panic.

Midnight lowered her head. "Is great trouble coming. Many of my kin with Clans are angry," she rasped. "Cats drive them out of their place. Now they come to attack and drive you out, take back what once theirs."

Leafpool drew in a sharp breath. "We drove a badger out of our territory," she remembered. "A female with kits."

"And Hawkfrost chased one out of RiverClan," Crowfeather meowed.

Leafpool hardly heard him. Her head spun as she plunged back into her dream of blood and slashing claws. "You say they're going to attack the Clans?" she whispered.

"And whose side are you on, Midnight?" Crowfeather added harshly.

Midnight's gaze met his. "I have no side. Cats, badgers, in peace could live. I speak against attack, but my kin not listen to me. For many days now they talk of blood and revenge."

Crowfeather drew closer to Leafpool. She could feel his body quivering. "What do they plan to do?" he asked.

"Many badgers gather. Your sets they will attack, kill many cats, drive out others."

Our sets . . . She means our camps. Leafpool's fur stood on end.

She and Crowfeather would be safe out here, but the Clans they had left behind would be destroyed, their Clanmates murdered.

"No . . ." she whispered. "It can't happen!"

"So what are you doing here?" Crowfeather asked Midnight.

"I go to warn Clans, tell them what is coming," the old she-badger replied. "Will you help?"

Leafpool opened her jaws to speak, but Crowfeather interrupted. "No. We have left our Clans for good. There's nothing we can do."

"Crowfeather, no!" A shiver of horror passed through Leafpool from ears to tail-tip. "We can't leave our Clans to die."

Crowfeather's amber eyes were full of pain. Gently he touched his nose to Leafpool's muzzle. "I know," he mewed. "But Midnight is going to warn them. They'll be safe if they listen to her. What more could we do?"

"We—" Leafpool broke off, not sure she knew the answer.

"We've come too far," Crowfeather insisted. "If we go back now, every cat will know what we've done. We won't be able to leave again. Things will be the same as they ever were—worse, because we won't be able to meet up like we used to. Every cat will be watching us, waiting for us to slip away. All this will have been for nothing."

Leafpool gasped with pain, as if the claws of the badgers in her dream had torn her pelt away. She knew Crowfeather was right; they would lose everything if they went back now. Yet how could they keep going, when they knew what terrible danger their Clanmates were facing?

Midnight looked from her to Crowfeather and back again. Leafpool didn't know how much the badger understood about the duties of medicine cats, or about the warrior code that said that cats from different Clans could not be together. But there was warmth and understanding in her gaze, as if Midnight somehow sensed the struggles they had gone through before they made the decision to leave.

"StarClan go with you," the badger murmured. "Future rests in paws of warrior ancestors. All I can I will do."

"Thank you," meowed Leafpool.

She watched as Midnight lumbered away up the slope in the direction of the territory they had left. Her paws trembled with guilt and sadness; her Clanmates were in trouble, and she was deliberately choosing not to help them.

Crowfeather nuzzled her ear. "Let's get some more sleep," he meowed.

Leafpool curled up beside him under the thorn trees, but sleep refused to come. Her mind was filled with images of snarling badgers bursting into the ThunderClan camp, ripping apart her Clanmates.

StarClan be with them! she prayed.

Her dream had shown her how savage the attack would be. She remembered the dreams that the other medicine cats had described at the Moonpool, dreams of darkness and slashing claws. And now she had received the same message from StarClan. Leafpool's pelt tingled; the starry warriors were still speaking to her. She hadn't lied to Midnight when she said she was still a medicine cat.

She could tell Crowfeather wasn't asleep either. He kept shifting restlessly, and once she heard him sigh. He pressed closer to her, as if trying to comfort her, or himself.

At last Leafpool drifted into a light, troubled sleep. She seemed to float in gray mist, with nothing to tell her where she was. Suddenly the emptiness was ripped apart by a shriek of agony.

"StarClan, help me!"

Leafpool leapt up, trembling, to see the thorn branches outlined against a sky growing pale with the first light of dawn. She had recognized the voice in her dream; it was Cinderpelt.

"Crowfeather!" she gasped. "I can't stay here. We have to go back."

Crowfeather lifted his head. His amber eyes were sad. "I know," he meowed. "I feel the same way. We have to go and help our Clans."

Relief flooded over Leafpool. She loved him even more at that moment because he understood, because he cared for his Clanmates as much as she cared for hers. Briefly she pressed her muzzle against his, with a purr that lasted no more than a heartbeat.

"Let's go," she meowed.

CHAPTER 21

✤

"Mouse dung!" Squirrelflight muttered. The starling she had just missed fluttered onto a branch above her head, while her empty claws sank into the moss. How was she supposed to concentrate on hunting when every waking moment was filled with worry about her sister?

I should have stopped her, she thought bleakly.

"Bad luck," Ashfur meowed, coming up behind her. "Should we call it a day? We've got more than enough to carry back."

"Okay." Squirrelflight followed him to the place under a thornbush where he had scraped earth over their previous kills. Spiderleg joined them, a squirrel dangling from his jaws, and the hunting patrol headed back to camp.

"Come on," Ashfur murmured to Squirrelflight when they had dropped their catch on the fresh-kill pile. "Leafpool will be fine."

"How can she be fine, when she's left everything behind?" Squirrelflight retorted.

"Why don't you rest for a while?" the gray warrior suggested, pointing with his tail at a sunny spot near the wall of the hollow. "You hardly slept at all last night."

"And I won't be able to sleep now. I'm going to make sure Cinderpelt has eaten."

Squirrelflight grabbed a vole from the fresh-kill pile and padded across the clearing to the medicine cat's den. Rounding the screen of brambles, she found Cinderpelt crouched in the opening of her den with her paws tucked under her. Her blue eyes were fixed on nothing. Squirrelflight shivered; it looked as though Cinderpelt were gazing at horrors that only she could see.

The medicine cat blinked and looked up at her. "Squirrelflight—is there any news?"

"About Leafpool?" Squirrelflight set the vole down in front of Cinderpelt. "No, nothing. I brought you some fresh-kill."

The medicine cat turned her head away. "Thanks, but I'm not hungry."

"You have to eat!" Squirrelflight protested. She wondered if Cinderpelt blamed herself for Leafpool's disappearance. The medicine cat seemed to have no courage or energy left. "We need you more than ever, now that Leafpool's gone."

Cinderpelt let out a long sigh. "But I've failed. Utterly failed."

"It's not your fault!" Squirrelflight wriggled into the narrow opening beside Cinderpelt so that she could press herself comfortingly against her. "You're a great medicine cat. What would ThunderClan do without you?"

Cinderpelt gazed at her, a searching look that made Squirrelflight feel like she was about to drown in the blue depths of her eyes. Cinderpelt seemed to be on the verge of confiding something to her, but all she said was, "I wish things didn't have to change."

"They don't have to. They *won't*. Leafpool will come back. We have to believe that."

Cinderpelt shook her head and closed her eyes.

Squirrelflight stretched out a paw and nudged the vole a bit closer to her. "Come on, you'll feel better when you've eaten."

Cinderpelt hesitated, then bent down to sniff the fresh-kill. "Squirrelflight, will you go and check on Sorreltail?" she meowed after a moment. "I'm worried about her. You know what good friends she and Leafpool were."

"Does Sorreltail know what's happened?" Confined to the nursery because her kits were due any day, the young tortoise-shell warrior might not have heard the news.

"Yes, I told her last night." To Squirrelflight's relief, Cinderpelt was beginning to sound more like her normal self. "She was upset, and I gave her some poppy seed to help her sleep."

"Sure, I'll look in on her. On one condition—that I see you eating that vole before I go."

A faint gleam of humor crept into Cinderpelt's eyes. "You never give up, do you? All right—and call me if Sorreltail needs anything."

As Squirrelflight slid out of the den, the medicine cat sniffed the vole again, took a bite, and then began to eat more quickly, as if she had suddenly realized how hungry she was.

Squirrelflight left her to it and headed for the nursery. Just outside, Brightheart was bending over Berrykit. She straightened up as Squirrelflight approached.

"There!" she mewed. "That thorn won't bother you again. Give your paw a good lick now."

"Thanks!" Berrykit looked up admiringly at the ginger and white she-cat. The horseplace cats seemed to have stopped noticing her scars. "You're the best medicine cat ever!"

"I'm not a medicine cat," Brightheart corrected him, with a sidelong glance at Squirrelflight. "ThunderClan already has two medicine cats. I'll never be one."

"Well, *I* think you are," Berrykit meowed, licking his paw vigorously.

It's a pity Brightheart couldn't have said that while Leafpool was here, Squirrelflight thought. "Hi," she mewed. "Cinderpelt sent me to check on Sorreltail."

"Sorreltail's fine," Brightheart told her. "She and Daisy shared a rabbit earlier, and now she's asleep again. Great StarClan, she's *huge,*" she added. "It can't be long before she starts to kit."

"That's good." Squirrelflight tried to summon up enthusiasm, but she couldn't get excited about the first kits to be born in their new home when her mind was filled with worrying about Leafpool and Cinderpelt.

She poked her head into the nursery and saw a tortoise-shell mound of fur sleeping peacefully among the moss and ferns. Daisy and Ferncloud were close beside the young warrior, sharing tongues and mewing softly to each other. Both of them glanced up and twitched their whiskers in greeting to Squirrelflight.

Brightheart had gone by the time she backed out again; Squirrelflight caught a glimpse of her tail whisking behind the bramble screen in front of Cinderpelt's den. Trusting Brightheart to report about Sorreltail to the medicine cat, Squirrelflight headed for the fresh-kill pile to find a piece of prey.

Firestar was there, sharing a squirrel with Sandstorm, while Brambleclaw devoured a thrush a tail-length away.

"I want you to lead the dawn patrol tomorrow," Firestar was meowing to Brambleclaw as Squirrelflight came up. "Have a good look along the WindClan border. It's possible you'll come across more traces of Leafpool."

Brambleclaw swallowed a mouthful. "I'll take Cloudtail. He's one of our best trackers." Hesitantly, he added, "But we followed her trail quite a long way into the hills. I don't think we'll find anything else now."

"You might," Firestar insisted. It was as if he couldn't admit they might never see Leafpool again.

Like Graystripe? Squirrelflight suddenly wondered.

Sandstorm lifted her head. "You might meet her coming back," she mewed. "If you do, don't be angry with her."

Brambleclaw nodded. "Don't worry. If I see her I'll make sure she feels safe to come home."

Squirrelflight could tell he didn't hold out much hope of setting eyes on the missing medicine cat. She was beginning to agree with him. Even though she clung to the hope that her sister would come back, she knew how hard it would be for Leafpool once she had made the impossible decision to leave.

She chose a magpie from the pile and settled down to eat it.

"Are you okay?" Brambleclaw asked quietly.

"Not really," she replied.

"You shouldn't blame yourself," Sandstorm assured her.

"But it's my fault!" All Squirrelflight's worries spilled over and she had to stop herself from wailing like a lost kit. "I knew Leafpool was leaving the camp at night and I didn't do anything."

Firestar leaned over to give her ear a comforting lick. "We should all have seen that there was something troubling Leafpool."

"Yes," Brambleclaw put in unexpectedly. "If you *had* done anything, you might have driven her away sooner. No cat knows."

His gaze slid past her to the camp entrance, where Ashfur had just appeared with his apprentice. They headed for the fresh-kill pile; Brambleclaw finished his prey, swiped his tongue around his jaws, and stalked off before the gray tomcat came up.

"That was good work," Ashfur meowed as he and Birchpaw approached. "Take some fresh-kill to the elders, and then you're done for today."

Birchpaw grabbed some prey from the pile and dashed off across the clearing, while Ashfur padded over to Squirrelflight. Firestar and Sandstorm got up and left the two of them together.

"I just gave Birchpaw a training session," Ashfur told Squirrelflight. "He learns really fast."

"That's good," Squirrelflight replied, trying to feel pleased that Ashfur's mentoring was going well.

"You look exhausted." Ashfur touched his nose to her ear. "This time you *are* going to rest, so don't try to argue."

Squirrelflight felt as though ants were crawling through her pelt; the last thing she wanted to do was lie down, unable to sleep. But seeing the concern in her Clanmate's eyes, she sighed and gave in. Finishing her prey, she padded over to the sunny spot near the wall, where she stretched out on her side and let the rays of the setting sun soak into her fur.

Ashfur crouched close beside her and began to lick her shoulder soothingly. In spite of the thoughts that buzzed in her mind, Squirrelflight began to drift into sleep. But the buzzing grew louder, and she realized it wasn't inside her head after all. A low, grumbling roar was approaching through the trees.

Irritated, she raised her head. "What in StarClan's name is that?"

Before she had finished speaking, the startled wail of a cat came from outside the clearing. The thorns rustled violently and Whitepaw skidded out of the mouth of the tunnel, her ears flat to her head and her eyes huge with fear. Brackenfur was hard on her paws.

Squirrelflight jumped up. The roaring grew clearer: it was the sound of many creatures, growling and snarling. It became louder still, until it seemed to fill the whole forest, and with it came snapping noises of breaking twigs, as if something were trampling down the barrier across the entrance to the hollow.

Suddenly Squirrelflight saw an enormous creature thrust its way through the branches. The dying sunlight showed her a broad head with a narrow, striped snout, massive shoulders, and strong, blunt claws.

"Badger!" she yowled.

Cats ran out from all around the clearing. Firestar emerged from his den on the Highledge and launched himself down the rockfall. Brambleclaw pushed his way out of the warriors' den, closely followed by Sandstorm and Cloudtail. Cinderpelt and Brightheart brushed past the bramble screen in front of the medicine cat's den; Brightheart's good eye narrowed and she snarled at the intruder.

The badger had paused just inside the barrier, swinging its head from side to side as it scanned the clearing with small, bright eyes. Squirrelflight was about to hurl herself on it when more trampling noises kept her paws frozen to the ground in horror. Other badgers were breaking their way into the camp, more than she could count, crushing the thornbushes like blades of grass.

With a roar that seemed to come from all their throats at once, the badgers surged forward. In an instant, the hollow was filled with gaping jaws and slashing claws. Squirrelflight glimpsed Rainwhisker being caught by one leg and tossed into the air; he landed with a dull thud a fox-length away, and didn't get up.

Suddenly a striped face loomed in front of her. Squirrelflight backed up against a clump of brambles, hissing as she lashed out with both front paws. The badger's rank scent stung in her throat. "Get out, or I'll claw your fur off!" she rasped.

Then she felt herself shouldered aside, stumbling to keep her balance as a streak of gray fur flashed past her. Ashfur had thrown himself between her and the badger.

"I can take care of myself!" she hissed, but Ashfur had already leapt forward, plunging his claws into the attacker's pelt while he fastened his teeth into its ear. The badger let out a hoarse bellow, shaking its head from side to side to dislodge him.

"Squirrelflight!" a voice meowed in her ear. It was Brambleclaw, bleeding from a long scratch down one shoulder. "Help me—we've got to get Daisy and the kits out of the hollow. Sorreltail, too."

Without waiting for her response he turned and raced toward the nursery, skirting the edge of the clearing. Squirrelflight darted after him, dodging a couple of screeching cats—Spiderleg and Sootfur—who darted in from opposite sides to claw one huge female badger; the great beast swung her head to and fro, jaws snapping, frustrated that she couldn't catch either of them.

Brambleclaw plunged into the nursery while Squirrelflight waited at the entrance, ready to defend it. The clearing heaved with cats fighting for their lives, and badgers fighting to kill them. Squirrelflight realized that the walls of the stone hollow, which had seemed to offer such good protection when they first found the camp, were trapping her Clanmates now. They couldn't run away, or avoid their enemies by climbing trees. Squirrelflight watched Birchpaw scrabble a few tail-lengths up the rock wall, only to fall back into the claws of a badger. The apprentice saved himself by squeezing into a narrow crack at the foot of the cliff, just out of reach of the swiping black paw.

How will Daisy and Sorreltail and the kits escape? Daisy would never be able to defend herself against something like a badger, and Sorreltail was too close to giving birth to fight well.

Could they climb to the Highledge, Squirrelflight wondered, *and take shelter in Firestar's den?* But the fallen rocks were too easy to climb, easy enough for a badger, and they could all be trapped up there.

More badgers were trying to enter through the wreckage of the thorns. At least that was their only way in. Firestar flung himself at the barrier, fighting furiously, with Dustpelt, Sandstorm, and Thornclaw beside him. Thornclaw was picked up by a massive paw and sent spinning into a clump of nettles; the trembling stalks closed around him, and he didn't reappear.

Squirrelflight glimpsed her father clinging desperately to a badger's shoulder while he clawed at its eyes. Then another of the huge creatures pushed in front of him, and she couldn't see any more.

"Where's Daisy?" a hoarse voice meowed. Squirrelflight turned her head to see Cloudtail limping toward her; the white warrior's pelt was covered with dust, but the light of battle still gleamed in his blue eyes.

"In here," Squirrelflight meowed, nodding to the bramble thicket behind her. "Brambleclaw's fetching her."

The tabby warrior appeared as she spoke, pushing Daisy in front of him. Berrykit squirmed in his jaws, wailing.

Daisy's eyes were stretched wide with horror. "They'll kill us all!" she yowled. "What about my kits?"

"We'll save your kits." To Squirrelflight's surprise, Brightheart had made her way across the clearing from the medicine cat's den. "It's not their fault their mother brought them here," she muttered fiercely as she vanished into the nursery. Cloudtail followed her to fetch the third kit.

"But we'll never get out!" Daisy wailed, staring at the fight still going on in the camp entrance.

"Yes, you will," Squirrelflight meowed. She suddenly remembered how Leafpool had sneaked out of the camp to meet Crowfeather. "I know a way."

"Show us." Brambleclaw managed to speak around the kit in his jaws.

Squirrelflight glanced into the nursery to yowl, "Hurry up!" Brightheart appeared at once, but she wasn't carrying a kit. "Fetch Cinderpelt," she snapped. "Sorreltail's kits are coming. *Now.*"

Panic swept through Squirrelflight. *Great StarClan, no!* Scanning the clearing, she couldn't see Cinderpelt, but she caught sight of Sorreltail's mate, Brackenfur, battling furiously with a badger only a few tail-lengths away. He was obviously trying to reach the nursery.

"Brackenfur, run!" she yowled, launching herself at the badger and clawing at its haunches.

The creature swung aside, batting at the air, giving

Brackenfur the chance to dodge around it.

Squirrelflight let go of the badger and raced back to the nursery. "Sorreltail's kits are coming," she gasped. "No!" she added, blocking Brackenfur as he tried to dive into the bramble thicket. "Find Cinderpelt."

Brackenfur shot her a look from eyes glazed with fear; then he turned and plunged across the clearing toward Cinderpelt's den. A gap opened up among the battling animals, just long enough for Squirrelflight to see him meet the medicine cat. He gestured frantically with his tail, then both cats headed back toward the nursery. They arrived just as Cloudtail and Brightheart appeared from the brambles, each with a kit in their jaws.

"If Sorreltail's kits are really coming, she can't be moved," Cinderpelt meowed. "One of you must stay to guard the entrance. The rest of you, do what you can to save yourselves and the kits." She vanished into the nursery without waiting to see if her order was obeyed.

"I'll stay," Brackenfur offered instantly.

"I'll come back and help you," Squirrelflight promised. "As soon as I've shown the others how to get out. It's this way . . ."

She glanced from side to side, trying to judge the safest way to reach Leafpool's escape route. *It's all the way on the other side of the clearing!* At least darkness had fallen, and although the center of the clearing was lit by the faint light of the crescent moon, shadows lay thickly around the edges. Badgers could see well in the dark, but Squirrelflight hoped that they were too distracted by the battle to bother with a few cats slipping along beside the walls.

"Stay close to me," she warned Daisy.

She padded around the edge of the hollow, sheltering as well as she could beneath brambles and clumps of fern. She could hear the quick, terrified breathing of the horseplace cat behind her, and farther back the faint mewling of her kits, almost drowned out by the snarls and screeches of battling animals no more than a couple of tail-lengths away.

"What's happening?" Mousekit asked plaintively. "What's all the noise about?"

"Yes, and why do we have to be carried?" Berrykit complained. "I'm big enough to walk by myself!"

"You're being carried because badgers are such big, clumsy creatures," Daisy told them over her shoulder. "They might tread on you in the dark." Squirrelflight felt a flash of admiration for the way she was hiding her fear from her kits.

"If a badger stepped on me, I'd bite it!" Hazelkit boasted.

"You won't get the chance," his mother mewed. "Now keep quiet and stop wriggling, and we'll be perfectly safe." She caught Squirrelflight's eye as she spoke, as if warning her not to disagree.

They shrank back against the camp wall as a badger lumbered past, roaring furiously as it tried to dislodge Thornclaw, who was clinging to its shoulder and raking his claws over its ear. As they passed the hazel bush where the elders had their den, Squirrelflight saw Mousefur crouched in the shelter of the branches, her claws bared and her eyes gleaming with fury. Goldenflower and Longtail were just behind her.

"Come with us," Squirrelflight called softly. "I know a way to climb the walls."

Mousefur shook her head. "A blind cat can't climb rocks," she replied with a glance at Longtail.

"Then you go," Longtail responded. "I can still claw a badger if it comes near enough."

Mousefur hissed at him. "We're staying together and that's that."

Squirrelflight didn't have time to stand around arguing. Beside her, Daisy was shivering with fear, barely holding back panic. Brambleclaw, Cloudtail, and Brightheart had caught up with them and were shifting restlessly under the weight of the kits they carried; Squirrelflight heard Berrykit asking, "Why have we stopped?"

"You can hide on the Highledge," she suggested to Mousefur. "Longtail should be able to get up there if you guide him." She still had her doubts about how safe Firestar's den would be, but at least it was more sheltered than down here.

"Okay." Mousefur nodded. "Longtail, grab my tail with your teeth."

Squirrelflight led the way past the warriors' den, Daisy and the others following close behind her. She had to halt briefly as a badger broke out through the branches, blood pouring from its side; it looked ready to give up. Sandstorm shot out after it, yowling, "Get out and stay out!" Squirrelflight flicked her ears at her mother as the badger fled, but there was no time to stop.

When they were more than halfway around the hollow, a

pale gray shape slid out of the shadows. It was Ashfur; one ear was torn and a trickle of blood came from a deep scratch on his flank. He was breathing hard, but he didn't seem to be seriously hurt.

"Squirrelflight, are you okay?" he exclaimed.

"Yes, fine. I'm going to show Daisy and her kits a way out."

"I'll come with you."

Squirrelflight twitched her whiskers impatiently. "No, go to the nursery and help Brackenfur."

For a heartbeat Ashfur hesitated, and Squirrelflight thought he was going to object. Then he slipped past her and the rest of the cats and vanished into the darkness. A badger spotted him, let out a roar, and gave chase, but Squirrelflight couldn't stop to help.

"Come on," she muttered. "It's not far now."

Her belly clenched as the shriek of a cat in pain rose above the clamor. Turmoil filled the clearing, the huge shapes of badgers lunging after their prey, with the small, lithe forms of her Clanmates flitting between them, dashing in to strike a blow, then darting off again. Squirrelflight couldn't see the thorn barrier from here, but she realized even more invaders must have broken through.

Great StarClan, is this the end?

CHAPTER 22

♣

Squirrelflight shook her head to clear the numbing horror that had gripped her. Her first task was to help her Clanmates before she thought about going to join the fight at the entrance to the hollow. Flicking her tail, she led them on again, the noise of the battle battering her ears.

To her relief the brambles that shielded the escape route had not been trampled down, leaving just enough space for them to hide. The cats huddled together in the thorn-circled gap and gazed uncertainly at the wall that loomed above them.

"It's not that difficult to climb," Squirrelflight promised. "I'll show you. Here, Brambleclaw, give me that kit. If a badger spots us, keep it busy." A pang shot through her as she realized how absolutely she trusted the tabby warrior to guard them while they retreated.

Brambleclaw flicked her ear gently with his tail and set down Berrykit so she could grip its scruff between her teeth. The tiny scrap had stopped complaining; now it looked stunned with terror.

Squirrelflight clenched her jaw and launched herself upward, scrabbling out of the brambles and digging her claws into a bush rooted a couple of tail-lengths up the wall. Berry-kit let out a squeak as she accidentally let him bang against the rock.

"Sorry," she mumbled.

Pushing madly with her hind legs, she reached a ledge where rock had fallen away, and from there she could scramble up with tussocks of grass for pawholds until she stood on the edge of the hollow.

She dived into the clump of ferns she had used to hide when she followed Leafpool and set Berrykit down, giving him a swift, rough lick. "There, little one, you're safe now."

She lifted her head cautiously above the ferns. The roar of battle in the clearing was muted up here, and the scent of badgers much fainter. She didn't think any of the hostile creatures were in this part of the forest. Keeping so low that her belly fur brushed the grass, she left the shelter of the ferns and peered over the edge of the hollow.

"It's okay up here!" she called. "You can come up."

Cloudtail was already climbing with Hazelkit in his jaws, dragging himself up without putting too much pressure on his injured foreleg. Squirrelflight showed him where to put the kit next to her brother and he let her drop into the soft ferns with a sigh of relief. Brightheart was right behind him with Mousekit.

"You stay here," Cloudtail told her. "Daisy and the kits will need some cat with them, in case the badgers come."

"You stay, then." Brightheart glared at him. "I'm going back to fight. You're injured."

"For StarClan's sake, this isn't the time to have an argument," Squirrelflight snapped. "We're all going back. Daisy will have to cope on her own. ThunderClan needs all its warriors down there."

Brightheart swung around and vanished over the edge. Cloudtail muttered, "She-cats!" and followed her. Squirrelflight checked the kits once more, saw them safe in a squirming heap among the ferns, and turned back to the hollow in time to see Daisy pull herself up and stand panting on the edge.

"Where are my kits?" she gasped.

Squirrelflight pointed with her tail, and the horseplace cat rushed over to the ferns.

"Thank you," she meowed, glancing back before she pushed her way among the stalks. "And good luck."

"We'll need it," Squirrelflight replied grimly as she gathered herself to scramble back down the cliff into the clearing.

Down on the ground Brambleclaw was still keeping guard. Ferncloud and Birchpaw were with him. The young apprentice had survived the badger attack, but part of the fur on his haunches had been ripped off and one eye was almost closed. His mother was bleeding from claw marks along her side.

"Look, Ferncloud, you can climb out here," Brambleclaw meowed as Squirrelflight leapt the last couple of tail-lengths and landed neatly beside him. "Take Birchpaw with you."

Birchpaw looked too dazed to figure out the escape route, but Ferncloud nudged him gently over to the rock wall.

"Stay close to him," Squirrelflight warned. "Daisy and her

kits are up there already. They'll be glad to have a warrior to protect them."

Ferncloud gave her a grateful nod and followed Birchpaw as the apprentice began scrabbling upward through the thorns.

Brambleclaw was peering out from behind the screen of brambles. "I'm going to help Firestar defend the entrance," he mewed.

Squirrelflight drew her breath in painfully. "Is Firestar still alive?"

"I spotted him a few moments ago," Brambleclaw reassured her. "The battle isn't over yet. I'll see you later." He sped off with a twitch of his tail.

Squirrelflight's heart lurched suddenly as she saw him vanish into the thickest of the fighting. Would they really see each other again? Or was it too late to put right everything that had gone wrong between them?

Unable to bear the thought of losing Brambleclaw now, Squirrelflight was about to follow him when she heard a cat wailing somewhere close by. Staring around the hollow, she caught a glimpse of Sootfur, his gray pelt barely visible in the shadows. She could tell he was badly wounded, because he was dragging himself along the ground as if he couldn't use his back legs.

"Sootfur, over here!" she called.

The gray warrior raised his head, too confused by pain to know where the cry had come from. Squirrelflight darted out to him and managed to nudge him to his paws, letting him lean on her shoulder as she guided him back to the screen of brambles.

"You can get out this way," she meowed, gesturing with her tail to the route up the wall.

Sootfur blinked drops of blood out of his eyes. "Can't . . . can't climb . . ." he gasped.

"You've got to!"

Squirrelflight pushed him over to the wall. Sootfur clawed desperately, but both his back legs were broken and he couldn't use them to thrust himself upward. He managed to haul himself a few tail-lengths from the ground, then slipped back down again with a shrill cry of pain.

At the same moment a badger appeared, breaking down the bramble screen and lunging at Sootfur. Squirrelflight glimpsed healed scars running along its side; her claws flexed instinctively with the memory of tearing through that coarse black fur. This must be the female they had driven out of their territory. For a moment she locked gazes with the furious creature. *To think I felt sorry for you!* she thought. *Do we really deserve this?*

Sootfur lifted his head, snarling, and lashed out with one forepaw while Squirrelflight leapt on the badger from behind, biting down hard on its hind leg. It flung her off as if she were a fly; she crashed into the rocks and lay stunned for a couple of heartbeats. When she managed to scramble up again, the badger was lumbering off into the darkness, leaving the black warrior lying ominously still.

"Sootfur, no!" Squirrelflight staggered over to him. There

was a new gash in his throat and his eyes gazed sightlessly into the sky.

"Great StarClan!" Squirrelflight yowled. "Why are you letting this happen?"

But there was no time to grieve for her Clanmate. She had to get back to the nursery. Instead of returning the way she had come, she risked a dash across the middle of the clearing, skidding around screeching bundles of fur and claws.

We can't win! a voice shrieked inside her head. *There are too many of them!*

Refusing to listen, she slashed at the eyes of a badger that tried to block her way, spitting fiercely until it backed off. When she reached the nursery, she found Brackenfur crouched in the entrance, his lips drawn back in a snarl as he challenged a young badger. The creature hesitated, as if it thought there might be easier prey.

A couple of fox-lengths away, Ashfur was fighting with an older, bigger badger; Squirrelflight watched in dismay as it caught the gray warrior with a blow to the side of his head, throwing him to the ground.

Squirrelflight let out a screech. Springing forward, she hurtled into the badger's flank, forcing it off balance. It lurched sideways, leaving its underbelly exposed; Squirrelflight dived between its paws and raked it with her foreclaws. The badger let out a growl of fury. Pain flooded through Squirrelflight as she felt long claws sink into her shoulder and flip her onto her back. The weight of the badger forced all the breath from her chest as it landed on top of her. She felt as if it were pushing her into the ground; she could imagine her bones cracking. She choked on a mouthful of hot fur and fought for air as her senses spun away.

Suddenly the weight lifted and she could breathe again. Gasping, she staggered to her paws to see Ashfur gripping the badger's foreleg with his teeth, his body whipping from side to side as the badger tried to shake him off. With a yowl of fury Squirrelflight dashed in on the other side. The badger swung its head around, jaws snapping for her. She ducked away from it, slashing at its throat and dodging out of range before it could swat her with a paw.

Meanwhile Ashfur had dropped to the ground and darted forward, distracting the creature's attention from Squirrelflight long enough for her to dash in again and rake her claws over its shoulder. The badger wove back and forth, never managing to land a blow. Its growls rose to a roar of frustration and it turned tail, fleeing toward the entrance.

Squirrelflight exchanged a triumphant glance with Ashfur, then spun around to check the nursery. Brackenfur was still tussling with the young badger. His teeth were fastened in its ear; before Squirrelflight or Ashfur could move, it dislodged the golden brown warrior with one swat from its blunt claws, then thrust its way into the nursery.

Squirrelflight froze as a terrible shriek rose from the bramble thicket.

"StarClan, help me!"

CHAPTER 23

Leafpool and Crowfeather paused beside the stepping-stones that led across the stream into ThunderClan territory. Night had fallen, and a thin crescent moon rode high in the sky. They had traveled all day, only stopping at sunhigh long enough to devour a rabbit Crowfeather had caught on the moorland. Now Leafpool's paws were sore and her heart pounded with mounting fear.

"Good-bye," she murmured, pushing her nose into Crowfeather's fur. "I'll see you again when all this is over."

"What do you mean, 'good-bye'?" Crowfeather demanded. "I'm not leaving you when there are hostile badgers around."

"But you need to warn WindClan."

"I know, and I will. But I'll see you to your camp first. It won't take long."

Seeing the stubborn light in his eyes, Leafpool knew she would only waste time by arguing. Leaping swiftly from one stepping-stone to the next, she led the way down the slope and into the shelter of the trees.

It was a relief to enter the woods after traveling for so long under the open sky, but Leafpool's feeling of homecoming didn't last long. Almost at once a rank scent drifted around them, masking all the other scents of the forest.

"Badgers," Crowfeather growled.

Leafpool was too terrified to speak. Although she was exhausted from the long trek over the moors, she picked up her pace until she was racing through the trees, the gray-black warrior at her shoulder. As they drew closer to the Thunder-Clan camp, she heard the sound from her dream she had been dreading every pawstep of the journey: the yowls of fighting cats mingled with the deeper roars of her enemies. Badgers had broken into the camp!

When she reached the edge of the hollow, she heard a rustling among the ferns and a cat wailing, "Not more of them! Oh, help!"

Whipping around, Leafpool saw Ferncloud and Daisy peering out from under a clump of bracken. It was Daisy who had cried out.

"Leafpool!" Ferncloud exclaimed. "What—" She broke off and added, "No, don't stop. Go and help the Clan."

Leafpool and Crowfeather ran on, down the slope that led to the entrance. The thorn barrier that was supposed to protect the camp had been utterly destroyed, trampled down by monstrous paws. Beyond the scattered branches, badgers filled the hollow, their thick-furred shoulders heaving as they pounced and fought. Leafpool caught a glimpse of her father, a wild light in his green eyes as he rallied his Clan with sweeping gestures of his tail.

"Follow me! Drive them out!" he yowled as he leapt at the

nearest badger, a huge male with a scarred muzzle.

Dustpelt and Brambleclaw were hard on his paws. Dustpelt hurled himself at the badger's shoulder, scoring its pelt with outstretched claws. Brambleclaw flung himself at another creature that stood growling a tail-length away, springing up as it lowered its head and fastening his teeth in its ear.

Around the edge of the clearing, the dens that were barely two moons old were torn, their branches scattered so that Leafpool scarcely recognized her home. One massive badger was crashing through the warriors' den in pursuit of Rainwhisker. Another rolled around a tail-length from Leafpool, locked into combat with Spiderleg while Sandstorm sank her teeth into its hind leg.

I'm too late! Leafpool thought in dismay. She couldn't see Midnight anywhere among the badgers. Perhaps her vengeful kin had caught her on her way to ThunderClan and stopped her from warning the cats. Maybe they'd even killed her!

Throwing off the horror that froze her paws, Leafpool tore through the trampled thorns into the clearing. There must be *something* she could do to help her Clanmates, something more than just die at their side. She was about to hurl herself into battle when an eerie shriek rose above the rest of the clamor. It came from the nursery, the only clump of thorns that remained standing.

"Cinderpelt!" she gasped to Crowfeather.

As if her paws had wings, she streaked across the clearing, barely aware of a badger that lunged for her, only to fall back as Crowfeather flew at it, spitting and clawing. He was hard on her paws as she raced up to the nursery.

Just outside, a ginger cat was lying in the dust, a badger looming over her.

"Squirrelflight!" Leafpool yowled.

Her claws sank into the badger's leg. Its head swung around, jaws snapping. Crowfeather thrust himself in front of Leafpool, his claws raking at the badger's eyes. With a bellow of pain it reared back and lurched away.

Leafpool flung herself down beside her sister. Only the link that still connected them told her that her sister wasn't dead. Relief swept through her from ears to tail-tip as Squirrelflight raised her head, blinking confusedly. "Leafpool . . . you came back!"

"Yes, I'm here. Are you hurt?"

Squirrelflight took in a huge, gasping breath. "Only . . . winded. Leafpool, in there . . ." Her gaze flicked to the nursery. "In there . . . Cinderpelt, with Sorreltail . . . kits coming. Badger . . . broke in."

A fresh wave of terror flooded over Leafpool. *I'm too late.*

She plunged past Squirrelflight into the nursery. The shadows inside were filled with the sound of vicious snarling, cut through with a wail of terror. Leafpool recognized Sorreltail's voice. "Sorreltail, it's me, Leafpool. Where's Cinderpelt?"

In the darkness she could make out nothing but a huge, humped shape. The stench of the badger filled the whole nursery. She hurled herself forward and collided with a solid flank covered in coarse fur. Raking her claws down the

badger's side, she gasped, "Out! Get out!" The invader turned
its head toward her; she caught the gleam of bright, malignant
eyes and knew she was living out her nightmare of the rolling
black mist.

Lashing out with one paw, she scored the badger across its
nose and saw blood spatter out, its hot scent mingling with
the reek of badger. A paw swept up to batter her, but before
the blow fell Crowfeather appeared next to her, slashing at the
badger's muzzle.

The badger let out a howl of pain. Turning, it thrust Leafpool aside and made for the nursery entrance, breaking down
more of the brambles as it went. Watery shafts of moonlight
filtered through the gaps, revealing the horrified faces of
Squirrelflight and Ashfur looking in.

"What's going on? Is Cinderpelt hurt?" Squirrelflight
asked hoarsely.

"I don't know yet," Leafpool replied. Her voice shook with
fear. "I'll look after her. You stay on guard."

Her sister nodded and went back to the entrance with Ashfur. Crowfeather touched noses briefly with Leafpool before
following them. "Call me if you need me," he meowed.

The floor of the nursery was covered with a thick layer of
moss and fern. Sorreltail lay at the far side, her head raised
and her eyes staring in terror. A powerful ripple passed along
her belly, and Leafpool realized that her kits were about to be
born. She started to cross the nursery, but stopped when her
paws brushed against a broken, motionless body.

Cinderpelt lay on her side in the bed of moss, her paws and tail limp, her eyes closed. Blood spilled slowly from a gash in her side.

"Cinderpelt . . ." Leafpool whispered. "Cinderpelt, it's me, Leafpool. Wake up."

The medicine cat's eyes twitched open and she gazed up at Leafpool. "Leafpool," she rasped. "I prayed to StarClan you would come back."

"I should never have left you." Leafpool crouched beside her mentor, breathing in the familiar comforting scent. "I'm sorry, I'm so sorry. Cinderpelt, please don't die!"

She scooped a pawful of moss from the floor and pressed it against the wound in Cinderpelt's side. "You're going to be fine," she mewed. "As soon as the bleeding stops I'll fetch some marigold to make sure the wound doesn't get infected, and some poppy seeds for the pain. You'll be able to have a good long sleep, and you'll feel much better when you wake up."

"Stop it, Leafpool," Cinderpelt whispered. "There's no point." Leafpool saw her eyes gleam dully in the shadows. "I'm going to join StarClan."

"Don't say that!" Leafpool protested, clawing up more moss and thrusting it against the tide of blood that showed no sign of stopping.

The medicine cat tried to lift her head, but the effort was too much for her, and she let it fall again. "It's all right," she murmured. "StarClan told me they would come for me soon. This is the fate they have laid down for me."

"You knew?" Leafpool felt as though a dark chasm had

opened up in front of her paws and she was crashing helplessly into its depths. "You knew you were going to die and you didn't tell me?"

"It was my destiny, not yours."

"But you knew I was meeting Crowfeather! You knew that if I went away ThunderClan would be left without a medicine cat! Cinderpelt, you should have *forced* me to stay."

Her mentor blinked slowly. Her blue eyes were very bright. "I would never force you to do anything, Leafpool. I didn't want you to stay if it was going to make you unhappy. You must want to be a medicine cat with all your heart."

"I do," Leafpool whispered. "I do." *Follow your heart*, Spottedleaf had said.

"You are a wonderful medicine cat," Cinderpelt told her.

"No, I'm not. I went away and left you, and my Clan. Oh, Cinderpelt, I'm so sorry!"

The tip of Cinderpelt's tail gave a tiny, restless twitch. "There's nothing to forgive. I am happy to join StarClan, knowing that ThunderClan will be cared for."

"No!" Leafpool cried, as if by sheer force of wishing she could turn back time and prevent her mentor's death. "This is all my fault. I should have been here. I should—"

Cinderpelt shook her head. "It would have made no difference," she mewed. "We cannot change our destiny. We just have to have the courage to know what it is, and accept it." She let out a long sigh. "StarClan is waiting for me. Good-bye, Leafpool."

Her eyes closed. Her body jerked once, then lay still.

"Cinderpelt!" Leafpool pushed her nose deep into her mentor's fur. She felt as if all the frosts of leaf-bare were gathered in her limbs.

A few moments later she felt a warm pelt brush against her side and realized that Crowfeather was crouching beside her. "I'm sorry, Leafpool," he murmured. "I know what she meant to you."

"She taught me everything, and now she's dead," Leafpool wailed. "I don't know what to do. I trusted Spottedleaf. She told me to follow my heart, but she knew Cinderpelt was going to die! How could she do that?"

Crowfeather pressed closer to her and drew his tongue over her face and ears with gentle, comforting strokes. "You did follow your heart," he meowed. "Your heart told you to come home. You could never be happy away from your Clan."

Leafpool turned her head and saw pain glisten in his amber eyes. "But what about you?" she whispered.

Crowfeather bowed his head. "Your heart lies here. Not with me. It was never truly with me."

Leafpool felt as though she were being torn in two, but she knew Crowfeather was right. She loved him, but not enough. For a few heartbeats she leaned into him, feeling his warmth and strength for the last time. Then she touched Cinderpelt's fur with her nose.

"It's all right," she murmured. "I'll stay here and take good care of the Clan, I promise. One day we'll meet again, walking among the stars."

For a moment she thought she felt the brush of two pelts

against hers, and she smelled two familiar scents as Spotted-leaf and Cinderpelt wound around her.

"StarClan is with you, Leafpool," Spottedleaf murmured, and Cinderpelt added, "We will always be watching over you."

Then they were gone. Leafpool was crouching on the floor of the nursery, with the roar of battle still outside and Sorrel-tail gasping in the far corner as her kits fought their way into the world.

"Your friend needs your help," Crowfeather meowed. "Can I do anything?"

"Just help the others keep the badgers off." Leafpool was amazed at how calm her voice sounded. "If you get the chance, ask some cat to show you Cinderpelt's den and fetch me some watermint. But if you can't, I'll manage without it. It's more important to keep the badgers out of here."

The gray-black warrior dipped his head and slipped away. Leafpool picked her way around Cinderpelt's body and across the mossy bedding until she reached Sorreltail's side.

"Don't worry," she reassured her friend. "I'm here now. Everything's going to be fine."

CHAPTER 24
♣

Squirrelflight leapt around at the sound of pawsteps behind her. Crowfeather was emerging from the nursery.

"What's happening in there?" she demanded.

The WindClan warrior stared at her as if he were looking straight through her. "Cinderpelt's dead," he meowed hoarsely.

Squirrelflight's belly clenched. It couldn't be true! StarClan couldn't be that cruel! She wanted to rush into the nursery to see for herself and comfort her sister, but she knew she had to stay where she was, guarding Sorreltail while her kits arrived.

In front of her, the hollow was emptying as if some of the badgers had been chased off, but the cats still weren't winning the fight. There were too many unmoving heaps of fur sprawled on the ground, too much blood sinking into the paw-trodden earth.

A few fox-lengths away Squirrelflight could see Firestar and Brackenfur battling a long-legged male badger, darting forward in turn to confuse it. The badger swiped at them with massive paws; it couldn't be long before one of the blows landed, hard enough to smash a cat's skull or break a limb.

Her belly churned as she looked for Brambleclaw, but she couldn't see him.

Crowfeather crouched beside her, his amber eyes burning as he gazed across the clearing.

"You wouldn't think he'd be so upset about the death of another Clan's medicine cat," Ashfur muttered into Squirrelflight's ear.

Squirrelflight didn't say anything. She knew the gray-black warrior wasn't just grieving for Cinderpelt.

Another badger lumbered out of the shadows, its jaws open to reveal two rows of pointed yellow teeth. It was bleeding heavily from one shoulder; Squirrelflight's belly twisted as she imagined what might have happened to the warrior who had inflicted the wound. Ashfur leapt out to confront the creature before it got too close to the nursery, and Squirrelflight sprang up to follow. "Crowfeather, guard the entrance!" she yowled.

But before she could join Ashfur, she was distracted by a terrified wail. Glancing over her shoulder she saw Whitepaw flat on the ground by the trampled barrier, frozen with terror as a badger loomed over her. Squirrelflight swerved and pelted over to the apprentice's side. She aimed outstretched claws, then pulled back without striking and stared up in disbelief.

"It's okay, Whitepaw," she choked out after a moment. "This is Midnight."

"Greetings, small warrior," Midnight rasped.

Squirrelflight's instinctive reaction had been relief, but then her suspicions flared up. Was Midnight here to fight on behalf of her kin? Squirrelflight took a pace backward until she was standing protectively over Whitepaw.

"What are you doing here?" she demanded.

"No need for fear," Midnight reassured her. "My way is not fight. I bring help."

She cocked her head to one side as if she were listening to something, then stepped aside to let a river of cats stream into the camp: strong, fresh warriors who fell on the badgers with yowls of fury. Tornear, Ashfoot, Whitetail, Onestar . . .

WindClan had come to help them!

The badger that had been fighting with Firestar and Brackenfur staggered back, turned tail, and ran. Firestar and Webfoot chased after it, hissing. Nightcloud and Onestar joined Ashfur to chase off the badger that had come too close to the nursery. Squirrelflight dashed forward to help, but she realized all the invaders were fleeing from the clearing. She skidded to a halt and watched them blunder through the broken branches that lay across the entrance to the hollow.

Relief stabbed Squirrelflight as she spotted Brambleclaw standing a little way off, his sides heaving with effort. She caught his eye and saw her own surprise reflected at the arrival of the Clan who had so recently rejected their friendship.

Ashfur's badger lumbered past her with Nightcloud and Onestar hard on its paws. Onestar halted in front of Brambleclaw as the badger scrambled over the remains of the thorn barrier and vanished into the trees.

"You came," Brambleclaw meowed.

"Of course we came." Pride kindled in Onestar's eyes.

"There are *four* Clans in the forest, but we can still help one another."

Ashfur staggered to a stop beside Squirrelflight, and she turned to lick his wounds. He had lost fur from his shoulder and one side, and there was a deep gash on his foreleg. Even as she took care of him she tried to push aside the thought that she hadn't been as frightened for him as she'd been for Brambleclaw.

"You'd better let Leafpool have a look at that," she told him. She'd almost said "Cinderpelt."

"Later," he meowed. "It's nothing serious. I couldn't believe it when I saw Onestar and his warriors," he added. "I thought we were all going to join StarClan."

"Not yet," Squirrelflight assured him. But the grim truth of what had happened swept over her, and she felt like wailing aloud. How many cats were dead besides Cinderpelt and Sootfur? How many more would die of their injuries?

The last of the badgers were disappearing with WindClan in pursuit. The exhausted ThunderClan warriors began to gather in the center of the camp around Midnight. Their eyes were stunned with horror, as if they couldn't believe the battle was over.

Whitepaw scrambled to her paws and ran over to Cloudtail and Brightheart, who were slowly approaching from the direction of the elders' den. Cloudtail's white fur was caked with blood and dust, and he leaned heavily on Brightheart's shoulder. Mousefur guided Longtail down from the Highledge, glancing around with narrowed eyes as if she wasn't sure all their enemies had gone. Goldenflower followed a moment later; Brambleclaw, Thornclaw, and Sandstorm joined them.

Dustpelt limped up, fear in his eyes as he scanned the clearing. "Ferncloud?" he rasped. "Birchpaw?"

"They're fine," Squirrelflight reassured him. "They got out of the camp. They're looking after Daisy and her kits."

The brown tabby warrior visibly relaxed, collapsing on the ground to lick a wound on his shoulder.

Firestar staggered up and halted in front of Midnight, gazing up uncertainly as if he wondered why this badger wasn't fleeing. As he tensed his muscles, ready to attack, Squirrelflight stepped forward quickly.

"Firestar, this is Midnight," she meowed. "The badger we met at the sun-drown-place. Midnight, this is our Clan leader, Firestar."

Relief flooded Firestar's green eyes. "The badger who warned us to leave the forest?" He dipped his head. "You're welcome here."

"Good is it to be here," Midnight told him. "And to see again friends from journey. Yet I wish time was happier."

"So do we all." Firestar let out an exhausted sigh. "You knew about this, then? You came to warn us?"

"No, she came to warn *us*." Onestar padded up to Firestar's side. "And to ask for our help."

"Attack come before I expect," Midnight explained. "No use come alone to ThunderClan. Best to find more fighting cats first."

Firestar blinked gratefully. "We're very glad you did. Thank

StarClan you found out what your kin were planning."

"First in stars I see it," the old badger told him. "Then I go to my kin, try to speak of peace, but they not listen, and little they tell me. They call me 'cat-friend,' and other insults more worse."

Squirrelflight flexed her claws. "I wish I'd ripped a bit more fur off, just for you, Midnight."

The badger shrugged. "Is not important. Except I might have got here more sooner. RiverClan they hate most," she added. "Warriors there drive them out first."

"We'd better send a message to Leopardstar," Firestar meowed. "The badgers could still attack there."

Squirrelflight's shoulders sagged at the thought of trekking all the way around the lake to RiverClan.

"No need," rasped Midnight. "My kin in no state fight more. They think twice before bother cats again."

"Thank StarClan for that," Squirrelflight murmured. She was wondering how soon she would be able to crawl into what remained of the warriors' den to sleep when she heard her sister's voice behind her. "Brackenfur? Is Brackenfur here?"

The golden brown warrior was lying in a patch of ferns at the edge of the clearing. His blood was trickling into the dust and he looked barely conscious. He lifted his head as Leafpool came up to him.

"Sorreltail?" He lurched unsteadily to his paws. "It's Sorreltail, isn't it? Is she all right?"

Leafpool brushed against his pelt. She looked exhausted too. "She's fine. She has four healthy kits."

"Four?" Brackenfur's tail curled up. "That's great! Thanks, Leafpool." He raced across the camp and into the nursery.

Squirrelflight watched him go. Thanks to WindClan they had won the battle. ThunderClan had survived greater disasters than this, and sooner or later the Clan would be as strong as ever. The four scraps of new life in the nursery seemed like a promise from StarClan.

Yet life had ended too. ThunderClan would mourn Cinderpelt's death for a long time. But it would have been even worse if Leafpool hadn't returned.

Squirrelflight rasped her tongue over her sister's ear. "I'm so glad you came back."

Leafpool glanced over at Crowfeather, who was still crouched outside the nursery, then turned back to her sister. "I'm glad to be back, too."

Crowfeather stood up as the WindClan cats came back into the camp.

"Look, it's Crowfeather!" Whitetail exclaimed. "What's he doing here?"

Onestar stalked over to stand in front of the gray-black warrior. "Crowfeather, you came back . . . but not to your own Clan."

Crowfeather looked at him steadily. "I wanted to bring Leafpool safely to her own camp first. I'm ready to come home now."

"We have things to talk about, but now is not the time," Onestar meowed.

Crowfeather dipped his head and fell in behind his leader

as Onestar padded over to Firestar.

"Onestar, every cat in ThunderClan thanks you," Firestar meowed. "Without you, StarClan would have gained many more warriors."

"You've helped WindClan in the past," Onestar replied. "It's only right that we should come and help you."

"We won't forget—" Firestar began.

He was interrupted by a startled yowl from Thornclaw, who was closest to the camp entrance. Squirrelflight stiffened. Had the badgers come back? She didn't think she could lift a single paw now, even to save her life.

But her exhaustion vanished when she saw two cats carefully picking their way through the scattered thorn branches. The first of them, a powerful warrior with a thick gray pelt, stopped at the edge of the clearing and looked around.

"This isn't what I expected to find," he meowed. "What happened?"

Squirrelflight stared in disbelief. After the badger attack, she had thought nothing else could shock her, but for a heartbeat she forgot how to breathe.

Gazing curiously around them, sleek furred and calm among the shattered Clan, were Stormfur and Brook.

ERIN HUNTER

is inspired by a love of cats and a fascination with the ferocity of the natural world. As well as having great respect for nature in all its forms, Erin enjoys creating rich mythical explanations for animal behavior. She is also the author of the bestselling Seekers and Survivors series.

Download the free Warriors app and chat on Warriors message boards at www.warriorcats.com.

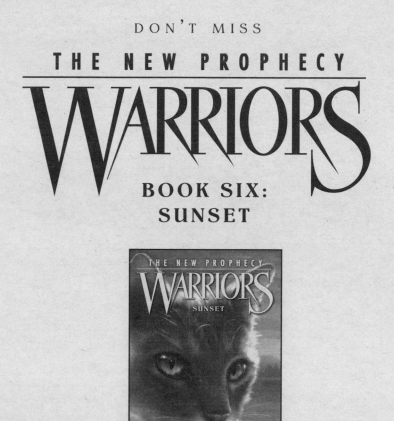

CHAPTER 1

❧

Brambleclaw stood in the middle of the clearing, gazing at what was left of the ThunderClan camp. A crescent moon, thin as a claw, drifted above the trees that surrounded the stone hollow. Its pale light revealed the dens trampled down, the thorn barrier at the camp entrance broken and tossed aside, and the wounded cats of ThunderClan slowly creeping from the shadows, their fur bristling and their eyes stretched wide with shock. Brambleclaw could still hear the trampling of the badgers as they lumbered away. The undergrowth beyond the entrance quivered where they had pushed through, driven off with the help of Onestar and the WindClan warriors who had come just in time to help ThunderClan.

But it wasn't the sight of devastation that pricked Brambleclaw's pelt and kept his paws frozen to the ground. Two cats he had never thought he'd see again were picking their way carefully among the scattered thorns of the entrance barrier. They were uninjured, their pelts sleek and their eyes alight with alarm.

"Stormfur! What are you doing here?" Brambleclaw called.

The powerful gray tomcat paced forward until he could touch noses with Brambleclaw. "It's good to see you again," he meowed. "I . . . I wanted to see if you'd found a place to live. But what has happened here?"

"Badgers," Brambleclaw replied. He glanced around, wondering where to begin helping his wounded and frightened Clanmates.

Beside Stormfur, the slender brown tabby she-cat brushed her tail against a long scratch on Brambleclaw's shoulder. "You're hurt," she mewed.

Brambleclaw twitched his ears. "It's nothing. Welcome to ThunderClan, Brook. I'm sorry you had to travel so far to find us like this." He paused and looked from one to the other. "Is everything all right in the Tribe of Rushing Water? I never expected you to come visit us so soon."

Stormfur shot a glance at Brook, so swift Brambleclaw almost missed it. "Everything's fine," he meowed. "We just wanted to be sure you had found a new place to live, like StarClan promised."

Brambleclaw looked around the devastated camp, the stricken cats stumbling through the remains of their home. "Yes, we found it," he murmured.

"You said *badgers* attacked you?" Brook prompted, sounding puzzled.

"They came here on purpose," Brambleclaw explained. "StarClan knows where they came from, more badgers than I've ever seen in my life. They would have killed us all if WindClan hadn't turned up." His paws trembled, and he sank his claws into the bloodstained earth to keep himself steady.

Stormfur nodded. "Don't worry about telling us everything now. What can we do to help?"

Brambleclaw sent a silent prayer of thanks to StarClan that they had chosen this moment to send his old friend back to the Clans. He and Stormfur had been through a lot together on the first journey to the sun-drown-place, and he could think of few cats he'd rather have beside him now.

He turned his head as a thin wail came from a trampled clump of ferns at the edge of the hollow. "We need to find all the cats that have been badly wounded. Some will be on their way to join StarClan," he warned, glancing at Brook. "The badgers came to kill, not drive us out."

Brook met his gaze steadily. "Whatever they have done, I want to help. I have seen this kind of savagery before from Sharptooth, remember?" Sharptooth was a giant mountain cat that had terrorized the Tribe of Rushing Water for many moons, until the cats from the forest arrived. Stormfur's sister, Feathertail, had died in the fall that killed the savage animal.

"We'll do whatever we have to," Stormfur promised. "Just tell us what to do. Are you ThunderClan's deputy now?"

Brambleclaw studied a fragment of moss that was trapped under his front paw. "No," he admitted. "Firestar has decided not to appoint another deputy. He wants to give Graystripe more time to come back."

"That's tough." There was a note of sympathy in Stormfur's voice that made Brambleclaw wince. He didn't want any cat's pity.

Suddenly Brook froze. "I thought you said the badgers had gone," she hissed.

Brambleclaw whipped around, then relaxed as he saw a familiar, pointed, black-and-white face pushing its way out of a clump of dead bracken.

Stormfur touched Brook's shoulder lightly with his tail. "That's Midnight," he meowed. "She wouldn't hurt any cats." He bounded forward to meet the elderly badger.

Midnight peered at Stormfur with shortsighted eyes. Then she gave a small nod. "Cat friend from journey," she rumbled. "Good it is to see you again. And this cat from mountain Tribe, is she not?" she added, gesturing with her snout toward Brook.

"That's right," Stormfur meowed. "This is Brook, a prey-hunter from the Tribe of Rushing Water." He beckoned Brook forward with his tail; she went over reluctantly, as if she couldn't quite believe this badger was friendly. Bramble-claw understood her feelings; he knew Midnight as well as any cat, but it was hard not to look at her bulky shape without remembering snapping jaws, fierce gleaming eyes, and claws that shredded cats' fur like leaves in newleaf. . . .

There was the sound of heavy paws, and he looked up to see Midnight standing beside him. Grief and anger sparked from her berry-bright eyes. "Too late my warning," she rasped. "Not enough could I do."

"You brought WindClan to help us," Brambleclaw pointed out. "Without you, our whole Clan would have been wiped out."

Midnight bowed her head, the white stripe that ran the length of her snout gleaming in the faint moonlight. "Shame for my kin I feel."

"Every cat knows this attack had nothing to do with you," Brambleclaw told her. "You will always be welcome in this Clan."

Midnight still looked troubled. Behind her, Brambleclaw spotted his Clan leader near the center of the clearing, with Onestar and the WindClan warriors. He padded toward them, motioning with his tail for Stormfur and Brook to follow. A fox-length away, in the shelter of an upturned thorn-bush, Leafpool was bending over the limp body of Ashfur. For a heartbeat Brambleclaw wondered if the gray warrior was dead, until he saw Ashfur's tail twitch. *StarClan shall not take all our warriors tonight*, he thought determinedly.

Firestar's chest still heaved from the effort of fighting. His flame-colored pelt was torn, and blood was oozing from a long scratch along his flank. Brambleclaw felt a flash of concern. Had his leader lost another life? Whether he had or not, he was badly hurt. *I will help him until my last breath*, Brambleclaw vowed. *Together, we can bring the Clan through this until we are even stronger than before.*

In spite of his injuries, Firestar's eyes were bright and he sat up straight as he faced the WindClan leader, Onestar. "The thanks of all ThunderClan go with you," he meowed.

"I doubt you'll have any more trouble with the badgers," Onestar replied. "But I can leave a couple of warriors behind to keep watch, if you like."

"No thanks, I don't think we'll need them." The warmth in Firestar's eyes revealed the long friendship between these two cats. Brambleclaw silently thanked StarClan that the tension between them, which everyone had felt since Onestar became WindClan leader, seemed to be over at last. "Do your warriors need the help of our medicine cat before you go?" the ThunderClan leader added. "If any of them are badly injured, they're welcome to stay here."

Brambleclaw glanced across at Leafpool, who was still crouched beside Ashfur. When she heard Firestar, she raised her head and stared across the clearing at the WindClan warriors. Brambleclaw felt a stab of sympathy as her gaze sought out one in particular. Two days ago, Crowfeather and Leafpool had abandoned their Clans so that they could be together, but news of the badger attack had brought them home again. Brambleclaw hoped that Leafpool had come home for good; ThunderClan needed her more than ever now that so many cats had been wounded in the badger attack.

Crowfeather was staring down at his paws as if he was deliberately avoiding Leafpool's gaze. Fur was missing from a broad scratch on his flank, but the wound had stopped bleeding and he stood with his weight on all four paws. Webfoot had a torn ear, and the WindClan deputy Ashfoot was bleeding from one shoulder, but none of the wounds looked serious enough to stop the warriors from returning to the WindClan camp.

"I think we're all fit to travel, thank StarClan," Onestar answered the ThunderClan leader. "If you're sure you don't need our help anymore, we'll return to our own territory now."

Crowfeather raised his head and shot one despairing glance at Leafpool. She scrambled to her paws, leaving Ashfur, and padded across to meet the WindClan warrior. They stood a little way from the other cats, their heads close together. Standing in the shadows, Brambleclaw couldn't help overhearing, but he didn't want to disturb them by moving.

"Good-bye, Crowfeather," Leafpool murmured, sounding choked with pain. "We . . . we'd better not see each other again."

Crowfeather's eyes flashed, and for a heartbeat Brambleclaw thought he was going to protest. Then he shook his head. "You're right," he meowed. "It would never have worked. I will never mean enough to you."

Leafpool sank her claws into the ground. "You mean more to me than you will ever know."

The tip of Crowfeather's black tail twitched. "You're a medicine cat. I understand what that means now. StarClan go with you, Leafpool. I'll never forget you."

He and Leafpool touched noses, a delicate contact that lasted less than a heartbeat. Then Crowfeather turned back to his Clanmates. Leafpool watched him go, her eyes clouded with loss.

Webfoot gave Crowfeather a dark look, and Weaselfur pointedly turned his back on him, but Onestar said nothing, only gathering all his warriors together with a sweep of his tail before leading them out of the camp.

"Thank you again!" Firestar called after them. "May

StarClan light your path."

Leafpool stood motionless until Crowfeather's gray-black figure had vanished into the shadow of the trees, then padded across the clearing toward Cinderpelt's den. On the way she flicked her tail to summon Brightheart, who had helped Cinderpelt with medicine cat duties in the past.

"Are you sure?" Brightheart asked hesitantly.

"Of course I'm sure." Leafpool's voice was ragged with exhaustion and grief. "Every cat in the Clan is wounded. I'll be glad of your skills."

Brightheart's remaining eye gleamed, and she seemed to shake off some of her own weariness as she followed Leafpool to the den.

"Is that Stormfur and Brook?"

Brambleclaw jumped as a hoarse voice spoke in his ear. Squirrelflight had appeared beside him. Her dark ginger fur was matted with blood and the tip of one ear was torn.

"Can't you see that it is?" Brambleclaw replied, realizing too late how abrupt he sounded. "Sorry—" he began.

Squirrelflight took a pace forward so that her pelt brushed his. She touched the tip of her tail to his mouth to silence him. "Stupid furball," she whispered.

Brambleclaw tensed, wondering if he was imagining the affection in her green gaze. Glancing past her, he saw Ashfur glaring at him with narrowed eyes.

Squirrelflight didn't notice Ashfur. She limped past Brambleclaw to touch noses with the visitors. "Thank StarClan you have come," she meowed, echoing Brambleclaw's thoughts. "We need all our friends right now."

Brambleclaw felt his shoulders droop in exhaustion just thinking about how much had to be done. Injuries to treat, dens to rebuild, fresh-kill to gather . . . "We'll speak to Firestar and then get started."

As they approached the Clan leader, Thornclaw staggered up to them. Blood trickled from a deep gash above one eye. "Stormfur?" he muttered, shaking his head in confusion. "No, it can't be." The golden brown warrior slumped to the ground, where he lay panting.

Squirrelflight rested her tail on his shoulder, urging him to lie still until his injuries could be treated. Brambleclaw led Stormfur and Brook up to Firestar.

The Clan leader's eyes stretched wide in surprise. "Stormfur . . . and Brook! What are you doing here?"

"There'll be time to explain later," Stormfur meowed. "For now, Firestar, put us to work."

Firestar stared around the clearing as if he wasn't sure where to start. "We should sort out the warriors' den so the cats who have been hurt most can get some sleep . . . but we need to get the entrance barrier back in place, too."

The whole camp was devastated, and few of the Thunder-Clan cats were in any shape to start rebuilding. Ashfur was slumped on the ground, bleeding from flank and foreleg, while Leafpool patted cobwebs onto his wounds. Cloudtail limped up to her, holding one forepaw off the ground; blood trickled from where a claw had been torn out. "Hi, Stormfur," he mewed as he passed, as if this had been such an extraordinary night, the sight of an old friend was no longer a surprise. "Leafpool, can I have a piece of that cobweb?"

Sandstorm was close behind him, her head bent with exhaustion and her tail dragging in the dust. She stopped dead when she spotted Leafpool, then swung around to face Firestar, her green eyes questioning.

"Leafpool's here?" she meowed. "What happened?"

Firestar shook his head to silence her. "We'll talk to her later," he promised. "For now, she's home, and that's all that matters."

"Firestar!" A yowl came from across the clearing. "Firestar, have those crow-food eaters gone?"

Brambleclaw turned to see the three elders, Mousefur, Goldenflower, and Longtail. In the darkness they had to pick their way carefully down the tumble of rocks that led to the ledge where Firestar had his den. They had taken shelter there while the battle raged below. It was Mousefur who had called out; she had lost some fur from one shoulder, Longtail's tail was bleeding, and Goldenflower had a deep scratch down one side. She was guiding Longtail with her tail across his shoulders.

"Are you all right?" Brambleclaw asked, going to meet them.

"Fine," Mousefur growled. "A badger tried to climb up to the Highledge, but we sent it back down the rocks faster than it intended."

"What if they come back?" Goldenflower sounded distraught.

"They'd better not." Longtail flexed his claws, and

Brambleclaw saw dark tufts of badger fur caught in them. "I don't need to see to fight badgers. I can find them by their disgusting scent."

"Better let Leafpool look at those scratches," Firestar meowed.

"Leafpool?" Mousefur's voice was sharp as she swung around to stare at the medicine cat. "She's back, is she? For good—or until that WindClan warrior starts sniffing around again?"

Brambleclaw bit back a sharp retort. He knew Mousefur sounded so harsh only because she was shocked and hurt.

"And who's this?" Mousefur padded up to Stormfur and examined him with narrowed eyes. "Stormfur? What's he doing here?"

"Just paying a visit." Stormfur sounded uncomfortable at the brown elder's suspicious tone.

Mousefur grunted, as if she wasn't completely convinced that Stormfur was a friend. "You were a RiverClan warrior before you left us. Why are you here and not over there?"

"Mousefur, don't be so ungrateful!" Squirrelflight meowed indignantly. "We need every cat who's prepared to help. Besides, Stormfur is half ThunderClan, remember?" Stormfur's father was Graystripe, the ThunderClan deputy who had been captured by Twolegs before the cats left the forest.

Mousefur bristled at Squirrelflight, but before she could reply she was interrupted by a cry from Ferncloud, racing through the broken thorns that were strewn across the entrance to the hollow. "Dustpelt, where are you?"

Brambleclaw bounded over to her as she stopped just inside the entrance, gazing around the dark camp and yowling her mate's name.

"Brambleclaw, have you seen Dustpelt?" she demanded.

"No, not yet," he admitted. "Come on, I'll help you look."

"I should have stayed with him!" Ferncloud wailed. "I never should have left the camp!"

THE TIME HAS COME
FOR DOGS TO RULE THE WILD

SURVIVORS

BOOK ONE:
THE EMPTY CITY

Lucky is a golden-haired mutt with a nose for survival. Other dogs have Packs, but Lucky stands on his own . . . until the Big Growl strikes. Suddenly the ground splits wide open. The longpaws disappear. And enemies threaten Lucky at every turn. For the first time in his life, Lucky needs to rely on other dogs to survive. But can he ever be a true Pack dog?

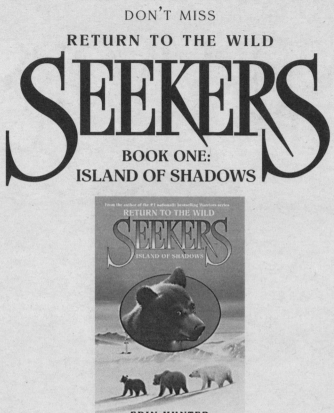

FOLLOW THE ADVENTURES!

WARRIORS: THE PROPHECIES BEGIN

In the first series, sinister perils threaten the four warrior Clans. Into the midst of this turmoil comes Rusty, an ordinary housecat, who may just be the bravest of them all.

WARRIORS: THE NEW PROPHECY

In the second series, follow the next generation of heroic cats as they set off on a quest to save the Clans from destruction.

HARPER
An Imprint of HarperCollinsPublishers

www.warriorcats.com

WARRIORS: POWER OF THREE

In the third series, Firestar's grandchildren begin their training as warrior cats. Prophecy foretells that they will hold more power than any cats before them.

NEW LOOK COMING SOON!

WARRIORS: OMEN OF THE STARS

In the fourth series, find out which ThunderClan apprentice will complete the prophecy.

NEW LOOK COMING SOON!

These extra-long, stand-alone adventures will take you deep inside each of the Clans with thrilling adventures featuring the most legendary warrior cats.

WARRIORS: MANGA SERIES

The cats come to life in manga!

HARPER
An Imprint of HarperCollinsPublishers

www.warriorcats.com

ALSO BY ERIN HUNTER:
SEEKERS

SEEKERS: THE ORIGINAL SERIES

Three young bears . . . one destiny.
Discover the fate that awaits them on their adventure.

SEEKERS: RETURN TO THE WILD

The stakes are higher than ever as the bears search for a way home.

SEEKERS: MANGA

The bears come to life in manga!

HARPER
An Imprint of HarperCollinsPublishers

www.seekerbears.com